MW00985043

THE LONG SHADOW

THE LONG SHADOW

BETH KANELL

FIVE STAR
A part of Gale, a Cengage Company

Farmington Hills, Mich • San Francisco • New York • Waterville, Maine
Meriden, Conn • Mason, Ohio • Chicago

LIBRARY OF CONGRESS CATALOGING-IN-PUBLICATION DATA

Names: Kanell, Beth, author.
Title: The long shadow / Beth Kanell.
Description: First edition. | Waterville, Maine : Five Star Publishing, [2018]
Identifiers: LCCN 2017047958 (print) | LCCN 2017059830 (ebook) | ISBN 9781432837594 (ebook) | ISBN 9781432837556 (ebook) | ISBN 9781432837631 (hardcover)
Subjects: LCSH: Vermont—History—19th century—Fiction. | Fugitive slaves—United States—Fiction. | Bounty hunters—Fiction. | Families—Fiction. | Domestic fiction. | BISAC: FICTION / Historical. | FICTION / General. | GSAFD: Historical fiction.
Classification: LCC PS3611.A5492 (ebook) | LCC PS3611.A5492 L66 2018 (print) | DDC 813/.6—dc23
LC record available at https://lccn.loc.gov/2017047958

First Edition. First Printing: April 2018
Find us on Facebook–https://www.facebook.com/FiveStarCengage
Visit our website–http://www.gale.cengage.com/fivestar/
Contact Five Star™ Publishing at FiveStar@cengage.com

Printed in Mexico
1 2 3 4 5 6 7 22 21 20 19 18

ACKNOWLEDGMENTS

History can be explored in books and other reference materials, and in newspaper articles, letters, diaries, and more. But when questions arise about things that happened more than a hundred and fifty years ago, the help of experts is deeply appreciated. Historian Barbara Clark Smith searched her resources at the Smithsonian Institute to help work out some of the kitchen tasks in 1850. Archivist Lynn Bonfield pointed out the possible Underground Railroad connection of Thaddeus Stevens to our region of Vermont, long before Stevens's Pennsylvania home was confirmed to have connections to such rescues. Bruce Brink, horse lover and expert with horse-drawn vehicles, gave details of speed and how much travel a horse might accomplish in varied weather. Although this novel is set in the "real" Danville and St. Johnsbury and Coventry, Vermont, the characters are fictional, not to be confused with the region's historic leaders—political, spiritual, and economic. I sought and valued Elye Alexander's editorial eye for pacing and adventure. Thanks also to early readers Cheryl and Lois, and to Dave, who wished I were in the kitchen more than at the desk, but didn't complain (much).

CHAPTER 1

North Upton, Vermont, March 1850

Uncle Martin wiped his plate with a thick slab of graham bread and pressed the gravy-soaked slice all into one mouthful, brushed his hands off on his jacket, and pulled a rustling handful of newsprint out from under his chair with a flourish.

"Your man's gone soft of thinking," he told my father as he shoved the pages toward him. "Webster, the golden orator, has turned coat on us. What use is the Union to us all if we let the stinking reek of slave-holding move into the territories after all?"

My mother made a small sound of protest. *Thump,* came my uncle's fist on the table, and the dishes rattled. At the same moment, I heard a light tap at the kitchen door. At my mother's nod, I rose to see who had arrived.

Standing in the dooryard, faces flushed with cold, were my two sweetest friends, both speaking at once. "Alice, school's finished for the week, the doctor said it's too close a space, and the Hopkins twins are fevered," Jerushah announced in a burst, overcoming Sarah's softer voice. "So, will you come across after supper to sew with us? We've only one guest at the house, you know, and there's no stage arriving until Monday, and my mother said to ask your mother."

Jerushah is the most beautiful girl in North Upton, Vermont. Her hair shines like black silk, and her clothes are always the latest styles. I love the way her eyes crinkle with merriment, and

7

her mouth smiles naturally, even when she's at her books. And Sarah, well, she is our adopted sister, we say: a sister dark as tanned deerskin, with deep-brown eyes that hold the hurt and horror of all the Africans pressed into Southern slavery. The moment we saw her, bundled off the stagecoach into the inn as a frail armful, Jerushah and I had pledged ourselves to her. Sarah's parents still lingered under the wicked South's cruel lash. But transported north, Sarah stays safe with us. Though, as best anyone can tell, she is only some twelve years of age, she has brightened and sharpened in our care so that she studies with Jerushah and me at the schoolhouse. And we are both more than fifteen years of age ourselves, nearly out of the schoolroom and into an age of preparing our womanly selves for the years ahead of us.

I held up a hand to my friends for their patience and slipped back into the steam-fragrant house to ask my mother's permission. Distracted by a loud interchange between my father and his brother, she gave a short nod and told me to send the others on their way, for my own dinner lay cooling on the table. This I did, dashing back out the kitchen door to brush a quick kiss onto Jerushah's cheek and then Sarah's, promising I'd be at the inn across the road as soon as the day gave way to dark evening.

A roar and more table thumping came from within the house, and I told my startled friends, "It's news of the Senate and Daniel Webster himself. I'll tell you everything, later." They laughed with me, knowing how men love to argue, and I watched them pass back to the road before I took a final thirsty breath of the clear March air and returned to the family dinner within.

Inside, I found my mother in retreat, her back turned to the brothers at her dinner table. Anger snapped in the air. My father scowled at the broadsheet laid out on the table. Standing lopsidedly next to him and leaning on the table, my over-excited uncle stabbed the page with a thick finger.

"Webster proclaims the South to stand in the right, in its complaint that the Northern states fail their Constitutional duty to return the escaped slaves. See, see it here. He calls the South right, the North wrong."

My father grunted in acknowledgment. I knew he cared more for Union than for Abolition—what use would it be to insist that all the Southern slaves receive freedom, if in the process so many landowners in those distant states lost the value of their goods and took measures to secede from our young nation? I poured the molasses in a steady stream into the cornmeal mush as my mother stirred it.

Uncle Martin stabbed the page again. "But here! Here, Webster proclaims that our government has trodden down no man's liberty, has crushed no State. Ephraim, can you not see the false thinking? How can any man say there's been no loss of liberty, when men whose only difference lies in their skin are in turn bound and flogged and treated as no more than the beasts of the field?"

Of an instant, Sarah's small, dark face hung before me in my thoughts, and I turned toward the table without further thought, saying, "Sarah's father, then. And her mother. Is Senator Webster saying they'll not ever live unslaved, unbound? Papa, is that what it means?"

My mother tugged at my arm and hissed at me to hush. My father's dark-red forehead warned me I'd said too much, had given too much advantage to my uncle in the argument.

"Compromise," my father growled. "There's no Union without compromise."

"There's no Union without a Constitution that honors what we all know to be true," Uncle Martin responded. "Your daughter sees it before you do, man. Is the dark-skinned child less of a daughter than yours? Is she a pup or calf, to be whelped

9

and stolen from her milk and mother, and from the care of her father?"

My mother intervened. "Hold now, Martin, give way for others to sample this thinking. You're in such haste, but Ephraim and I cannot act on your Abolitionist thinking. That's not to say the time won't come, but it isn't our time yet."

With a sudden shove, Uncle Martin launched himself away from the table and denied my mother the honor of calling a truce. "No time for me," he confessed. "I'm for the territories, come the next stage. I've found a printing press, and I'm sending it West to meet me in Illinois. There's justice and the Constitution and the good law of the Gospel to stand for. I thank you, Abigail, for the dinner, and . . . and I ask your pardon that I've overset your peace. But I'll ask no pardon for standing up for natural law and God's own."

With a flourish of his long coat, my uncle swung open the kitchen door and left us, all standing, all staring at the door panels as they swung back, cutting the cold and the light. My mother was the first to regain her voice.

"Ephraim! What can we do to stop him?"

"Stop him?" My father's eyebrows crouched together in a dark warning. "There's no stopping Martin. He wouldn't take advice about the militia, nor the war, and he'll not take it now." He thumped the table again, before stamping out of the house and slamming the door behind him.

I asked the question that burned hottest for me: "Will Sarah's mother and father ever reach the North? Will there be war, instead of freedom for them?"

"I can't say," my mother sighed with deep fatigue. "God save us indeed from a war for the Union, for I know your father would take the uniform himself, if that's what's at stake."

Only the belated arrival of my grown brother William, passing a packet of shop goods through the kitchen door before tramping out to the sugar-camp, kept us from that dark and lingering thought.

The sun's setting left a blush across the western sky that lit the grainy snow in soft rose, darkening even as I stepped down from the doorway. Wood smoke hovered close to the handful of houses that made up North Upton; cold night air pressed it close to the rooflines and held it in a mist among the homes. Between the steepled church at the southwest end of the main street, and the sawmill to the northeast, a dozen homes stood. Light flickered softly at a few windows. Whitewashed board fences lined the roadway, to restrain cattle and sheep within it when they moved through the village. The scent of horses and cows mingled with the smoky air, so familiar as to almost be unnoticed.

Moving as quickly as I dared, I slipped and slid down our long lane to reach the rutted village road of ice and thickened mud. I picked my way across, ignoring the wide solid door of the Clark Tavern, heading to the narrower house doorway.

A loud groan erupted from the shadows by the tavern door, along with a slither of boots on the frozen ground. I jumped backward, making space between my feet and the wriggling bundle of dark clothes. Just in time, too, for the man on the ground gave a rattling cough and hawked a great gob of spittle toward me.

Even from the sound of it, I knew it had to be Old Mo— Moses Cook, the old man who walked among the villages each day. In the same moment, a gust of the man's stench reached me, and I pulled back further, covering my nose and mouth with one hand. Strong fumes of spirits mingled in the reek of him. Entering the tavern? Leaving it? I asked aloud, "Mr. Cook, are you all right?"

Another groan. I edged closer, trying to see in the settling darkness and not step where either the man or his spittle might lie. Holding my basket like a shield, I also tried not to inhale as I reached across to the door and seized the tavern's brass knocker.

From the ground came a harsh repeating heave of sound. A cough? No, it was a laugh. Oh, that horrible man, he had seized the hem of my skirt and was pulling on it, forcing me to grab the doorframe to avoid toppling over onto him. I pounded the knocker again, frantic. A voice inside called, "Come," and I pounded a third time while I stamped my foot against the arm and hand. Old Mo's laughter increased as he caught hold of my petticoat, too, and tugged harder.

At last the door opened, and Jerushah's father, Mr. Clark, a questioning smile on his wide face, peered down at me, then realized the situation.

"Here, Moses, let go now, let the girl go," he said quickly as he crouched and took hold of the old man's fingers, forcing them to release my clothing. "Come on, you can't go to sleep out here, can you? Better come in and wait until your wife arrives. Up you go."

As Jerushah's father lifted the man, a powerful smell of soiled clothing and urine assailed me, and I gagged, pulling back sharply, shaking my skirt to settle it back into place.

"Go along to the other door, Alice," Mr. Clark told me over his shoulder as he half lifted Old Mo and took him inside, depositing him on a chair that instantly toppled with the limp body, clattering and thudding onto the tavern's wooden floor. "You want the kitchen door, child," he added.

Jerushah answered my knock at the house door and pulled me close to the kitchen's widest fireplace, where Sarah and Mrs. Clark sat hemming sleeves with small careful stitches. Sitting next to Jerushah on the padded settle, I took one side of her woolen skirt onto my lap while she spread out the other; we could work toward each other as we turned the inner seams. My toes tingled as they thawed. The moment outdoors fell from my thoughts. All was peace and gentleness and the sweet goodness of a clean home. And so quiet! The three smaller children of the house must already be snug in the big bed upstairs.

"How is your mother?" Mrs. Clark asked softly. Like her daughter, her hair gleamed in dark braids, pinned into careful round coils at the sides, and she wore a tidy and matronly lace cap over them. Her eyes were dark as Jerushah's, but her face was so much smaller that she seemed all made up of deep gazing and a small gentle mouth.

"She does well, thank you, and she asked me to tell you we'll start sugaring-off next week, most likely." Half the village traded with my mother for maple sugar each spring, often bringing their own pans to form the boiled-down syrup into sugar cakes.

"Thank you, Alice. We'll be ready, and your mother must tell me if she requires extra hands for the boiling. She has William, I know, but your older brothers—Has she heard from them this winter?"

"No, ma'am." I kept my gaze down toward the stitching. Everyone wanted to know whether Charles and John were making their fortunes in the gold fields in California. Two others from the village had gone West also, the Staunton boys, and it was whispered that they were rich as kings and might never return. It was embarrassing that Charles and John had not found gold, or any other riches, so far. But our family didn't speak about such things. "It takes so long for the letters," I said aloud, and everyone nodded.

"That's what I was just telling Sarah," Jerushah said. "She sends a letter each month to her mother, but it must take months for those to arrive, and more months to get a reply."

I nodded politely. I wasn't convinced that Sarah's parents could read or write at all. "Sarah, what about the lady who

13

brought you here, that Miss Farrow? Does she ever write to you?"

"Only once," our dark sister whispered. "With no news."

Mrs. Clark reached a half-gloved hand across to pat Sarah's. "We say, 'No news is good news,' dear," she offered encouragingly. "Somehow bad news always arrives safely, but good news isn't in such a hurry."

Jerushah glanced sideways, and I knew what she thought, too: that Sarah might never hear from her family, so far away and so powerless. I struggled to find something to cheer everyone—surely talking about Senator Webster's betrayal was not the topic. I felt a second wave of discomfort, knowing my father favored Webster, not Uncle Martin's abolitionist position. And here was Sarah in front of me, the very proof of Uncle Martin's argument.

Jerushah changed the topic, asking instead, "Is it true, Alice, that your uncle is headed West? He was at the store talking about it when I went for more thread this afternoon."

"I didn't know until today," I admitted. Every turn of the talk came back to what I didn't want to think about. "He says he leaves on Monday's stage. He'll have a printing press taken West to meet him in Illinois."

"Illinois!" Sarah squeaked. "It's dangerous in Illinois! There are rough people, and wolves, and the rivers!"

"Not all at once," Jerushah teased. "Besides, if Martin Sanborn is setting up a printing press, I'll be bound to say he's headed for a large town. Would it be Springfield, Alice?"

"I should think so. He'll want people to subscribe, and shops to market their goods. Mrs. Clark, how many people live there?"

Jerushah's mother paused to think. "My husband's cousin lives in Springfield, you know. I believe she said it was twice the size of Upton Center or St. Johnsbury already. And it is growing rapidly, since so many settlers must pass that way. You must all be so eager to see him succeed, Alice."

"He always finds a way," I admitted. In fact, all the Sanborn men prospered. Everyone said they had a sixth sense for how to choose their way. Look at my father's well-set sugar woods, and my older brother William's business in rakes—both thriving. I wondered, "Perhaps he'll also find a wife in Illinois." And we all giggled, even Mrs. Clark. Uncle Martin's limp never interfered with his attraction to young women. But he swore he'd never marry until a woman could be trusted not to slow down his work! So far, no candidates for marriage had convinced him they'd enhance his efforts.

"He'll leave a large position open at the *North Star* newspaper," Mrs. Clark mused. "I suppose the editor will have to find two people to do the work your uncle has done."

I blushed at the compliment to my uncle and was about to reply when shouts from the dooryard made Jerushah and me start up—and Sarah gave a squeak of fear.

Mrs. Clark only clucked with annoyance. "Some fool's drunk and seeking a fight," she guessed. "Girls, go to the back bedroom and close the door—be sure to latch it—while I see what's to be done to sort this out." She tugged her dark skirt straight, buttoned a woolen jacket over her blouse, and headed for the door, as the three of us scurried through the shadowy kitchen, baskets and sleeves and skirt left behind us.

Dropping the heavy bar across the back bedroom door, we gave ourselves a safe barrier. Then we all pressed close to the unshuttered upper half of the window to try to see whether there was indeed a brawl in progress. I wondered whether Old Mo had something to do with it.

The sky hung dark beyond the barn, sprinkled with cold stars that gave little light. Jerushah positioned herself at the far edge of the window for a tighter angle, toward the wing of the building where the tavern door stood partly open and a spill of candlelight and fire-blaze flickered golden on the soiled snow of the path. Two men, one bulky and dark, the other rail-thin, stood shouting at each other. Neither could be Old Mo. When the larger one moved, I could tell from the tilt of him that it was my uncle.

"He'll not go with you," the thin one, Jerushah's father, declared. "What's more, I won't have you ask him again. His place is here, and you know it."

"And you know this town's already half empty," my uncle roared back. "Between the gold out West and the fact that only rocks grow here, it's no place for a young man to make his way. Let him loose, if only for a few years. He'll be twice the man he is now, and"—my uncle's voice dropped to almost a plea—"he's a damned fine young man already, Ethan. Give him a chance to see a little of the world, and to make a difference for his own nation. Send him with me. You know I'd care for him as if he were my own."

Mrs. Clark came forward from the house, to stand next to her husband. "But you've had none of your own, Martin," we heard her say crisply. "And he's ours, not yours, and he stays." She looked behind her, and I realized Jerushah's tall, lanky brother Matthew stood listening at the doorway into the tavern. "There's a time to ride out, and a time to stay with your own. He stays."

My uncle's shoulders sagged in defeat—he couldn't argue with a lady. Next to me, I felt Jerushah's stiff frame soften with relief. Sarah, caught between us and too short to see the figures beyond, looked up at me and asked, "Are they angry at each other? Are they fighting?"

"No," I assured her with a quick hug. "Nobody's fighting. They're just loud, sometimes. Everyone's safe."

"Oh. I'm glad." She tucked her small hand into mine and squeezed. "Will you miss your Uncle Martin, Alice?"

"I will." Unspoken, I heard more of my own thinking: How could Matthew stay here, when Uncle Martin invites him to the great adventure of going West? If I were a young man, I'd be on that wagon. My fists clenched.

Jerushah turned to meet my eyes, over Sarah's capped head. "Matthew won't stay forever," she admitted. "He hates the tavern. He's told me. Most likely your uncle knew that and was being kind."

A thud from beyond the kitchen meant the house door had closed again. The three of us rejoined Mrs. Clark beside the fire, where she shook a handful of corn into a pan, inviting us to pop the kernels and turn the evening into something festive, a celebration of girls and women in the comfortable space we'd made our own. Most likely, I was the only one wishing to wander beyond its safe enclosure.

Then I remembered the presence of Old Mo in the night, and hoped his wife had taken him far from North Upton, back to Greenbanks Hollow or wherever it was he'd walked from.

CHAPTER 2

Later that night, restless, I slid out from the warm cocoon of my bedcovers and pressed up against the angled window that let the moonlight into my room. I breathed softly against the frosted glass. The heat of my breath melted the white rime. Cupping my hands, I forced a circle to open through which I could see the moon-bright farmyard.

A movement against the moonlit wall of the horse barn caught my eye. Had a horse been left loose? No, it was a person: a short man pressing aside the barn door and slipping quietly into the space where the animals stood. Far too short to be a Sanborn—my father and his brother Martin could never look so small. Nor would men of Jerushah's family, although they were all slender—and her little brothers were far too young to even be awake. I waited, unsure whether to wake my father. A moment later, the little man emerged, hands as empty as when he'd entered the barn, and walked away. A cap shadowed his face, and his long coat swelled over his shoulders with a short weather cape. I pressed closer to the window to catch the angle of vision down the drive and saw the moonlit figure cross the road and enter the Clark Tavern door, betrayed by a soft ruddy glow as he opened it—the dim red light of lingering coals in the fireplace, no doubt.

Of course: Jerushah had mentioned a guest at the house, most likely sleeping above the tavern, although I'd seen no other person that evening. Perhaps he'd been out late, on business in the distant town or at a farm outside the village. Though why that should lead him into our own barn, I had no clue. I watched the barn for as long as I could hold myself awake, fearful that perhaps the stranger had set a fire in it or left some other harm, but nothing changed except that the cold seeping around the window frame settled in my arms and chest, and at last I gave in and crawled back between the two layers of featherbed, to wait for morning.

When the rattle of the stove lids woke me, I tugged on my wool stockings, wrapped myself in the usual three petticoats, fastened the small buttons of my linen shirt, then slipped my long skirt on over the lot. The hem edge felt thick and uneven; brushing it nightly wasn't enough to rid it of the winter's accumulation of soiling, and I knew I'd be stitching a fresh binding for it soon. There seemed no escape from the chores of clothing and kitchen.

"Where's Father?" I asked urgently, taking over my mother's stance at the mixing bowl so she could start the griddle heating.

"In the barn," she replied, surprised. "Feeding the horses. What else?"

"Someone went into our barn last night. I saw him. A man, someone staying over at the tavern. I saw him in the moonlight."

In her long oval face, my mother's eyebrows rose, and she reached out a hand to test the heat of my forehead. "Are you certain? And why were you wakeful in the night? Bad dreams, any sweats or aches?"

I shook off her hand. "I'm not sick, Mama. I just didn't sleep right away, so I saw him. He went in, and out again."

"Not likely," she replied. "But you may tell your father when he comes in for breakfast. Give me the batter now and lay the table."

Cold wind stormed into the room, jamming the door part open as my father struggled to close it with one arm, the other holding my mother's egg basket.

"It's a northeast wind, a heavy storm coming in," he announced after he fastened the door and set down the basket. "I grained your hens, Abigail, and turned the rooster loose in the barn for the morning. There were four eggs."

That was good news. We hadn't had four eggs in one morning since October.

I knew I should wait until my father had a hot breakfast in him, but I lost patience and spilled out, "There was a man last night. I saw him. He went into the horse barn and back out again. He went to the tavern afterward. I saw him," I repeated. "In the moonlight."

"I daresay you did," my father nodded without looking at me. "He returned a hoof knife he'd borrowed. I found it hung properly in place this morning. Mind now, Alice, don't fuss." Dropping into his seat, he lifted a forkful of griddlecakes and added to my mother, "I've no time to spare, Abigail, I'm off to the mill for a fresh set of wagon boards. William won't come today, for he'll know the weather means we won't be boiling sap."

"And the sugaring-off," my mother pursued, asking no further about the man who had borrowed, and returned, the hoof knife. "Will there be enough for Saturday next?"

"I'm no weather prophet. I can't tell you that until midweek." He ate rapidly, a stack of hotcakes and a dish of side bacon, emptied his steaming cup, then scraped his chair backward again, before I even had my own plate full to settle with. "I'll head straight to the wagon work when I get back. Don't expect me in again until noon."

My mother and I exchanged glances across the suddenly emptied room.

"Borrowed a hoof knife?" I repeated. "Then why bring it back so late after dark?"

"Men's mysteries," my mother agreed. "We've enough of our own to pursue, so we'll leave them to theirs. Let's wash the sugar pans and count them up. I'm sure that there'll be syrup enough for the end of next week, even if your father won't risk saying it."

At mid morning, with three dozen assorted pans and a dozen wooden trays scrubbed and drying, I offered to check for more eggs. If they froze, they'd be of little use. Bundled in a wool coat shabby enough for the horses and chickens, and a pair of William's outgrown boots, I escaped the kitchen and pressed into the sharp March wind, with its grainy shards of snow driven against me.

Inside the barn, I shook back the wool covering from my head, letting the icy pellets fall to the sawdust-covered floor. The nearest horse, old Sam, snorted at me and shuffled backward in his wood-framed stall, then changed his mind and moved forward again, moist black nose sniffing for treats. I dipped a hand into the oats bin and offered him a taste from my flattened palm, and he picked off the kernels delicately, barely wetting my fingers. I did the same for Ely, whose thick brown coat had patches of loose, shedding hair—another true sign of spring.

Pressing past the horse boxes, and then the lambing pen with six enormous ewes stuffed full of the earliest lambs to come, I reached the nests where my mother's prize brown Leghorn hens brooded warmly. If I were blindfolded, I thought, I could tell where in the barn I was, just by the scent of it: the cedar and pine aroma of clean sawdust at the door, the thick dark comfort of horse bodies and their gleaming round droppings, then the sour smell of the sheep, and at last the chickens—whose aroma took on an acid sourness in the late winter months but who also scented the air with feather and cracked corn and something clearly of birds, not of beasts. I closed my eyes for a moment to

21

pay more attention, turning in a circle, sampling the air in each
direction.

A cold gust of outdoor air whipped my face, and I opened
my eyes at once, looking toward the doorway. William? Or my
father? No, it was the man I'd seen from my bedroom window
the night before. His back toward me, he struggled to hold the
door against the storm. When he turned my way, he gave a
small jerk of surprise.

"I beg your pardon. I wasn't expecting anyone here," he said
politely. In the soft light of the barn I could see he was young,
about the age of Jerushah's brother Matthew. "You'll be the
daughter of Ephraim Sanborn, then? My name is Solomon. I'm
only leaving for him some papers he was expecting." His voice
came fluid and soft, the words spoken more slowly than those
of our own village might say them.

I nodded and said, "I came for the eggs."

Sam's massive head and neck extended out of the front box,
stretching for the stranger, who took time to scratch the big
horse's face before setting a canvas bag down next to the door.
When he looked into our horse's eyes, a wide gentle smile
stretched across the man's face. With one hand he still held the
door behind him. "That's a fine old fellow," he said with a nod
toward Sam, then added, "I won't stay. Would you kindly let
your father know the bag is here for him?"

The young man retreated and, after one more flashing smile,
backed out the door, shutting it snugly behind him.

I hurried to check the nests, reaching under each hen in turn,
finding two more eggs and adding some clean straw to cover
them and hold them in the bottom of my basket. Jerushah must
know more about this man, or boy; I needed to ask her. I headed
for the door, then stopped and looked at the canvas satchel with
its buckled leather strap.

What was in it? What papers would my father need? Although

I knew in that instant that I'd regret it, I crouched down and tugged at the buckle.

Inside the satchel was a rolled bundle of clothes, and inside the clothes, I felt a square of oilcloth wrapped around something that indeed felt like papers. Dare I investigate further? The thump of Sam's leg and a short neigh of welcome startled me, and I thought all at once that my father might be coming. I turned the bag swiftly toward the wall to hide the open strap and rose to stand with my basket.

It was a false alarm—no person entered the barn, though I stood still for a long moment. So I crouched again to fasten the buckle closed, shaken at the thought of how my father would have scolded me if he'd seen me opening the bag. Already, I felt dishonest. I left the satchel in the barn, battled the wind across the dooryard to the warmth of the house, delivered the eggs to my mother's delight, and begged permission to step across the road to speak with Jerushah.

"Just a few minutes," my mother warned me. "Hurry home so you can set some dough to sour for Sunday's bread and biscuit. Mind your manners, and don't wear that old coat, put on your own."

She allowed me to continue to wear William's cast-off boots, however, though they looked far from ladylike. And she wound a woolen muffler around my face, across my mouth and nose. The kitchen darkened even as she did so, for the storm's thick walls of snow cut the daylight. From bright March to gray November in a matter of minutes! Or so it seemed.

I eased my way across the road at last and toward the faint shadow of the Clark home and tavern. The wind hurled me against the first door, and it opened abruptly to let me in—but it was the tavern door, not the house, and the same young man held it.

"Gracious heavens, come in, come in," he urged and tugged

at my arm. William's long bootlaces betrayed me, catching one foot against the other, and I tumbled through the opening. *Bang,* went the closing door, and the golden light of a hearth fire threw shadows dancing in the room.

"I've come the wrong way," I explained when I'd caught my breath and tugged the muffler away from my face. "It's the house I want."

Another door flapped open and shut, as Mr. Clark appeared to the rear of the tavern space, arms full of split wood. "Lord preserve us, just look at the snow on you," he exclaimed. "Shake off your coat, young Alice, and you can use the back passage to the kitchen, where Jerushah and the others are. Be sure to shut the kitchen door snugly behind you." And he pressed me forward into the dark hallway. I'd missed a second opportunity to discover more of the young stranger. Well then, Jerushah must tell me herself.

Only the smallest of windows lit the passage between public room and private home, and there were two doors to my left. The first, latched with a simple iron bracket, appeared to lead to the cellar and might offer access to both the beverages of the tavern and the root cellars for the house. The second door shook with a blast of wind, and I realized it was the house door where I usually entered. And there in front of me was the way to the kitchen, with the warm scent of roasting potatoes passing toward me. I rapped on it and lifted the latch, stepping into a bright candle-lit space where Jerushah and Sarah sat at a table, reading aloud turn by turn, and Mrs. Clark bustled among the pots and kettles on her wide cast-iron cookstove.

"Alice! Did the storm blow you over to us?" Mrs. Clark laughed and waved me toward the table. "The girls are reading to me from a wonderful story. You may join them, my dear. Or did your mother send you for something? Can I help you?"

"No, thank you, ma'am. I've only come to ask—to ask Jerushah something." I fumbled, not sure how to begin the subject in front of Mrs. Clark.

"Ah, you girls! Well, I'm in the midst of frying salt pork for tonight's beans, so you'll have to talk with the cook in the kitchen, so to speak."

Jerushah stood to take my coat and laid it near the stove to dry. "Come sit with us. It's the most marvelous story, tragic and tender, about a boy in England, named David Copperfield. We have ten chapters of it already, thanks to Aunt Mary Clark's packet."

Sarah stood also, bouncing on her tiptoes. "And we can start the first chapter again so you'll hear all of it, can't we, Jerushah?"

"Yes, yes, let's start again. Mother won't mind."

"Start again if you like, I'll fetch my butter and beets from the cellar for your father's noon meal and catch back up with you." Mrs. Clark bustled out through the door I'd entered, basket over one arm.

I leaned forward, and the other girls leaned toward me, catching my urgency. "Tell me," I asked, "who is he? The guest? He's been over to our horse barn twice, looking for my father."

Jerushah laughed. "Solomon. Solomon McBride, all the way from Connecticut, and headed to Montpelier on Monday's stage. So you've seen our bonnie Prince Charlie himself. And my, doesn't he know he's handsome!"

"And sweet!" chirped Sarah. "He brought us the post, and lemon drops and cinnamon sticks as well." She scurried to fetch one of the sweets for me to sample.

Jerushah leaned closer. "He probably thinks every girl longs to follow him," she added with merriment. "But he'll never be as lovely a man as this kitchen of girls would need, will he?"

Confused, I laughed uneasily and replied, "Handsome is as handsome does, don't you think?"

"And what does Handsome Solomon McBride do here in North Upton?" Jerushah pressed. "He's talked with your brother William, and with Matthew, and spent time at the store, too. But not with us girls. He's a mystery indeed."

My heart seized up. "Could he be an informer?" I whispered. "Could he be taking word that Sarah's here, telling the slave-catchers in Connecticut or further south?"

Jerushah shook her head briskly. "No, I'm certain he's an abolitionist himself, and he's been nothing but courteous to our Sarah. In fact, to judge by the time he's spent with your uncle Martin, too, I'm guessing he's recruiting for either the Anti-Slavery Society or the colonization groups. Or both." A scuffed footstep from the hallway sent her scrambling to open the pages of the magazine in front of her.

"By Charles Dickens," she read aloud, winking at me. Gossip was ungodly; Mrs. Clark would scold if she knew we'd been talking about the guest. " 'Chapter one. I am born. Whether I shall turn out to be the hero of my own life, or whether that station will turn out to be held by anybody else, these pages must show.' "

Sarah snuggled against me, pressing a lump of horehound candy to my lips, and I kissed her palm, warm and tinted as cocoa, and held her securely as we listened to Jerushah. But my thoughts lingered on the mystery of Solomon McBride. So few men now for anyone to recruit in North Upton, and nearly everyone here was already a member of the Anti-Slavery Society. Did the stranger tell my Uncle Martin something that made him so determined to leave for the West? He wouldn't coax our William off with him, would he?

Restless, anxious, I listened to only the first chapter of the story, then excused myself to return home and help my mother's Saturday baking tasks. The storm couldn't last all that long, and on the next day, there'd surely be guests at our own table, perhaps even the minister himself. I whispered to Jerushah as she helped me with my coat, "No matter who he is, we'll keep Sarah safe."

Wordlessly, she squeezed my hand in agreement, and a solemn vow between the two of us knotted itself in that moment.

CHAPTER 3

"It's a grand holiday in the city of New York," the visiting minister continued, as my mother heaped second helpings on his plate. "When the seventeenth of March falls on the Lord's Day, as it does today, there's a parade that takes hours to march round about the city, and even those who have no Irish in them attend and salute the saint of that foreign island. And you'll know, I'm sure, Mrs. Sanborn, that the island's potato crop has failed for these past five years, so its starving remnants are more and more often among the masses in New York, striving for a new life in this great nation."

"Not only to New York," my father commented, and the minister took back the conversation again.

"Indeed. Our railroads benefit directly from these hard-working men who give their lives to supporting their large families," began the long-winded response. "In my town of Quechee, we see already the arrival of workers to lay the rail bed and prepare the way for the tracks to come. I must confess, I have little to do with the Irish workers, for they are Catholic to a man. And they live close to their labors, mingling very little in the towns that are not directly along the Connecticut River."

My mother asked, "Are they godly people, then, the Irish? In spite of their popery and rituals?"

"Godly, hmm . . . Each of us shall be judged by the Lord," the pastor intoned. "But I have grave doubts that Our Savior will look kindly on those who bend their lives to the instruc-

28

tions of a Pope in a foreign land. I have heard that the Irish women raise their children strictly according to their church, which cannot help but be of some good, but the use of fermented spirits is so widespread among the menfolk that I suspect God's judgment is already revealing to us the weak rod of popery's leadership. A godly man, if you'll pardon my saying so, ought to care more for his soul and his home than to indulge in taverns and nightly drunkenness. I fear we'll see too much of such behavior as the railroads advance northward."

"There's time to prepare," my father noted. "The rails aren't likely to approach us for another few years. Temperance in a man . . ."

I stopped listening as closely. I knew my father's views on temperance, the forsaking of strong brews. I noticed he'd forsaken his usual mug of hard cider with the noon meal, too, in consideration of the dinner guests. Slipping one hand behind my back, I fidgeted with the tight binding of my corset, trying to breathe more comfortably. No use: the Sunday garments constricted relentlessly. God must prefer shallow breaths and low voices.

Pressed up against the kitchen table, covered with an embroidered cloth to mask its makings, was an improvised extension of boards and legs, to seat the gathering of sixteen. At the farthest end, closest to the door to the parlor, sat my young cousins: Charles Junior, Janet, Orra, George, and Ida. My uncle Charles shot them stern glances from time to time, but only the smallest one, Ida, who was barely four years old, took notice of her father's attention. The others wriggled and talked in low voices, and I saw the younger two boys exchanging something across the table. I was almost sure it was a glass marble, slipped from one boy's hand to the other's. I suspected it was rolling from place to place.

Charles's wife, Julia, my mother's younger sister, sat next to our own minister, the Reverend Alexander, whose poor health made necessary Mr. Dudley's sermonizing today. Poor Aunt Julia—Mr. Alexander kept sneezing, and I doubted if she had much appetite left, after listening to him relieving his congestion repeatedly in his large and not very white handkerchief. As I looked again, she rose suddenly and said, "I'll fetch more from the stove. Let me help a bit, Abigail, you've already invested your labor in this fine meal." She rustled across the kitchen, her blue wool skirts held stiffly by a full set of hoops, far more elegant than my mother's crinoline petticoats.

My mother smiled at her sister but continued to listen attentively to Mr. Dudley. His response to a question from Uncle Martin returned the discussion to slavery and abolition and the effects of the Mexican war. My brother William's wife, Helen, excused herself to rest in the other room; she was so far along toward their first child that it seemed almost shocking to have her sit at the table among us. Discretion was more the rule for such a condition. But I supposed William wanted her to enjoy our mother's cooking and be off her feet for a bit. I felt relieved that she'd exited the room.

Thump! Uncle Martin pounded the table. "As long as one man dares imagine he can own another, this nation shows itself a land of cowardice and immorality. Taking the whip to women and children, breaking apart families, killing men for the dark stain of their outer skins, abusing them as no man in this village would even treat a weak-minded horse: it's a tragedy and a sin of enormous proportion."

An answering thump of agreement came from the Reverend Dudley. "But you'll note that Seward has taken up the challenge to resist that scoundrel Webster in the nation's capital. It was a terrible mistake to allow Texas to be declared a slave state, and the Slave Power of the South must be stopped."

Uncle Martin and the other men scraped their seats eagerly

forward. "Seward has spoken? We've heard nothing of this," Uncle Martin said quickly. "The news comes late here sometimes. Tell us more." My father nodded, too.

I straightened against the chair back and tried to pay attention as my mother and slender, youthful-looking grandmother did. Over and over, the men turned the morality, the politics, the news. Didn't they see that it all came down to one person's safety at each moment? Trapped between the table and the window, I recalled how Sarah had arrived in North Upton.

It had been a golden day in October, early in the afternoon, with school having finished at noon because so many of the children needed to help with the last haying and harvesting. A warm autumn had stretched the season, but frost could come any night, so pumpkins, other squashes, beets, turnips, carrot, onions, all must be under cover in the cellars and back rooms, clean and dry and ready for wintering over. The older boys drove horses and oxen, guiding the high-piled wagons of hay up the laid-stone ramps into each barn, while the men kept forking the stacks of dry hay onto other wagon beds. My mother, anxious because the clear sky meant a cold night ahead, labored steadily to fill baskets with root crops, and I struggled to tighten the strings around clusters of onion tops, hanging each bundle separately in the dim shed. It was a relief to step back into the golden light of the afternoon and breathe the dry leaf-and-soil scent of the nearly emptied vegetable patch.

A cloud of dust over the far stretch of the road, where it came from Cabot to our west, sent me calling to my mother. "The stage is arriving," I told her. She wiped her hands on her long apron, rubbed her back, and asked me to carry two full baskets of beets into the kitchen, as she stepped toward the board fence lining the roadside.

Only by being quick with the carrying could I join her there, waiting for the arrival of the brightly painted yellow stage with its bundles of letters, its parcels and passengers. Would they all stay over for the night? Mrs. Clark let out rooms over the tavern if the stage arrived so late that its driver wouldn't press on toward the large town of St. Johnsbury, seven miles east along the route to Portland, Maine.

Snorting and tossing their foam-flecked heads, the big stage horses pulled up next to the tavern, and the driver, Young Sam Walker, jumped down from his perch to loosen their tack and allow them to drink from the stone water tub in the yard. Within the coach I saw three persons, and the first one to emerge was a young man who gallantly held the door open. He reached up to take a bundle of clothes, it seemed, from the arms of a tall colored woman cautiously maneuvering her hoopskirts so as to neatly emerge without showing much more than her booted ankles as she stepped down. A small whimper came from the bundle, and making a hushing sound as to an infant, the woman took the wrapped child back into her arms, where I realized a bonneted face had pressed itself to the ample chest of the woman.

My mother, less stunned by the sight than I, opened the gate in the board fence and stepped across the way. Mrs. Clark joined her, and the two of them spoke in low voices with the colored woman. Disregarding whether I'd be scolded for it, I left our gateway myself and crossed the dusty road to see the child.

My mother had eyes in the back of her head. "Alice," she spoke, "help Mrs. Clark. Mrs. Clark, should Alice fetch some milk for the little one?"

"Yes, please do, Alice," our neighbor agreed, and so I had to fetch and carry again, this time from the Clark kitchen, with Jerushah following me back out into the yard, before I could see the small brown face at last.

My mother introduced me, my reward for obeying promptly. "Miss Farrow, may I introduce my daughter, Alice?" I gave a

32

half bow from the waist and halfway held out my hand, unsure what to do. The tall woman nodded graciously and loosened the clinging hands of the little girl in her arms, turning the child to face us all.

"And this is Sarah Johnson, who has come all this way from Virginia to wait for her parents and her brothers and sisters to join her," Miss Farrow said softly. "Our good friend Mr. Thaddeus Stevens, the great senator in Philadelphia, has commended her to our care."

"Yes, indeed," Mrs. Clark said almost as softly, reaching out to stroke Sarah's damp, dark cheek. "My husband told me she would arrive this month, God willing. Let's bring her into the house, for I'm sure you are both weary and ready for some relief."

With Jerushah following them, Mrs. Clark and Miss Farrow and the trembling child who was our Sarah stepped away from the road toward the house, and my mother drew me by the hand, back to our side of the road. We watched the stage driver remove several parcels and a sack of letters from the inside of the coach, and my mother called across, "Will you be staying the night, Mr. Walker?"

"I think not," he called back cheerfully. "It's a clear fine evening, and I've a mind to make sure Miss Farrow reaches her home tonight. I'd best be headed on to St. Johnsbury while the going is good."

"Well and good," my mother agreed. She turned to me. "We'll carry the other baskets into the kitchen, Alice, and lay the table for supper. But your father and William are sure to come late, so we'll sort the beetroots and carrots and bed them into the cellar while we wait."

I followed her lead, not asking for more information until we reached the kitchen together.

"Mother, who is Miss Farrow? And is that her child?"

"Miss Farrow lives with Judge Paddock and his family in St. Johnsbury," my mother replied. "She is a good lady, and active in the church there. You know," my mother lowered her voice, though nobody could have overheard, "Dr. Arnold's family brought Miss Farrow and her aunt north with them from Connecticut, where the aunt had been enslaved. But in Vermont, of course, the aunt was as free as any other soul and raised her niece as a true New Englander. For a young woman, Miss Farrow is quite outspoken, and she's spoken in a most moving way of the moral need to end the institution of slavery in all other states of the Union."

A slave! I had no idea that someone who had grown up with her aunt being a slave could look as elegant and imposing as Miss Farrow. But why not, indeed? I asked again, "And is that her child?"

"No-o," my mother said slowly. "Since the child's been sent by Senator Stevens, I suspect she's a fugitive from the South. We'll pray for her and her family tonight, and tomorrow Mrs. Clark is sure to tell us the story. Such a small child to travel so far without her mother!"

And that was the truth: that Sarah, being the oldest of a large family of children in a slave-holder's retinue, was due to be torn from her parents and sold away from the only home she'd known. Through friends among the northern Virginians, her parents had sent her north to safety, at last hidden in a cannily crafted double cellar near the law office of Senator Thaddeus Stevens in Lancaster, Pennsylvania. And since the senator was a Vermont son of Upton Center, still well connected there, our Sarah came north in the hands of Miss Farrow, with false papers that said she was the free-born child of the St. Johnsbury lady. It was clear to me that day that Miss Farrow had shepherded more than one child along the route north.

But it was only Sarah that I cared about at that moment. The scent of autumn leaves, the golden afternoon, the sense of safety and safe harvest, all of them glow inside me again as I think of her arrival.

Thump! Uncle Martin's customary emphasis in the argument at the Sunday dinner table broke into my reverie. I came back to myself and asked my grandmother Palmer, sitting closest to me, "If there's to be no more slavery in the new territories, will Sarah's mother and father travel freely North soon?"

My grammy shook her white-haired head and patted my hand. "Even with the Lord's strong arm of blessing, the Slave Power won't let go of the South yet, Alice. You'd best teach young Sarah patience, and teach her also to trust in Providence. Now hush, and let the menfolk sort things out."

What good was sorting things out among the menfolk, if it didn't bring relief to Sarah's situation?

Aunt Julia asked a question we'd all avoided through the dinner. "So, Martin," she inserted, with her head cocked to one side, "is tomorrow truly the day you'll leave us?"

The chatter of the children on the floor echoed loud at the silenced gathering around the table. Uncle Martin's dark wedge of furry beard worked for a moment with emotion. Slowly he said, "There's no pleasure in leaving family, Julia. And I don't expect such a fine meal again unless Ephraim brings Abigail out to the territories." My mother blushed and brushed the compliment aside. Uncle Martin leaned forward, heavy arms on the table, and turned his head to look at each of us in turn. "However, the time is upon us when each God-fearing man, and even woman, must rise and speak the truth. If slavery spreads to the territories, this nation shall never free itself from the enormity of its sins. I'm off on the stage tomorrow, and with the Lord's help and a few good men in Springfield, I'll have a newspaper in print by the end of April, perhaps sooner. There's no time to lose."

My father leaned heavily against the table, and the wood groaned. He countered my uncle: "You're feeding a wildfire of dissent that can only do evil for the nation, Martin. It's the Union that matters. Press the South toward freeing the slaves all at once, and there's sure to be chaos and ferment. A mere thirty years ago, it took the Missouri Compromise to hold the slave states with us. What price will you charge us now?"

"It's the price of salvation or damnation," cut in our minister, the Reverend Alexander. "Slavery's the deepest of sins, destroying human souls. Not only the souls whose bodies are beaten and chained, but the souls also of those who hold the whip."

"No doubt," my father agreed, and I saw my mother nodding vigorously from where she stood by the dry sink. "No doubt that slavery's a terrible sin. And it's our task to tutor the South, that she be weaned from this darkness. But let no man provoke the failure of the bonds that hold our states together!" He glared at Uncle Martin.

My mother spoke. "Is there no hope of peaceful change? With the territories open to settlement, the freedmen already move West with their families."

I nodded, and murmured my mother's earlier conclusion, "One man at a time, we can save them."

But my brother William and my uncle raised their voices together, and, to my surprise, William's was the louder. "One man at a time will not save the nation. God's burden is on our shoulders now to act. Thousands upon thousands of men, women, and children live under the lash and in conditions of degradation and dread."

Uncle Martin cut back in. "Alice, and Abigail, to save one at a time is what the Clark home does, keeping the little colored child safe, and what Miss Farrow does, as she brings one at a time to Vermont's free hills. But can you not see the failed reasoning already? Where is that child's family? Torn apart, sold like beasts at the auction block? We have already failed for lack of taking the stand we should have taken thirty years back. And our slowness is costing us lives and souls in each hour of each day."

Embarrassed, I pulled back from the table and carried a stack of plates to my mother, who wrapped an arm across my shoulder. My mother leaned close to me and whispered, the warmth of her breath against my cheek. "You and I and the other women, we'll carry forward, taking care of each soul that comes our way. God may save us from a bitter war, if we can tame the passions of our menfolk."

Unexpected tears sprang to my eyes, and I buried my face for a moment in my mother's shoulder to hide them. She curled her arm more tightly around me, then pressed a cloth into my hand. "There's work to be done," she suggested gently. "Each clean dish, each fresh meal, is a little place where goodness may grow."

Overhearing the words, William's wife, Helen, came back from the parlor and took up a cloth herself, and the men rose to take their conversation to the parlor. But Uncle Martin stood stiffly by the table. "I have packing to complete. Abigail, Ephraim, I'll come tomorrow at mid-morning. The stage is due at noon."

"I've papers for you to take to Montpelier if you would," said my father, awkward with half a thought, more of it hanging unspoken.

"Then I'll stop again this evening for them," Uncle Martin quickly responded, a short shake of his head cutting off further mention of what the mysterious papers might be. He touched my mother's arm and said a short thanks for the good meal and fine company, then tramped heavily out the door.

On the floor, the children lay silent, watching. As the men moved into the parlor and stirred the fire on the hearth there, I saw Charles Junior slide away from the younger children to join his father. Janet, already maternal at the tender age of eight, pulled from a pocket a Bible tract and began to read a story from it to the younger three, who snuggled against her in a mound of tired but willing little bodies.

Helen asked my mother, "Have you met that other man who'll take the stage tomorrow with Martin? The young man from Connecticut, Mr. McBride? They say he's wrapped the girls around his finger in the week he's stayed here." She eyed me with a teasing gaze.

"Not I," I protested. "He's too pretty. Mother, that's the man who was in our barn the other evening, and again last night, first with a hoof pick to return, then to leave something else for Father."

"We'll not discuss your father's business on the Sabbath," my mother said firmly. Helen and Aunt Julia looked disappointed. My mother added, "Helen, tell us instead about the child you're bearing. How much movement? Is it the movement of a boy or a girl, do you think?"

And so we were back to womanly conversation, speaking of children and birth and cooking and clothing. But I slipped outside after all the family and the ministers left and sampled the evening for myself. The sky had cleared, and, although a hint of pink light hovered to the west, in the east a scattering of stars already prickled above the trees. Equally out of my reach, since I had no permission to go there, glowed a curtained light at the Clark home and another over the tavern. Under foot the ground ridged and sank unevenly, patches of ice amid troughs of half-thawed, half re-frozen mud. From the distance, I could hear the rush of the swollen river beyond our fields, and the crashing of the waters at the mill dam not much farther off. Close to the house, there were few sounds; the dripping icicles had frozen again in the cold night air, and the handful of spring birds kept silent in their hidden places. Up in the hills, a chorus of barks and wails rose all at once: coyotes hunting together. Over the sound, a louder, deeper one rose and cried to the skies. A second joined it. Wolves. I shivered and turned to go inside, to tell my father that there were wolves nearby.

At least, I reflected, the wild creatures around us would keep humans out of the northern woods at night. No slave-hunter or bounty seeker would track our Sarah to the safe haven of North Upton, Vermont. Or so I believed, that March evening. Only Uncle Martin's impending departure disturbed my part of the village.

Of course, I wondered once more about Solomon McBride. I would have to ask my uncle to write to me during his journey, to share what he'd discover about his fellow passenger on Monday's departing stagecoach.

CHAPTER 4

Cold nights and warm days make the sap flow in the maples. Monday morning, I woke almost as early as the sun itself, from the bang and clatter of someone shoving split wood into the cookstove. If I rose promptly and helped my mother all morning, surely she would let me visit Jerushah and Sarah in the afternoon.

And at noon, the stage would come through town—and Uncle Martin would depart! It was an important day. I flung off the bedclothes and scrambled from my nightdress to my workday shift, petticoats, skirt, and blouse. My hair, still snugly braided from the day before, demanded only a quick adjustment to smooth its surface, and I hurried down the narrow staircase.

My mother sat at the kitchen table, her journal of recipes spread open in front of her, a wood-cased pencil in her hand. She lifted an eyebrow at my hearty "good morning" and asked me to stir the oats simmering on the stove.

My father arrived in a gust of cold air, stamping his boots and then scraping the mud off them outside the doorway while he held the door open a long moment. I poured tea from the enameled pot, one cup for each of my parents, one for myself. My mother rose to take over the stirring, with a practiced scrape of the spoon to clear the bottom of the pot, and I laid the table with spoons and knives, placed the bowls at the side of the stove, and sliced the last half loaf of bread from yesterday's gathering.

"Cream," my mother reminded me, so down the cellar steps I hurried, skirt clutched to one side to keep it clean. Next to the root boxes, a small covered can of cream sat, a treasure that William had brought the day before, and I lifted it carefully to carry upstairs. Oatmeal with cream always tasted better than without! Spring had surely eased into the village, with William's cow bearing a healthy little heifer, and new milk to enjoy.

At the top step, I caught the toe of my shoe in my skirt hem and lurched forward, barely saving the can of cream from toppling. With one hand, I caught myself on the doorframe and with the other I maintained my grasp on the wire handle. I quickly stood straight again, foot untangled, second hand now supporting the base of the precious container of cream. Behind me I heard a small clatter, and realized I'd lost a sleeve button from my blouse.

My mother took the cream from me, and I told her that a button had bounced down the steps behind me. "Find it later," she said, urging me toward the table, "and sit with your father. First things first, and today the first thing is breakfast." I slid into my seat and accepted a steaming bowl of oat porridge, pouring fresh maple syrup liberally into the dish and topping it, after my father topped his own, with a splash of the benefits of William's milk cow. My mother joined us at the table, a contented silence settling over us all as we ate.

Warmth and savory aromas blessed the morning that I spent in the kitchen with my mother. Shortly before noon, I saw through the window my father and Uncle Martin come out of our barn, partway toward the house, then stand talking. Each carried a heavy leather satchel, and both seemed to be speaking at once.

My mother saw the direction of my gaze, and we pulled on

our jackets to step out into the dooryard. A basket topped with a linen cloth, filled with food to start the journey, came with us from the kitchen.

Sun heated my face, but the air nipped at my fingers, and I thrust them into my jacket sleeves. The men stopped talking; all I overheard was something about the mails. Cued by the phrase, my mother tugged two letters from her pocket: "One for Charles, one for John," she told Uncle Martin. "You'll be sure to see they go into the post?"

"I will," my uncle promised. He threw one bear-size arm around my mother's waist, and the other around mine. "I'm leaving Ephraim with the two most lovely ladies of the East," he continued. "Small wonder that I can't persuade him to come with me." His beard, lowered suddenly in emotion, scratched against my cheek.

I wriggled to press a quick kiss to the patch of skin above the beard. "Write to us often," I suggested. "Send us a page of your newspaper, too." I choked, unable to say more.

My father stepped close and drew my mother out of Uncle Martin's arm, into his own, so the two of them stood together. My uncle released me also, to take the strap of the second satchel. One bag to either side of him, he resembled a peddler.

With a cough first to clear something from his throat, my father growled, "The Lord bless you and keep you, Martin."

"The Lord bless you also, Ephraim. Remember, He who gave us life, also gave us liberty," Uncle Martin pronounced. His eyes flickered to the inn across the way. At that moment, Mr. Clark and Solomon McBride came out from the tavern door, and Mrs. Clark followed Jerushah and Sarah out the kitchen way. They joined us at the roadside, bundles and baskets and another satchel among them.

The bright jingle of harness bells interrupted the leave-taking, and Mr. Clark offered a pail of water to the steaming horses.

Jumping down from his seat in a flourish of bearskins and blankets, Young Sam, the red-cheeked driver, seized two satchels in one hand, the third in the other, and flung them up onto the roof of the stage. "A good day for travel," he called out, "but let's be on our way west, gentlemen, before the sun loosens the roads into deep mud."

And just like that, with the creak of the wheels, the stamping of the two horses, and the bells again jingling, the newly loaded stage was under way. My uncle, seated at the far side of the coach from us, thrust an arm up in farewell. I couldn't see his face—just the suddenly serious face of Solomon McBride, peering out the back of the coach, giving a small wave that I thought, without much reason to think it, might even be meant for me.

A hand on my shoulder turned me from the road. My mother said firmly, "Set your hands to work, and let God hold your heart. Go lay the table for dinner, Alice. I'll speak a moment with Mrs. Clark and will follow you inside directly."

With a start, I realized my father had already returned to our barn, where the door thudded as he closed it behind him. Mrs. Clark shooed Jerushah and Sarah back toward their house, although a nod from each, toward me, made me sure we'd all find time to talk later in the afternoon. My mother's hand squeezed harder and pressed me on my way. "Now," my mother instructed.

I slid along the icy ruts toward the house. The sooner our dinner was laid, eaten, and done, the sooner I might have leave to see my friends. The clang of the school bell for the end of noon recess reminded me that most of the other children of the village were in the classroom. Thank goodness for my mother's concern about fevers and spring colds—I had another week of freedom at least.

"He who gave us life, also gave us liberty," I repeated aloud as I laid out the spoons and forks at each of three places at the kitchen end of the big table. Uncle Martin was reminding us all of why he was headed West—to fight the Slave Power and see that the territories, and someday our nation, would see no more slavery.

I should be doing more to fight the good fight, myself. I resolved to ask my mother later: Could we shelter another child like Sarah, in our own home? Or find a way to help Miss Farrow with her work?

After the meal, my mother, it seemed, had little time to spare for larger conversations, and instead more items on her list to pursue. "Set aside thoughts of your Uncle Martin until your prayers tonight," she instructed me. "For the moment, I need you to fetch apples from the attic, and two pumpkins, and I want a bunch of dried thyme and some mint as well."

I knew better than to complain; with sugaring-off just a few days away, every minute must apply wisely to preparing the food. Our neighbors would surely bring more, but as the hosts, we took pride in setting a full table to start with.

Up the steep stairs to the attic I scrambled. I caught my skirt on the point of a nail as I swished over the last step. Dislodging the fabric carefully to avoid a tear, I remembered the lost sleeve button from the morning and resolved to look for it on my next errand into the cellar.

Lit from a window at each end, the long attic captured a peace that no other part of the house held. Baskets of apples, pumpkins, and other squashes sat in a neat line down the center of the long room. Gaps in the line proved that nearly half a year had passed since harvest. I ducked so as to not brush against a paper-wrapped bundle of thyme hanging from a nail in the ceiling, then remembered my mother had asked for some. After nudging a half-empty apple basket toward the space at the top of the stairs, I added two pumpkins to the basket and laid a bundle of thyme on top. And mint? Ah, there above the shelves where the outgrown shoes were stacked. A few dried leaves fell out of the bundle as I unwound its string from the overhead nail, and I rubbed one between my fingers, savoring the scent.

With my basket piled high, I took a moment to peer out the farther window. Smoke rose from a handful of house chimneys, and also from the schoolhouse, at the end of the village. Pressing my face against the cold glass, I wriggled to see up on the ridge and spotted a column of steam from the sugar camp. Was William already there with my father? No, there he was—walking briskly along the road toward our farm. I scurried to the east end of the attic to see him turn toward our house, but he wasn't in view.

Angling from the other direction, I spotted him, standing in front of the Clark house, talking with Matthew. Jerushah's brother looked upset, his dark brows lowered in his thin face, and he gestured toward the ridge, then pressed his thick hair back irritably from his forehead, and he spoke again. William patted his shoulder and leaned close. I wished I could hear them.

A moment later, they separated, with Matthew headed into the tavern. I pulled back from the window, and, as I did, Matthew suddenly looked up toward me. The movement must have caught his eye. One hand shielding his gaze, he stared toward me, his face knotted again with concern or perhaps anger.

I seized my basket and carefully descended to the kitchen, in time to see William enter with another can of fresh milk. Although I carried it at once to the cool cellar, this was no time to linger for searching out my sleeve button. I bolted back to the kitchen, where my mother offered to cut William some bread and ham, but he said he had already eaten and was headed for sugaring.

"William," I interrupted, "what did you and Matthew talk about? Is something wrong?"

My brother shrugged. "Nothing. Matthew wanted some milk, too, and I said I'd have more this evening." He edged toward the door. "Father's waiting, I'd best get up the hill. Mother, Helen said to tell you she thinks tonight might be the night."

"I'll be ready," my mother promised. "I'll look in on her after supper."

William nodded and backed out of the kitchen.

I asked, "Mother, does she mean the baby? Is it coming tonight?"

"I should think Helen is hoping so, but first babies often take a long time to arrive," came the reply over one shoulder. "Fetch the long knife, Alice, and start cutting the pumpkins, while I set these apples to stewing. They're too soft for pie, but they'll make a good sauce."

By mid-afternoon, we had bowls of stewed pumpkin cooling, and two large pots of applesauce, as well as a fresh batch of bread dough rising. The list for Saturday's sugaring-off grew ever longer, though, as we thought of more items that mustn't be forgotten.

"Should I go across the road and borrow Mrs. Clark's big stew pot, the way we did last year?" I offered.

"Not yet," my mother said as she scratched off one task and added another. "That will be for Thursday. And I know she has cups, but those can wait until Friday evening." She looked up at me. "You need an errand to run, don't you? Well enough, you may tell Jerushah's mother that Helen's baby may come tonight, and would she kindly join me in a visit there, after supper. Come home in an hour, to mix tonight's biscuit."

Without even pausing for a jacket, I stuffed my feet into William's cast-off boots and splashed through the mud and snow-melt of our dooryard. At the Clark house, an unmistakable aroma of raisin cakes met me, along with my friends.

So that I wouldn't forget, I gave Mrs. Clark my mother's

message right away, and she told Jerushah to finish wiping the dishes clean, so she could inspect her basket of birthing needs. Of all the women in the village, Jerushah's mother was the one everyone wanted for a baby's birthing.

Sarah wriggled in excitement as she threw her arms around my waist. "You'll be an aunt, Alice. Aren't you glad?"

"I suppose so!" A person couldn't help smiling at Sarah's enthusiasm. "I feel like I've been an aunt to my cousins, though, because they're so young. Charles Junior, Janet, Orra, George, and Ida," I rattled off. "God willing, this will be an easy birth. My mother says Helen is built for having babies. But because it's her first, it could still take a long time." I squeezed Sarah and nuzzled the top of her head, noticing the lavender scent of her cap. Then I took up a cloth to help Jerushah.

Sarah scrambled for her book and announced that she would read the second chapter of *David Copperfield* to us as we worked. Mrs. Clark bustled back and forth, up the stairs to her bedroom, back to her large covered basket, and up again.

As Sarah leafed through the pages to find her place, I said to Jerushah, "William told Matthew he'll have fresh milk for you tonight. Did Matthew tell you? I'm so glad to have cream again, aren't you?"

Jerushah agreed, but added, "I don't think we need more milk just yet, for your brother brought us nearly a gallon last night. Boys and men, they don't remember these things."

"No, they don't," I agreed. But I was puzzled. William always knew where he'd delivered milk, and how much. He could rattle off his business numbers readily. Why did he say he'd been talking with Matthew about bringing more milk? "Maybe I heard him wrong," I added. But I knew I hadn't. I suspected William of barring me from some form of adventure. Didn't he realize I needed something more than kitchen labors in my days?

We covered the stacks of clean dishes so no dust would land

on them, and Jerushah poured hot water from the simmering kettle into a large brown teapot. I offered to go down to their cellar to fetch some milk. Cup in hand, so I wouldn't have to bring up the large milk can, I stepped into the hallway between the house and the tavern, where I'd seen the cellar door before. Behind me, Jerushah called out, "Be sure to set the brick against the door to hold it open for light—it's so dark down there!"

The air in the Clark cellar smelled musty and damp, as if the floor wasn't properly frozen. But it was cold under my stockinged feet. I found the covered box where the milk and butter were stored and reached in for the milk. Sure enough, there were two large milk cans there, quite full, and a smaller one from which I filled the cup to take to the kitchen. Cream floated on the surface, thick and golden even in the dim light.

I closed the box and looked around me. Bins of vegetables in sand and sawdust lined the walls, as they did at home. Shelves of canned goods caught the light, reflecting it. Barrels that must be ginger beer and other beverages for the tavern sat on brick-and-board platforms to hold their taps well above floor level. At the far end, several baskets seemed to hold just dirt; I walked closer to look and could see nothing poking up from the earth in them. Next to those baskets was a door, latched not with the customary shed latch of bar and ledge, but with a proper door latch that could be thumbed open from either side. Why?

Jerushah called from the top of the steps. "Alice? Did you find the milk?"

"Yes, I did," I called back, and scurried to pick up the cup and scramble up the stairs. "Sorry to take so long, I was daydreaming."

"Daydreaming? About what?" Jerushah took the cup, latching the cellar door shut and gesturing for me to precede her into the kitchen.

"Oh, just about cellars and food and such," I said awkwardly.

It would sound very odd if I asked why the door in her family's cellar had a thumb latch, wouldn't it? Besides, it probably had something to do with having a tavern. To change the subject, I asked, "Where did Mr. McBride head toward yesterday? I know he took the stage with my uncle Martin. Is he headed West, too?"

"Not him! He said he has business at the state capitol, and he's likely to be back again on Friday," Jerushah reported. "Although I don't know why he comes to North Upton. Wouldn't you think he'd want to stay in Upton Center, by the courthouse, if he's working for the governor or legislature?"

"He's our mystery man," I agreed. "What do you think of him?"

"Not much! Too pretty by half and thinks enough of himself so there's no need for anyone else to think of him. Oh, Alice," Jerushah teased as she poured tea for the four of us—Mrs. Clark bustled past again, dropping a soft roll of cotton into the basket and then clucking to herself and whirling back toward the upstairs bedrooms—"Alice, don't say you're taken by the looks of Mr. Solomon McBride?"

"Of course not!"

Jerushah seized my face between her two hands and tilted her own to look more deeply into my eyes. I blushed in spite of myself and squirmed. "At least he's somebody new to look at," I admitted. "Better than the Wilson brothers!"

We all laughed, Jerushah and Sarah and I, but Jerushah held my face an extra moment before saying, "I can't imagine settling for any man, from North Upton or Upton Center or even Montpelier. Life is sweeter and more sensible with women, don't you think, Alice?"

I shook my head to say no, and she let go, an unexpected sadness in her gaze. I countered, "We all marry, don't we? It's good to look around and see what might be on hand. Love isn't always blind."

"Love isn't always judged by the eyes, either," Jerushah retorted. "The heart is connected to the hands and the ears and even the mind, as well as the gaze!" Suddenly she set her hands to her waist and gave a forced little laugh. "What nonsense! It's your sister Helen's birthing time that's making us all soft in the head. Sarah, read us another chapter from your London story. We country girls need to hear more about the city, so that we may remain grateful for our places."

Mrs. Clark landed in the kitchen again, picked up her cup of tea, then said, "Mint! That's what I need," and trotted away, this time headed for the attic, as her footsteps overhead soon proved.

A momentary darkening at the window caused me to look that way, and I saw Jerushah's brother Matthew stepping past, escorting Old Moses Cook. I shuddered, remembering the filth of the man and his foul laugh.

A thump from outside signaled the opening of the heavy tavern door as it banged against the outer wall. Men's voices spilled out for a moment, until the door closed again. Milk, and the damp basement, and the door latch, all buzzed in a restless distraction in my thoughts. In spite of what I'd said to Jerushah, I found myself thinking again about Solomon McBride. If a girl had to marry, as we all would someday, she needed to look around and think about her choices. A passion for disturbance rose up in me, and perhaps it, too, was a sign of spring.

CHAPTER 5

In spite of my mother's visit, with Mrs. Clark, to William's wife, Helen, that evening, no baby emerged. My cousin Charles Junior, the oldest of my aunt Julia's children, stayed at William's house, to be sent as a messenger if needed. Taking advantage of the calm, clear evening, my father and William boiled sap until nearly ten p.m. Likewise, my mother and I continued our kitchen tasks through the after-supper hours. Reaching my bed some four hours later than usual for a winter night, I slept soundly, without dreams.

When Charles Junior arrived after lunch on Tuesday, unable even to speak from such hurry and excitement, my mother seized her basket and a shawl, calling out to me to mind the bread still baking and see that the stewed fruit didn't scorch. Through the front room's window, I watched for a moment: with my cousin racing ahead of her, my mother strode briskly across the road, tapped at Mrs. Clark's door and exchanged a quick word, then hurried down the road and around the corner, toward William's home beyond the millrace. A few minutes later, Jerushah crossed the road to deliver a corncake from her mother, for tea.

"I can't stay," she said quickly. "My mother's gone to the birth, too, of course, so Sarah and I are watching the little ones." She flung her arms around me, her hair damp with the mist of rain just starting outside. "Come see me later, if you can!"

I doubted that I'd be able to do so. Four loaves stood cooling from the morning's baking, two sat in the oven now, and two more, covered by a cloth, waited their turn and must not be bumped or chilled, lest the tender risen dough collapse.

With care, I chose some splits of maple to feed the firebox and tucked them in among the searing hot coals. I needed to pay close attention.

I looked at the list of other preparations to feed our neighbors on Saturday and set the dried beans soaking. Then I slipped my feet into my old thin shoes, lit a candle stub, and headed down to our cellar, to search at last for my missing button.

After the steamy warmth of the kitchen, the cellar felt cold and clammy. Even the wooden steps, damp and slippery underfoot, chilled me. I shivered, almost went back up for a shawl, then determined instead to get the task done. First I looked all around the foot of the stairs, holding the candle as close to the floor as I dared without the melting wax dripping on me. I looked in the top of the closest vegetable bins, too, where the sand kept the carrots and beets cool and moist. No button.

So I dripped some wax onto a stone ledge at one side and set the candle stub into it to hold. Then, with a quick trip back to the kitchen and a check that the woodstove had enough coals to radiate a steady heat, I took a twig broom back down to the cellar and began to carefully draw it along the cellar floor, from the foot of the steps onward. By this means, I found two nails and a chip of pottery, as well as several dead beetles. But still, no button.

I returned to my candle stub and dislodged it, meaning to set it again into wax at the far end of the cellar. My button must have rolled quite far.

In the far wall of the cellar, with the candlelight, I noticed a section of wall paneled in wooden boards. Moving closer, I saw a pair of strap hinges and realized I'd found a door. A door in the cellar wall? Instantly I thought of the door I'd seen in the cellar at Jerushah's house. This door now in front of me did not have a thumb latch, or any other obvious way to open it. But it had hinges.

I made another trip to the kitchen, this time for a sturdy knife. I wedged the candle between two bricks to hold it upright. Testing along the wooden surface, I found the outlines of the door and began to clean the grooves around it. Surely this door had not been opened in some time. In fact, I could not open it; no matter how far I slipped the knife blade into the slit along the edge, the boards stuck tight in place.

Boot steps above me signaled an arrival. I called up the stairs, "Father?"

"No, it's William," came the reply. "Where are you?"

"Down here—in the cellar." I raced up the stairs, heedless of my skirt hem. "William, is the baby born? Is it a boy or a girl?"

"A boy," my older brother said cheerfully. "I've come to tell Father. But I can't spare the time to go all the way to sugar camp. When he comes down to the house, let him know, won't you, Alice?"

"I will!" And as William turned to leave, I asked urgently, "His name, William? What's the baby's name?"

An enormous grin split his face. "William Junior, of course. Tell Father!"

I was alone again, but being alone with news is entirely different from being alone and waiting. Should I ring the dinner bell to call Father down from camp? I dithered for a moment. Then the chill in the room made me realize I had ignored the fire in the stove, while seeking my lost button. Best not to call Father until the fire picked up again. And oh, my candle!

As I added a few small splits, and slid open the iron panel for air to draw into it, the fire caught almost at once. I added a larger split of maple, then went down the steps to fetch my candle stub. When I bent to pick it up from where it flickered, I spotted my button at last and pocketed it. There!

Just as I returned to the kitchen, my father indeed arrived. Outside, the gray sky and drizzling rain had brought an early darkness. "Too wet to keep boiling, and I'll be glad of some hot tea," admitted my father as he shook his coat and hung it to dry. "Any word from your mother?"

"William was just here! It's a boy!"

After that, even hot tea wasn't enough to hold my father in the house. Flinging his wet coat back over his shoulders, he stopped only to check the wood box and say he'd be back to fill it again in an hour or so. "And then," he offered, "I'll take the fire and you can visit your brother's son. A son," he repeated as he swung out through the doorway. "A grandson! William Junior!"

I glared at the woodstove holding me prisoner at the house. Resentfully, I jammed another split of wood into the firebox and stared out the window at the darkening landscape. A light flickered in the window at Jerushah's house and made me lonely once again.

Although I knew I shouldn't, I took the black iron poker from beside the woodstove, re-lit my candle stub, and went directly to the cellar, where I pried open the almost hidden door and discovered what, in the back of my mind, I had begun to suspect might lie beyond it: a cave . . . no, a tunnel, a tunnel leading toward what must be the road and then the cellar of my best friend Jerushah.

Only the shortness of my candle, and a trace of common sense, prevented me from plunging into the space beyond the cellar door.

CHAPTER 6

Bright sunshine the next morning warmed my walk to William and Helen's house to see their baby—my first nephew. I carried a basket of bread and jam and a meat pie, so heavy that I moved it back and forth from one arm to the other as I stepped cautiously along the frozen mud of the village road.

As soon as I'd walked round the curve of the road by the church, I could see through the windows of the schoolhouse. A few children sat at their desks, facing the teacher; Miss Wilson, head bent over something at her high desk, did not look up to see me pass. I worked at keeping my footsteps quiet, not wanting to be questioned about why I wasn't inside with other students! How long would my mother and Mrs. Clark agree to keep Jerushah and Sarah and me at home, instead of completing the last weeks of school?

William and Helen's house stood just beyond the village cluster of homes, next to and a little above the mill where William's rake factory took power from the Sleepers River. The waters, swollen from the rain and recent snowmelt, overflowed down William's dam as well as through the penstock that fed the millworks. Their pounding shook the small brown mill building. I supposed William to be inside, taking advantage of the high waters to drive his saws and such. Oh—if William must nurse his millworks, Helen and the baby might be without assistance. I increased my pace, though my arms ached as the basket swung from them.

When I opened the door at the little whitewashed house and stepped into the steamy heat of its kitchen, I saw there was no need to worry: Mrs. Clark stood at the stove, stirring porridge with one hand and lifting the lid of a soup kettle with the other.

"Good girl. Put your basket on the table, and rinse out this teapot for me, would you please, Alice? Yes, and there's the kettle; here, take the porridge spoon while I measure out the tea and herbs for the tisane," she rattled cheerfully. "Keep stirring. That's right, good. Now I'll take it, and you may kiss your brother's wife and see the baby, but hands in your pockets. Yes, best to wait a few days before too many people touch the babe; let him grow strong and wake up to the world a bit."

Helen lay half asleep in her bed, one arm curled around the baby, whose eyes didn't open even as I leaned across to leave a soft kiss on Helen's cheek. She smiled crookedly, adjusted her legs, and winced. "Isn't he beautiful?" she whispered to me. "He looks just like your brother, doesn't he?"

"Just like him," I whispered. If Helen thought the two looked alike, it would be kind to concur. I struggled to see some likeness and guessed the delicate eyebrows and deep-socketed eyes might support the assertion enough to keep me honest.

I inhaled the scent of the baby, faint but different, like all newborn creatures, catching at the back of my throat. Helen's strong sweated scent also spoke to me of the hard labor of bearing a baby. A hint of sour blood rose with the smell. I backed away, trying to breathe only through my lips, not my nose.

"Mother and Mrs. Clark said you did really well," I offered. A faint smile rewarded me as Helen closed her eyes again, one arm drawing the small bundled baby closer to her.

In the kitchen, steam and the clean scents of mint and lemongrass mingled. Mrs. Clark patted my shoulder and said, "Stop to check on Jerushah on your way back home, will you, Alice? Tell her I'll be back to make the noon dinner. And tell your mother her bread looks delicious. Off you go, now!"

In the short time I'd been in the house, the weather had shifted: a sharp wind tossed thick clouds, some edged with dark gray. Cold rain? Snow? I saw a trail of chimney smoke from the rake mill building and, on impulse, bolted inside to see William.

The rumble and banging of the building assaulted my ears. It shook with the force of the river passing through the penstock and turning the machine shafts. At the far end of the building a massive saw blade growled through trunks of maple that William fed to it, trimming each length. Matthew stood at the other side of the blade, catching the trimmed trunks and feeding them back to William for each surface in turn until a squared-off beam had formed.

William tugged at a long iron lever to disengage the saw from the river power. Matthew looked over his shoulder and saw me also and set down his half-trimmed length of wood. Both of them shook their heads a moment, to shake back the ability to hear. They took out cottony earplugs, each pocketing the soft clumps and moving toward me.

"It's Aunt Alice," William said with a grin, tossing a gentle fist at my shoulder. "Been paying a call on William Junior? What do you think of him?"

"He's a wonder," I replied, surprised to discover that, in fact, I meant it. "Does it amaze you, William, to see him alive and perfect like that?"

"It does indeed, though I've felt him alive and kicking well enough before now," my brother teased. His face settled into a quiet solemnity, his eyes moist. "What Nature does with such care, God blesses into our hands and hearts. An infant is proof of the truth and goodness that are born within us."

Matthew nodded. "As God the Father leads us, so we lead the children," he said softly.

The mention of truth reminded me of what I wanted to know.

"William, why did you tell me that you and Matthew were talking about more milk the other day, when you can't have been? Mrs. Clark said you already delivered the milk before. Is there a secret? I want to know!"

When my brother answered, he spoke half toward Matthew, half to me. "I'm not trying to deceive you, Alice," he said slowly. "But it's not something I want to burden Father with just now, and, if you knew, you'd feel you had to tell him."

"Are you in trouble, William?" My throat tightened. "Is it something bad? I don't have to tell everything to Father. You could tell him yourself later, when things are right again. Tell me what it is, so I can help."

"It's not that kind of secret, or that kind of trouble."

Matthew cut in, his voice harsh and sure. "You'd be telling it to Jerushah, too. It's not that we don't trust you girls, but there's danger involved, even though it's about doing what's right. You can't step into this kind of matter. Leave it in our hands, Alice. Your brother and I both know you girls will help if we need you, but for now, hold off—'discretion is the better part of valor,' " he quoted.

"Girls can be valorous, too," I argued.

"Wait," William urged. "Wait for the right time. Go home, Alice, and remain silent, as a favor to Matthew and to me, as we do our Christian duty. There's nothing wrong in this. But wait. And," he added more quickly, "there is something you and Jerushah can do to help, in the next few days. No matter what you see or hear, ensure the kitchens stay busy and active and don't let anything change. Help us to shelter our effort under such sounds and activity. Can you do that, if I promise you it's to meet the needs of others?"

Matthew clicked his tongue to say "hush," but it was too late: My brother's phrasing told me a great deal. "You're helping with a fugitive," I whispered in excitement. "Oh, William, let me help, too!"

"You see!" Matthew's arms were crossed now, as he scolded William. "They're all the same, girls are; they work it out of you if you speak at all. Now she'll be telling all the others, and the whole village will come to know."

"I won't!" I was furious. "I've kept William's secrets whenever he asked me to do so, if they were good and right. I won't say a word!"

William came close and placed both hands on my arms. "Promise, Alice? I know it's a lot to ask of you. You mustn't say a word, at least until he's safely away. Can you promise?"

"I can, and I do," I returned. "Is he here now?"

"Not now." William paused, reading Matthew's angry face, then continued: "We won't tell you when. You shouldn't have to bear that knowledge, Alice. Just help us by doing your best not to see, not to notice, and encourage the others to gaze at ordinary life events. Will you do that for me? For us? For him?"

A vision of a terrified fugitive, wounded and frightened and lost, filled me with certainty: "I'll do it, William. I will." I turned to Matthew. "And I won't say a word even to Jerushah until you say it's safe. Will you tell me straight away when it's safe?"

Matthew shrugged, then nodded reluctantly, and William squeezed me against him for a moment. Courage and excitement blazed in me. I could do anything for this good cause.

I pulled away, straightening my jacket and hat. "I'll return home right away, so Mother won't ask what has kept me so long. God bless and keep you both!"

As I hurried home, I brushed off bits of sawdust clinging to my woolen sleeves, thinking that if I had to explain about stopping at the mill, it would be harder to hold silence about William and Matthew. As I passed the tavern portion of the building, I edged to the further side of the road. A gust of wind laden with sharp icy pellets of hail followed me up the drive to the house, and the warmth of my mother's kitchen.

"I've just fed the stove," my mother said immediately. "Take off your jacket and boots and come here so I can show you how to turn the pies while they bake. Then you can help me peel potatoes."

I groaned. Peeling potatoes for so many people—and then surely carrots and turnips as well. As I hung up my things, I repeated my mother's favorite saying aloud, though I resented it at that moment: "Set your hands to work, and let God hold your heart."

Hail beat on the windows for much of the morning, changing eventually to thick, wind-blown snow. When my father joined us for his noon dinner, his exhaustion from working the horses up and down the ridge sat with us at the table, silencing us all to the level of passing the bread and jam and slicing and chewing the mutton stew, bracing for a long afternoon of work to come.

At mid-afternoon, as I fetched the sixth or seventh pail of root vegetables from our cellar, I realized I needed to talk with William again. For if he and Matthew were conducting a fugitive toward the Canada border, shouldn't I tell him about the tunnel between our two houses?

Unless perhaps he already knew. I wondered.

Chapter 7

A warm Wednesday night and Thursday's fair-faced weather took my father and William to sugar camp. Because my mother made twice-daily visits to Helen and the baby, I found myself more tied to the kitchen stove than ever before. So it wasn't until Friday morning that I persuaded my mother to let me skip across to the Clark home for a short time while the kettles and vessels of the day heated up. It was just about eight o'clock, and the day would surely be interrupted by the arrival of the stagecoach from the west, headed toward Portsmouth, New Hampshire. Before any arrivals or news complicated my day and Jerushah's, I greatly desired time to talk with my friends.

Wrapped in a shawl, with my brother's old boots on my feet, I splashed through slush and puddles on my way. Despite my knocking, nobody came to the door at Jerushah's house. I stepped inside, set my soiled boots in the corner of the hall, and padded into the kitchen, where spirited singing filled the air. No wonder my knocking had not been heard! Mrs. Clark beat the butter and eggs in her mixing bowl in rhythm, and Jerushah and Sarah urged the little ones to join the hymn, "Love Divine, All Loves Excelling." I joined with them to finish the second verse: "Take away our bent to sinning, Alpha and Omega be; end of faith, as its beginning, set our hearts at liberty."

The third verse exalted the Almighty's perfect love, and the final one sang of the new creation, making us pure and spotless. Aside from mud, it seemed a perfect hymn for the turning of

61

the year and Easter's approach, and I said so—which made Mrs. Clark smile. "We are teaching it to the younger children for our Easter morning service at the Union Church," she offered happily. She bent to pick up the smallest child, deftly wiping his face with a corner of her apron. She added, "The children's hearts are pure and spotless, even when their faces are not!" And we all laughed together.

The aroma of baking beans warmed the wide room. I helped my friends butter the pans for the gingerbread batter that Jerushah's mother was preparing. The crocks of beans had to come out of the oven and sit in the heat at the back of the stove while the pans of gingerbread went in. Directed to stir each crock, we sniffed happily at their fragrance.

"And not a drop of molasses in any of them," Mrs. Clark announced proudly. "Onions and maple and a few little additions of my own, as well as salt pork, of course. Liberty beans, we'll call them."

Sarah clapped her hands together in appreciation. Jerushah and I nodded. Molasses went into many a recipe for beans, but not in our Vermont village, where everyone knew molasses was made by slaves. Determined to ignore the dark sweetener, all of us used maple sugar or honey instead, even if some of the cakes didn't rise quite the same. Upton as a town—Upton Center, North Upton, West Upton, and Greenbanks Hollow—made and sold maple sugar for much of Vermont and beyond.

With the gingerbreads baking, and plenty of hands to wipe the dishes and guide the little ones, Mrs. Clark excused herself to "refresh herself" and the three of us could talk about important things. Not about Helen and William's baby, for it was still too soon to talk about him. But Jerushah said right away, "Mr. McBride is coming back on the stage today! Papa heard it from the doctor's wife, who saw him in Montpelier. Alice, do you think he's sweet on you?"

"On you, perhaps," I suggested. "He's only seen me out in the barn. But maybe," I hushed my voice and whispered, "maybe he's coming back to see William and Matthew about something."

Sarah whispered, "About my mother and father? Could it be about that? Maybe he's seen them on their way north!"

Jerushah and I exchanged speaking glances. She replied soothingly, "They'll come someday, Sarah, but let us not raise our hopes too soon. We'll pray for their safety, and we'll pray that a letter may reach you from them. Who knows what may arrive on the stage?"

William's secret swelled inside me. But I'd promised not to tell. Instead I asked Jerushah, "Did you know there is a doorway in your cellar?"

She frowned in puzzlement. "Do you mean the doorway to where Papa keeps the extra barrels of cider? Back behind the stairs?"

"No, another one. I noticed it last week, and there is one in our cellar, too. I think they may connect underground. Can we test them?"

Jerushah flashed a look over my shoulder. "Mama is coming back inside. I can hear her in the passageway. Hush. We'll find a way later, after your sugaring-off. It's all too busy now."

Sarah agreed excitedly while placing a hand to her mouth.

All too soon I realized I should return home. I carried a sack of two dozen spoons, a large collection that the tavern provided. Borrowing them for the sugaring-off would make sure more people could eat at once. And my mother could mark another item from her list as "complete."

Passing our horse barn on my way to the kitchen door, I heard the squeal of a sheep in pain. One of the ewes, injured? Or lambing too soon? Arms full, I rushed to report the sound to my mother, and she pulled a pan of gravy off the heat in haste.

"Keep stirring," she ordered. "If I'm not back here in five minutes, ring the dinner bell for your father to come down from sugar-camp." Still in her apron, she hurried out.

I stirred and worried. Lambs too soon could happen by order of Nature, for sometimes the ram jumped the fence early and mingled with the ewes before the date planned. But more often it was a sign of trouble—and trouble for the ewe as well as the lambs, which we could ill afford.

Minutes later, the bell outside the kitchen door rang vigorously—my mother must have found the situation in the barn more than she could handle alone. By the thumps that followed, I guessed she had jumped down the steps and returned to the barn. I heard the sheep crying out again for a moment, while the barn door opened and then shut.

I moved the tea kettle onto a hot burner of the stovetop, set the gravy to one side where I could reach it easily to stir it again, and checked the firebox. A good bed of dark red coals hissed as I opened the small iron door. I added two small splits of maple but left the draft slide closed, not wanting the fire to heat up again too suddenly.

My mother reappeared, sleeves rolled high, arms wet and reddened. "Your father is easing the second lamb out. He'll need to go back up to sugar-camp to continue boiling with William. I can pack up dinner for the two of them."

She sent me to the barn to watch and learn. "Come back to fetch the dinner pail when he's ready to ride back up."

In the dooryard, Ely, halter rope looped around a fencepost, stamped one hoof and nickered at me as I came outside. I slipped quietly into the barn, trying not to disturb my father as he wrestled with the confusion of legs that were ewe and new lamb and lamb still only half born. I grabbed an armful of hay and dipped a pail of water out of the trough, and took them to Ely. Then I returned to my father.

Crouched against the outside of the sheep box, I watched between the rails and tried to keep my skirts on the dry straw. A tiny pair of legs protruded already from the ewe's nether parts. One handful at a time, Papa unfolded the other legs and small body of a dark lamb that had been stuck in the birth canal, and at last he eased its wide head out. A gush of red fluid and the white, worm-shaped afterbirth followed. The heavy tissue of the birth sac still covered the dark lamb's face, and it was not breathing.

My father pulled back the covering and wiped his large hand over the little nose and mouth, clearing away a thick wetness. He cupped his hand around the nostrils and blew gently into them repeatedly, until, with a little twitch, the lamb began suddenly to breathe on its own. I felt my own breathing start again—I hadn't realized I was holding it.

"Ask your mother for some warm rags that I can wrap around the first lamb," he told me quietly. "She's been away from her mother too long. Quick, now."

My mother must have expected the request—for in the kitchen she pressed into my arms a bundle of flannels, so heated that I could barely clutch them and held the door for me to exit the kitchen again. At the barn, I nudged the door with one foot, then angled my shoulder to pull it open further.

The dark lamb, pressed against the ewe, had already found the bag of milk and suckled as its mother licked its wool. The earlier one, white fleece matted with birth fluid, lay in my father's lap as he rubbed it vigorously with a handful of straw. I pressed the hot flannels through the slats into his hands, and he wrapped them around the small body, still rubbing steadily.

"Now can you put her with the other one, to suckle?"

"Not yet. She needs to be warmer first." Back and forth his hands moved, his body forming a cave of heat around the chilled animal.

I looked around me. The other five ewes, penned away from this one, ignored my father and snuffled along their feed box. "Should I give them some grain?"

"Half a box. They had grain this morning already. Give them some hay. And Alice, fetch some water for this pen also."

I looked at the hem of my skirt, thought about trying to tie it up for cleanliness, then realized it was already thoroughly soiled. So I fetched, filled, and poured without further regard for my skirt. Tonight, I'd have to brush and clean the bottom panel as best I could, to be presentable for the next day.

Sugaring-off! My father seemed to hear my thought, for he paused in his care for the lamb, then stiffly rose and placed it against the mother's side, tugging the flannel out of the way of the ewe's questing tongue and teeth. We watched together as the warmed lamb began its nuzzling of the teat. I sighed. My father smiled at me and handed me the pieces of flannel.

"Take these to your mother now. I'll check all the ewes while I'm here, but I need to ride back right away. Are you fetching dinner for me?"

Aside from a pointed glance at my soiled clothing, my mother refrained from scolding me and simply placed the dinner pail in my arms, wrapped in a strip of wool. "Careful, it's hot," she warned.

Outside, my father nudged Ely over to the porch steps to mount more easily, and he positioned the dinner pail in the leather sack hanging across the horse's back. Climbing up next to it and steadying the pail with one hand, he told me, "Check the lambs again every half hour, Alice. I'll come down around dusk for a bit, but it's going to be a long boiling. Tell your mother."

He turned the horse toward the track up to the ridge, where the smoke of the sugaring fire and the steam from the kettle poured upward in a thick swirling column. Just as I placed my hand on the door to step inside, I heard loud harness bells arriving in the village. The stage! I had completely forgotten. A quick glance downward, though, convinced me to first enter the house. Barn dirt and straw were not the way I cared to greet the arriving stage—especially if Mr. Solomon McBride was indeed riding it.

Oh, and would there be a fugitive as well? Heavens! My mother shook her head as I hastily brushed and sponged my skirt. "Handsome is as handsome does," she reminded me. "Wipe clean your hands, and then you can fetch me a cup of cream from the cellar. There'll be time for visiting, all day tomorrow. Today, my dear, you're mine in the kitchen. And with your father and William still boiling, you and I must set the tables into place."

Which was why, on this important Friday, I wasn't able to even watch through the window as the stage passengers disembarked and entered the tavern door across the road. And already, I knew, the time for checking the lambs again was racing toward me. Liberty and labor, I said to myself, as I eased my way down the cellar steps, wishing I had time also to explore what lay beyond the door at the far wall. Liberty and labor. Heavens!

All that afternoon, I ran from kitchen to barn and back again, with the barn visits shortening each time. Both lambs nursed from their mother, although the white one, the one that took such a chill, seemed slower to feed. I rubbed each lamb repeatedly, especially the white one, urging more heat and life into it.

In the house, my mother and I rolled up the two small rugs in the parlor and set the two cupboards well back against the walls. Using the boards and tables that had seated our sixteen on the Sunday before, and extending them to their fullest, all the way into the parlor, we laid out seating for two dozen. Latecomers would have to wait their turn for the second seating, and children could stand if need be. Of course, there would be more tables outside.

Daylight lingered, so when William appeared in the kitchen at nearly five in the afternoon, my mother and I jumped with surprise.

"I'll help fetch the two tables from the tavern," my brother announced. "Then I need to go home to my wife and son." A smile of pride creased his tired face. He added, "If you can spare Alice, Mother, she could hold the doors for Matthew and me as we haul over the tables."

I seized a woolen jacket and hurried out into the dooryard behind William, whose long legs set him well ahead of me. "Wait for me!"

"Hurry up, then!" He held the door wide for me, and I ducked my head under his arm to enter the fire-lit parlor of the tavern part of Jerushah's house. Of course, she wasn't in that room—but Matthew was, bending to add wood to the hearth. In a flash, I thought of the stagecoach.

Turning to my brother, I whispered, "Did he come?"

He nodded toward Matthew. Jerushah's slender brother stood up and pressed a finger to his lips. "He's asleep upstairs. Solomon McBride, too. They spent two nights in—in a hidden place in Hardwick."

I wanted to ask "what hidden place," but already I knew better. Even so, I wondered why there weren't several people for us to assist. I whispered, "Only one came here?"

"Only one," Matthew confirmed. "But Alice, this one is being hunted, and we know there are bounty-hunters in Boston with his description. They're blaming him for the way some others have taken courage, and calling it a riot, and saying it's his fault." He leaned close to me, eyebrows and lips scrunched together intensely. "So, you must not say a word, not even to the other girls. Promise?"

"I promise," I confirmed. The poor man! How terrified he must be. "What can I do?"

"Help to keep people busy and not curious," William suggested. "Matthew, my mother wants those tables now, for tomorrow's sugaring-off."

"Wait!" The two of them, hands on the first table to be moved, paused to hear me. "The doors in the cellars. Is there a tunnel between our houses? Do you know about it?"

Matthew let slip an angry exclamation, but William quieted him with a gesture. "I didn't tell her. I've kept it closed and dusty on our side. She must have found it on her own."

I wanted them to trust me. "I haven't told anyone," I assured them. "I just w-w-wanted to help you." I had no idea Matthew could look so fierce.

They both spoke at once. "Forget that you saw it." William added, "Help Mother. Help Helen. Keep everyone thinking about the sugaring-off, and other things. You've no cause to concern yourself in this other business. Matthew and I will see this man safely toward Canada by Monday. Hold the door open now; there's work for us."

As I tugged the door toward me, the foul smell of a body half tumbling into the tavern told me who was entering before I saw him: Old Moses Cook, squealing without words, lunging toward the nearest table and chair. Ugh. Irritation flashed across Matthew's face, quickly banished by a short smile and a shout down the hallway toward the kitchen. "Papa! Mr. Cook's here for his usual. Can you come out here? Will and I are toting tables."

Mr. Clark bustled into the tavern, and Jerushah's brother and mine seized a long table, while I held the door wide for them. I whispered to William, "Is it safe for that man to be here, when— you know, when the others are sleeping upstairs?"

My brother snorted as he blew away my concern. "Don't be

69

such a worry-monger, Alice. Old Mose doesn't see a thing besides his draw of cider, don't you know?"

I eased the door shut and watched William and Matthew lift the table onto the wagon bed then held it open again for them to add a second, a third, and a fourth, before we all climbed up and rode behind Ely's steady thumping feet, up the lane to my own home.

I turned my promise of silence back and forth in my thoughts. Could I tell my friends, after the fugitive was gone? They would want to know. This secret pounded in my chest. I pictured the sleeping travelers—the fugitive and the mysterious Solomon McBride—in the bedroom over the tavern parlor, and my face flamed in passion. The fugitive must be saved! No matter the cost. It was, I repeated to myself in William's words, "our Christian duty."

CHAPTER 8

A hint of dawn lit my bedroom early Saturday morning, as my mother tapped at the door a second time. "Alice! Wake up. Get dressed; I need you. Alice!"

I swallowed my sleepiness, called out that I was coming, and heard my mother hurry back down the stairs. Outside, the clanking and banging that had haunted my last dream before waking came together into evidence of a fire being made in the dooryard, where the syrup boiled up at the sugar-camp would be finished today and poured into the pans and boxes to set as maple sugar. At least two other families would bring syrup, too, for the get-together.

Downstairs in the steamy kitchen, kettles of stew and pans of beans simmered as my grandmother scraped and prodded. Weaving around the clutter of tables and chair and stools, I reached the door to the yard and called out, "Papa! Breakfast is ready! Mother says please to come in now."

My father waved an arm as he led Ely toward the horse barn. "Tell her I'll be right there."

Sunshine sparkled on a thin layer of fresh new snow. A small fire under a set of crossed logs leapt cheerfully, scenting the morning air with the smoke. The wagon stood next to the barn, loaded with barrels of syrup brought out from shelter, ready to be heated in the sugaring kettle on its heavy chain. Many families "finished" their boiling, from syrup to the stage that would chill to grainy sugar cakes, at their kitchen stoves; in

71

North Upton, if weather allowed, we gathered our neighbors together to heat and pour the thickest liquid outside, into the pans and boxes waiting, stacked on the bed of a second wagon.

I squinted up at the small window over the tavern. A fugitive slave, born and raised in the heat of the South, might find our springtime harsh. I wanted to see the man, to feel as though I was part of helping him to reach Canada.

I remembered what William had said: that my task was to keep the day and the visitors focused on the ordinary, so nobody would look for trouble. To the kitchen, then—where I donned a fresh apron, determined to do my best.

My mother pointed toward the table, urging me to eat quickly. "Pickles," she read aloud from her list. "Set out ten dishes of each kind, the sweet and the sour. And when you finish that, butter and jam, the same number. Mother," she added, speaking to Grammy Palmer, "we'll stack plates on the tables next, before there are too many people in the kitchen."

Arrivals began almost at once: William with an extra tablecloth from Helen, then Jerushah and Sarah, each with a basket of sliced gingerbread. "My mother's bringing her beans when she comes later," Jerushah explained. "She doesn't want to bring the little ones yet, they'll just be in the way." Baskets were set aside, then cloaks, and I admired Jerushah's apron, newly stitched with yellow primrose embroidery along the neck. Leaning close to see, I reached to touch the shining dark smooth curls of her hair, pinned up as elegantly as Mrs. Dolley Madison's would have been, I told her. She beamed with pleasure and brushed a light kiss onto my cheek.

Not to be left out of the exchange of compliments, Sarah approached the two of us and showed a delicate collar of lace, fastened with a bit of ivory on a pin. "I pressed it myself," she said with satisfaction, and below the chestnut glow of her throat, the lace seemed intricate and very white indeed.

"You'll have the boys all wanting to sit with you," I teased her.

A hot flush darkened her cheeks further. "I don't want to sit with any boys. I want to sit with you and Jerushah."

"Indeed you will," I agreed. "But first, there are bowls of pickles and such to fill and place, and we three ladies of the kitchen need to set our hands to work at once."

Even as we labored to set out dishes, the house filled with new arrivals. My aunt Julia in her hoopskirt took to stirring and moving kettles at the stove, since the width of her skirt barred her from almost any other space. Grammy Palmer moved to the hearth in the parlor, where she hung a pot for tea from the old hook over the fire. A family from Upton Center arrived, and another all the way from St. Johnsbury, cousins on my father's side.

Between the stove and the hearth, crammed with people and conversation, the air thickened with heat and steam and the savory aromas of the feast. Sweat dampened our faces, as it did those of the women in the kitchen. I wiped my forehead with a corner of my apron and inspected the tables. I tugged at Sarah's hand and beckoned to Jerushah.

"Let's go out into the dooryard," I suggested. Together we pressed between tables and chairs, working our way to the far side of the kitchen where my mother stood, opening baskets and bowls, lining them up for guests to sample the contents.

My mother nodded as I pressed past. "Go on out and look, the three of you, but mind you come in straight away when I ring the dinner bell."

We bolted for the door, slowing to steady our skirts as we emerged into the crisp outdoors with its crowd of men and boys.

Sarah shivered in the fresh air, and Jerushah hastily wrapped Sarah's thin shoulders in a woolen shawl. The relief of being outdoors evoked a wide smile for Jerushah and for me, and I let out a lung-full of stale, steamy indoor air and drew in the crisp and wood smoke-tangy day.

Bright sun overhead warmed my shoulders and seeped through the cloth of my cap. Linking our arms around each other's waists, Sarah at the center, the three of us proceeded with neat careful steps across the dooryard, to the cluster of neighbors gathered by the outdoor fire. My father held an iron ladle; when Aunt Julia's husband, Charles, lifted a plate of snow toward him, the ladle was allowed to drip a line of dark syrup over the icy mound. It soaked right down in, melting into the dish.

"Still a ways to go," Uncle Charles noted. "If we bank the fire down a bit, we can hold it until after everyone has eaten dinner."

Nods and murmured agreements signaled the gathering's willingness to wait until after the noon dinner to finish the boiling and pour the pans of sugar. A pair of men with long iron rakes drew the coals back in a circle around the dangling kettle. For good measure in slowing it down, my father dropped a handful of clean snow into the syrup, inspecting the way it hissed and bubbled in the sugary heat.

At the far side of the group, I saw Jerushah's brother Matthew talking with Solomon McBride. They stood a little apart, laughing. I marveled, unable to stop my own gaze from lifting for a moment toward the upstairs window over the tavern.

"Alice! Alice Sanborn!" The call distracted me, and I looked to see who was calling my name. Adeline Wilson and two of her cousins hurried toward us, and we released each other to gather in a knot of girls, admiring each other's nicest collars and brooches and catching up on each other's news.

"My little brothers are still a-bed with weakness and enervation," Adeline admitted when I asked about them. "But the fever is past, and I never caught it myself. My mother said I might as well come to the sugaring-off and be out from under foot. My father brought five barrels of syrup here," she added proudly.

That was a lot of syrup. I asked Adeline whether her mother had sent pie pans or sugar boxes, and she pointed to a stack on a nearby wagon. Her father emerged from our barn, having stabled his horse to keep the animal warm. Behind him, clutching a strip of leather in one hand, lurched the one person I didn't want to see—Old Moses Cook.

Before I could urge the girls with me to duck out of sight, the unpleasant creaky voice cackled in our direction, and Old Mo, arms waving in excitement, staggered toward us. I heard Jerushah draw a sharp breath of determination, then step forward with a pleasant smile. "Good morning, Mr. Cook. How are you today?"

In the daylight, the dirt on the man's hands showed a layer of mixed filth, including horse hairs and a smear of something brown and greasy. His face, toothless, hung in creases around his twitching mouth. Whatever he thought he was saying, I could hear no words to it, just a mumbled exclamation repeated. I backed away, looked down at where the old man was gesturing, and realized it wasn't me, or even Jerushah, but Sarah that he wanted to approach. She stood half sheltered behind Jerushah's skirt, eyes wide with apprehension.

"No, don't touch her!" I exclaimed. I moved in front of Old Mo, and he grabbed at my skirt with one of his soiled hands.

The word he was repeating came clear: "Darkie! Darkie!" Then it shifted into a low croon, bubbling from his loose mouth: "P'tty girlie, p'tty girlie." He was calling Sarah pretty.

"Leave her alone!" I dared to push against him, risking contact with those awful hands, whose fingernails curved long and thick and yellow.

My father appeared behind Old Mo and took his arm, turning him sideways. "Morning, Moses. Good to see you out this way so early. Been looking at the horses, have you? I always heard you were good with horses in the old days. Come over here by the fire so I can keep an eye on it, while you tell me what you think of my red cow in there. You think she'll be a good milker, do you?"

Some other men cut in as well, and Jerushah and I turned swiftly to Sarah. Shaking and pale despite her brown skin, our friend clung to us and said, "Don't let him touch me. Please, don't let him touch me."

"He's not going to touch you," Jerushah comforted Sarah, enfolding her and at the same time moving her away from the men and toward the kitchen. "He's just an addled old man who drinks too much. Come on, let's go help with the dinner."

I cast a glance over one shoulder as together we escorted Sarah away from the men and their fire. Was Old Moses dangerous? I'd always just thought of him as disgusting in his dirt and his drinking, but part of village life, walking into North Upton a few times each week, and he'd never said a word to me in all my life. I didn't like the way he singled out Sarah in the crowd. No, I didn't like it at all.

A clanging of the dinner bell at the doorway stirred up the gathering, which quickly sorted into first and second dinners—we girls hurried to enter for the first serving. I paused by the door to wipe off my hands on a towel, wishing I could wipe away all thought of Old Mo the same way.

The noise of so many people—there must have been twenty-five at least—inside our little kitchen assailed my ears. Sarah still looked distressed, but Jerushah kept an arm around her and whispered something that brought a small smile. Speaking to me over Sarah's head, Jerushah suggested, "We could wait for the second serving."

I shook my head. "Better to eat now, so we can start cleaning the dishes right away. Come on, if we sit in the parlor it will be quieter." Which proved, in fact, to be true, and Grammy Palmer appreciated the plate-full that we brought to her there.

The next time that I could press toward the window, I saw a saddled horse tied up in front of the tavern. Someone who didn't care to come to the sugaring-off? A moment later, two figures, clearly men, came out of the front door of the building. They shook hands, and one mounted the horse, settling a pair of large saddlebags behind himself. The other, after a wave, turned back, and I was sure it was Jerushah's father. Jerushah came to stand beside me and commented, "My father said he didn't want to leave the tavern empty on such a nice afternoon. It looks as though he chose wisely."

The rider and horse headed out of the village in the direction of St. Johnsbury, at a steady walk for the distance where I could see them, before the angle of the barn blocked my vision.

A few minutes later, with aprons rustling, my friends and I stood at the dry sink in the kitchen, accepting direction from my mother and several other women all at once. We scraped, brushed, rubbed, and wiped the endless stream of pewter plates, glazed bowls, and drinking mugs coming back toward us, as well as spoons and some forks. The door swung open and shut over and over—people coming in, people going out. Thank goodness, Moses Cook wasn't among them. Sarah glowed in the attention that the women gave her, all praising her attire and her modesty and saying how sweet she was. And if it hurt, as I'm sure it did, when some of them said "poor motherless child," our friend knew how to hold back her tears and fears and say "thank you" with a quiet nod.

William stepped inside, waving an enveloped letter in one hand and calling out for our mother. She turned toward him, saw the envelope, and wavered a moment on her feet—then pulled herself together and glided quickly toward him.

"From Charles? John? Is it . . . ?"

"They're well," William reassured her. "It's more news than that, but they're well, Mother."

Conversation rippled around us as others realized a letter had just arrived from my older brothers out West. I heard "California" and "gold mining" in varied voices around me. I turned to watch my mother's face as she parsed the crossed and re-crossed lines of writing on the paper. As her shoulders settled and her lips curved upward, so did mine.

A tap from Jerushah, and her careful gesture, took my attention to William, who stood by the door, staring at me fixedly. His lips mouthed my name, and "Come out." He slipped away, and, stopping only to set down my scrap of flannel and pick up instead someone's shawl at random, I followed him in haste.

Outside, he tugged at my arm and drew me quickly around the corner of the house. "A post rider just came through," he said urgently, "and he had news. There's someone asking about Fred, over in Upton Center. A bounty hunter. We need to move him north, tonight."

Fred? Ah, the fugitive. I understood. "What can I do?"

"Pack us food for the trip, for Matthew and Fred and me. Bread and sliced meat and whatever else you can manage. Two days' worth. See if you can find a hat and muffler for Fred, too." I nodded my understanding as William continued. "I'll have to bring Helen and the baby here at the end of the day, to stay with Mother until I'm back. Make up a bed for them someplace, would you? And the food, Alice, put it into the tunnel; it won't do for anyone to see you give it to me. I'll have Matthew slip into there from the Clark side before we leave. Food, clothing, bed for Helen . . . what am I forgetting?"

"Lantern," I said. "Grain for the horse? And horse blanket?"

"Yes, those, too. I'll have to tell Father so I can use his horse.

Best give me something to melt snow in, for water along the way. And sugar; add a cake or two of sugar. It will keep us going."

"William, I can't do that much alone. You have to let me tell Jerushah." And Sarah, I added silently to myself.

"Yes, yes, go ahead. We'll be well on our way north before any chance word can harm us. I'll slip down to the cellar and loosen the door for you."

And he was gone, leaving me with a list to keep rehearsing, a handful of unasked questions, like what to pack everything into, and a growing sense of alarm that suddenly shook me into awareness: Sarah! If a bounty hunter was as close as Upton Center, Sarah must hide, right away. The bounty hunter could see her as a fugitive slave, and take her! Oh, but even so, all the village knew she was here; could so many people possibly keep this knowledge away from any slave hunter?

My father would know what to do. The conviction came to me as if from above, and I searched the crowd in the dooryard, looking for him first by the sugaring kettle, which was boiling fiercely, watched over by several men. Then I looked by the wagons where the pans and boxes were stacked, and the other wagon with the barrels of syrup. At last, I spotted him slipping inside the barn. I followed.

In the half darkness of the barn, I blinked the snow brightness from my vision and looked around. "Papa! Oh Papa, what can we do about Sarah? Should she go north also, with the others?"

"Nonsense," my father snapped. His irritation calmed me like a dash of cold water. "Sarah's in no danger. There's no bounty for her, no owner seeking her. She's a child, and she's of little value to anyone but the Lord. Your brother's trouble is that he and Matthew are hiding a wanted man, one with a price, a reward, for his capture. That's the only reason for the man to travel further north. Now," he scolded, "don't you have tasks to do to help your brother? Don't let your mother know yet—she can't feed and manage so much with worries on her mind. I'll tell her later. Go!"

I gathered my skirts and shook out the barn straw, and hastened out into the afternoon light and spring-like warmth. Forcing a smile and giving short replies to people, I wove rapidly through the dooryard and made my way into the kitchen, looking for Jerushah. When I saw her, sitting with Sarah and replying to the Reverend and Mrs. Alexander, I stood on my tiptoes to catch her eye. With one finger to my lips and then away, I beckoned before I went into the cold hallway and opened the door to the cellar. I paused a short moment for Jerushah, with Sarah, to catch up to me. Refusing to reply right away to their questions, I led them down the rough wooden steps to the cellar, relieved to see a candle stub glowing at the far end of the room. William had done more than I'd expected and had vanished again, perhaps into the connecting passageway under the ground.

"Careful," I hissed. "The bottom steps are slick with damp." We helped each other, then stood together in the dim near-darkness, and, in a whisper, I explained the situation. I added what my father had said about Sarah being safe, but I could feel her shiver next to me. Jerushah wrapped her in a reassuring embrace.

"We'll never let anyone chase you," Jerushah promised. "Not a soul in this village would ever let a slave hunter even into a home here. Courage, courage. We're with you; don't cry."

I heard Sarah sniff loudly. Then, with Jerushah's arms around her and me kneeling in front of her, patting her hand, she straightened suddenly and made a decision of her own.

"We need to gather food for them," she announced. "I'm the smallest. I can slip among the tables. Will you fetch a sack for packing it?" She turned and led us back up the steps, firm and strong as if she'd left her lamb self behind and turned to something more stubborn and strong and ever, ever safe.

CHAPTER 9

In the kitchen, my grandmother and Mrs. Alexander were stacking plates from the second sitting, while heating more water to clean them. Several small children played on the floor nearby, and two very small ones slept, rolled in blankets and shawls.

There was no need for the three of us to talk about what to do. Jerushah joined the women, neatly positioning herself so that the conversation must face toward her, not toward the tables. Sarah swept up two linen cloths that had covered the baskets of sliced gingerbread. I noted her quiet movement toward the parlor, where platters partly emptied remained with their breads. For myself, I struggled with how to pack a substantial amount of meat for the three men. No whole roasted chicken on hand, no sliced lamb: Every meat dish for the sugaring-off had been a stew of some sort. I edged along the deserted tables, aware that everyone else must be in the dooryard now, taking part in pouring the well-boiled syrup into the forms for sugar cakes. Still, I found myself on tiptoe.

There! Two mutton pies with crumpled crusts sat neglected by the parlor hearth. Someone must have set them there to keep warm and forgotten them. I eyed the scorched edges of the lard pastry over them; most likely these failed to appeal, compared to better dishes. I stacked some soiled plates, nodding to Sarah as she gathered the ends of bread loaves and wrapped them in her pieces of cloth. "I'll be back straight away," I whispered, and moved toward the kitchen.

Setting the plates to one side of the kitchen table, I stepped behind Jerushah to grasp a pair of shallow baskets that had held the gingerbread earlier. "I'll brush these out," I said casually. Only Jerushah noticed me taking them toward the parlor, rather than outside. Her voice rose in a silvery laugh as she encouraged Grammy Palmer to talk about a long-ago sugaring party.

In the parlor, I tucked a pie into each basket. Whoever had baked them would miss their tin plates, but in the confusion of all the visitors, perhaps they would not guess at theft. I knew it was theft I committed in that moment, of the baskets, of the pie plates, of the pies, and wondered what judgment might fall on me for this transgression.

More theft followed, as I took a flour sack from my mother's sewing basket and set the basketed pies into the bottom of it. Sarah smoothly added her bundles of bread and gingerbread, two cakes of maple sugar, and a paper twist of tea. I knotted the sack—now, how could I transport it past Mrs. Alexander and my grandmother in the kitchen?

I began to whisper the problem to Sarah, but her newly formed resolve included much ability to take action. She beckoned for me to follow her. As she entered the kitchen, she lifted up a crawling child and carried the little one toward the women.

"Would you kindly look at Betsy's little hands," Sarah improvised as she held the wriggling child. "I think she may have a sliver of wood in her thumb."

While everyone bent to inspect the small hands and the suddenly wailing little girl, I dangled my sack against the more distant side of my skirt and stepped quietly past the huddled group, toward the short turn of hallway that led to the cellar stairs.

My heart beat hard in my throat so that I wobbled on the steps. I carried my important bundle to the mouth of the tunnel, opened the door, and thrust the sack into the silent darkness beyond.

The candle stump had nearly burned to the stone on which it perched. For safety's sake, I blew out the small flame and felt my way back to the stairs. A little light from above lit the higher steps, and in a moment, I stood again upstairs, closing the cellar door as quietly as I could.

In the kitchen, Sarah and Jerushah stood together, reviewing with my grandmother and Mrs. Alexander the list of families and children suffering from spotted fever over the winter. "I believe only the youngest and oldest are severely at risk," Mrs. Alexander speculated, "and even for these, the course of the disease must pass, now that the weather is moderating. Or has been," she added with a look toward the window.

The sweet sunshine that had bathed the day seemed dimmer now, as the sky clouded. Grammy Palmer recited, "March comes in like a lion and goes out like a lamb, but sometimes March comes in like a lamb and goes out like a lion. We'll have another six weeks of winter, no doubt. There's snow coming."

I shivered. A snowstorm, as William and Matthew and Fred the fugitive journeyed north in the night? Ah, but Ely would be strong, drawing a wagon on which they could ride along the coach roads, no doubt.

Resolving to be as brave as our Sarah, I pulled myself together and proposed that we all step outside to see the last of the sugar making, before completing our household tasks. Mrs. Alexander and my grandmother declined but, with much laughter and teasing, told us to go ahead out and see which young men had sweetened enough to smile at us. Wrapped in shawls, our caps snug on our heads, we stepped out into the dooryard, and I whispered to my friends, "It's all in the tunnel."

Now it was up to William and Matthew to see that our Christian effort would be put to good use. A quick search of the crowd around the kettles and boxes convinced me that both of them must be elsewhere, preparing to head north.

While Jerushah and Sarah stepped close to see the boxes of sugar being counted and the next row of pie pans being filled, I excused myself to visit the barn. There was no need—surely my father had prepared Ely, with blanket, grain, ready to hitch to the wagon as soon as our guests left for their homes—but the list of preparations rattled in my thoughts, and I needed to see for myself.

Inside the barn, I found my father and Solomon McBride.

"Then let me ride the older one, and you know I'll be gentle with him," Solomon was saying. "It's the best plan. If I'm at the inn at Upton Center by nightfall, I can tip the tavern talk toward saying Fred's been seen in St. Johnsbury, on his way up the Connecticut River valley. Doctor Jewett there would give any slave hunters a hard and stubborn time of it."

"That he would," my father agreed. "But you'll have to travel on foot. It's only two miles to Upton Center. Start now, before it's fully dark, and you'll reach there within an hour. I'll not send my old horse out at this time of day. Moreover, I may well need him tonight and tomorrow, with Ely gone in William's hands."

I didn't see Ely, the younger horse. "Where is he? Have they already left?"

My father scowled at me. "You've no call to be in the barn, Alice," he growled. "William's fetching his wife and child. Go make up a bed in the parlor for them. You can set up the trundle bed there, for this night and the next."

"I also came to check that the lambs are well," I protested, wanting to stay in the barn a little longer. I pointed toward the sheep pen. My father and I stepped up to see how the ewe lay. Sure enough, the two early-born lambs, white and black, nestled snug against her belly, an occasional snort and suck assuring us that they now understood their purpose at the milk bag.

Solomon McBride stood behind us and spoke in a low voice, far different from his earlier sharp plea. He said, "So Nature gives to us a rightness and a goodness, a balancing and a safety. The black lamb lies down with the white, and neither is more nor less than the other. The Boston writer, Mr. Emerson, has told us that man is born to be a reformer, a re-maker of that goodness of Nature among mankind." He quoted, " 'A renouncer of lies, a restorer of truth and goodness.' We are at our best when this is the spirit of our lives."

For a moment my father stood unmoving, gazing only at the lambs. Then he turned and slapped Solomon's slender shoulder. "By heaven, you've a silver tongue, no doubt about it. I'd as soon see the colored folk returned to Africa, to their freedom there, and that's where I've placed my money," he continued. "But I'll salute you and the others if justice is your aim. Still, you'll not take my old horse tonight. Instead I'll outfit you with a lantern and stick from my own. I'd even walk with you, if it weren't that I'm needed here."

This change in sentiment seemed to satisfy Solomon, though it startled me greatly. We all left the barn, my father to join the group pouring the last kettle of hot and fragrant maple syrup into the molds, Solomon McBride to his cold walk to Upton Center, and I to the dooryard for a moment to murmur the latest news to Jerushah and Sarah. Then I returned to the house, this time enlisting my grandmother's assistance in making a comfortable nest in the parlor for Helen and tiny William Junior—we had tables and chairs to move, the trundle bed to take in pieces from the upstairs bedroom, and blankets and featherbeds to carry and tuck.

Never before had there been a sugaring-off when I had not stood next to the great black kettles, counting the pans filled, waiting for chances to taste the grainy sugar as it formed in them or on an offered plate of fresh snow, from which to sample the first harvest of the year. Though I worked quickly and cheerfully with Grammy Palmer and Mrs. Alexander to equip our parlor for its arriving babe-and-mother residents, I felt the discomfort of change. Like clouds headed to the valley laden with snow and wind, appearing out of wilderness and blowing at last off toward the invisible distant Atlantic Ocean, the weather of the week mastered my life. My choices were small: to pack food, to keep others' secrets honored, to hold the list of tasks in my heart and see the items slowly completed. The immensity of risk and storm blowing into North Upton humbled me.

Under Grammy Palmer's instruction, Helen and her baby snuggled into their temporary nest. Mrs. Alexander retreated to the kitchen to make tea. My mother and father moved around the dooryard, thanking guests, making sure each took home some maple sugar, counting out filled pans and boxes to those who had brought their own. I offered to carry the borrowed spoons back to Jerushah's house and received a nod from my mother. My father's glance told me he guessed my other errand, but he didn't interfere.

Sure enough, when I reached the steamy kitchen across the way, fragrant with cornbread and the savor of stewed fruit for a light supper, I found Jerushah and Sarah impatiently waiting for me.

"I knew you'd come!" Sarah exclaimed. She crowded against me and whispered, "I want to see him before they leave." She meant the fugitive, of course. The man they called Fred.

I wanted to see him, too. Why were the slave hunters chasing him even up into our north woods? Was he of such enormous value to the Slave Power of some Southern plantation owner? Or only sought for the sake of punishment and example?

Politely, the three of us offered to sweep and wipe the tavern room, telling Mrs. Clark we would prepare the room for any evening customers. Rocking the smallest child and singing him a lullabye, Mrs. Clark nodded her assent, and we gathered flannels and a bowl of warm water. Jerushah said there was a broom already there, a good corn broom. Down the connecting hallway we swished, our voices hushed in anticipation.

William and Matthew stood at a high table in the tavern, packing a leather satchel with woolen blankets and an oilcloth. Each had wound his ankles with an extra length of wool to keep deep snow out of his boots. A third set of boots and woolen coat and muffler waited on a chair.

Sarah, in her new-found certainty, spoke first. "I would like to meet him and wish him Godspeed," she said simply. "May I?"

Our brothers exchanged long looks. Matthew spoke first. "He's not well," he explained quietly. "Go quietly and gently. Make sure you stop at the top of the stairs, where he can see you, before you go toward him."

Sarah nodded and climbed the stairs. Jerushah and I dipped our flannels in water and began wiping the other tables and chairs. The dim light of the hearth fire grew stronger as we worked, and some heat began to reach us. We strained to hear, but whatever Sarah and the fugitive were saying, it was too low for us to catch.

At last, the stairs creaked, and we looked up. One hand stretched behind her, our Sarah was leading a man down into the room.

Matthew had not exaggerated. The thin, half-starved face of the man had hollows that fear and hunger must have carved together. He moved slowly, like an old man, pain with each step. I thought he must be as old as Sarah's own grandfather.

And then he stepped to the floor, in front of the fireplace, and looked for the first time into our faces, two Vermont girls,

Jerushah and me, with our hands full of wet flannel and our eyes and foreheads furrowed in sympathy. And he gave a long sigh, and then, unexpectedly, a small laugh.

"I never thought to see two young ladies working, while I rested my head above them," he whispered hoarsely. He smiled and nodded toward us. When he smiled, I realized he was barely older than our brothers, perhaps in his early twenties.

"We're glad to help," I told him.

Sarah patted his arm. "You see? And in two short days you'll be safe in Canada. You're already a free man, Mr. Johnson. But in Canada you'll feel it all the way through. William and Matthew are good men. They'll make sure you reach sweet Canaan."

"Two short days," the man repeated wonderingly. "Surely spring itself is two days from here, on Canaan's shore."

We helped him into the warm outer garments, and Sarah wrapped the long muffler around his face and neck, until only his soft brown eyes shone over the edge of the wool. She patted his arm again, then turned to Jerushah and me and reminded us to carry the flannels and water back to the house with us. Each of us solemnly took the hand of Mr. Fred Johnson and wished him well, then pressed a kiss to our brothers' cheeks.

"Take good care of William Junior," my brother reminded me.

"I will," I promised.

As we three re-entered the hallway that led to the women's world of cooking and children, I looked over my shoulder and saw the cellar door opening, and William, Matthew, and the fugitive passing down into the underground room, toward the tunnel and our own house, where they could make their way to the horse and wagon waiting in the barn.

I reminded myself that Solomon McBride must be in Upton Center by now, laying a false rumor for the slave hunter at the tavern there. If I had realized how his misdirection could go awry, I would have bundled up our Sarah that very minute and pressed her into the arms of the men descending the stairs.

Ah, what a lot of pain and fear that might have saved for us all.

CHAPTER 10

Supper at my home was cold bread, hot tea, and slices of one last dried-apple pie somehow missed during the feeding of so many neighbors and friends during the day. My father vanished for an hour or so, to check the low banked coals at Helen and William's home and to settle the sheep in the barn. His nod toward me on his return conveyed the message that all was as well as it could be—with the wagon and its three young men headed north. I counted off the time: two days to the border, if all went well, and two days to drive home again. William and Matthew could be home as soon as Wednesday afternoon, God willing.

It was nearly midnight when I tumbled into my own featherbed, barely able to escape my skirt and petticoats and tug the covers over me. Sleep caught me and drew me down into dark places, where snow swirled and lightning flickered across cloud-swept skies. I shivered in my dreams, urging a tired horse northward but unable to see the road before us. I woke for a moment and felt a gust of wind rattle past my window frame and knife across the room, and I burrowed deeper in my bed., I shook the nightmare for a moment and thought of Jerushah, and comfort came to me, and a different kind of dream. Though my arms and legs ached, my heart slowed and gentled, and I did not wake again until my little room was bright with morning sun.

The skies had cleared. But the wind, if anything, had

strengthened through the night hours. Aware that it must be past the usual time to rise, I scurried into my clothes from the night before and padded down to the drafty kitchen. My mother poured a cup of tea and dosed it with maple sugar before pressing it into my hands.

"Your father's gone to the church to talk with the minister," she explained briskly. "If you'll wrap yourself around some breakfast, we'll meet him there. Grammy Palmer is already here to stay with Helen and the baby."

I wrinkled my face in disappointment. "I could stay with Helen and the baby," I suggested, "and Grammy Palmer could go to the service. It's Palm Sunday, and I know she loves the hymns."

"Not this time," my mother said. "We have God's work to do, you and I this morning. Your friend Sarah needs us all to stand together if trouble comes to North Upton. And that means we need to set an example of standing together as a family, as the minister delivers his sermon."

So with a lace collar pinned to my short wool jacket to honor the Sabbath, I found myself sitting straight and tall in the hard wooden pew near the front of the church, my parents to either side of me, listening to a two-hour sermon on the responsibilities of a Christian people, interrupted at the middle by a new hymn to learn: "Just as I am, without one plea, But that Thy blood was shed on me, And that Thou bidd'st me come to Thee, O Lamb of God, I come! I come!"

The back of my neck itched with awareness that Jerushah and Sarah must be sitting in the Clark family pew, three rows behind us. The phrase "lamb of God" always made me think of Sarah. Sarah's small size hid a growing flame of compassion and determination. Why, she had not even trembled to meet the stranger, nor had she drawn back from the tasks of sending him toward his freedom.

Next to me, my mother straightened her skirts in preparation for rising in a hymn at the end of the sermon. To my surprise, as the last verse of the hymn concluded, she left our pew, walking toward the pulpit where the Reverend Alexander stood expectantly.

"Our Sister in Christ, Mrs. Sanborn, wishes a word with you all on this fine morning of early spring. And then we will close the morning service with some thoughts for Easter, which is our next Sunday service."

My mother turned to face the congregation and took a deep breath. At first her voice was soft, but it rose as she warmed to her task.

"Brothers and sisters, neighbors, I know that many among you have embraced the Reverend Alexander's call to see justice in our land. We who treasure this Union of free people are all too aware that the stain and sin of slaveholding have marred even the New England states in the past, and we seek a cleaner, wiser Union of righteous action and liberty for all."

A murmur of agreement filled the sanctuary.

My mother continued: "And in the name of He who holds the keys to the Kingdom of true liberty and justice, we have welcomed a child among us whose parents still reside in one of those dark uncertain places where slaveholding continues. We pray daily for the release of Sarah's mother and father and her sisters and brothers, that they may join us in freedom and independence of body and soul."

"Amen," rippled from the pews around me.

"Last night, word came to us that a slave hunter arrived in Upton Center yesterday, inquiring about strangers and seeking a way to seize the pieces of silver that reward those who capture the innocent and return them to fetters and the scourge. I stand here today to ask you to join me in turning this man aside, should he reach North Upton in his search. There is no need for any to break from the truth, but there is pressing need for all to send this evil man elsewhere. I ask you to search your hearts and act from the goodness and kindness therein, so that we may all act to protect and cherish the child placed among us. Will you hold with me in this, for the sake of Righteousness and Justice?"

I trembled to hear my mother speak so boldly and ask so much of the village. And as the men and women and children around me rose to stand and affirm their agreement with nods and further calls of "Amen," I stood also, shaken and moved. My father's pride in my mother showed in a tear that coursed down his cheek as he too uttered "Amen." I marveled at the moment and risked turning my head quickly to search out Sarah in the congregation. Because she was so small, I could not see her face, but I saw Jerushah's, beaming and joyous, and the somber but sure agreement of her parents standing with their children between them.

Though the March winds bit and sliced at our faces on the walk home for noon dinner, I felt only the heat of my enflamed heart, stepping beside my mother and father, certain of what it was to act in the ways of the righteous.

Helen and my grandmother had laid the table, while the baby slept. My brother's wife looked happy to be among us, cosseted and nourished. Her own parents lived in Wheelock, nearly a day's travel to the north, and I thought for the first time how hard it might be for her to reside far from them. I resolved to be a better sister to William's family, and to improve what I offered to my family and friends.

Thinking of friends, of course, made me wish I could spend part of the Sabbath with Jerushah and Sarah. Our family would not return to church for the afternoon services, but it still would not be right to go visiting on the day of rest.

Just as the steamed pudding arrived to complete our Sunday

dinner, and my mother sliced into its hot and fragrant raisin-laden interior to dish out portions, a crisp set of knocks came at the kitchen door. My father went to open it and welcomed in Solomon McBride.

"Good afternoon, sir," the young man began, tugging his hat off his thick, dark hair. "I wonder if I might speak with you a moment, perhaps outside where the ladies need not be disturbed on this Sabbath day?"

My father looked around the room. "The ladies," he said dryly, "seem all to have committed themselves to disturbance of late, for the sake of duty. So take a seat, young man, and give your message to us all, while the pudding is passed and the tea is refreshed. What word do you bring from Upton Center? How went your journey and your task?"

"Indeed, sir, I thought all was well. I found the man we'd heard about," Solomon confirmed as he settled on a chair and accepted a spoon. "And he was indeed searching for the stranger among us, and I told him there'd been word of some such headed toward St. Johnsbury. And I found him a cousin of Doctor Jewett's to take him there on Monday, after the Sabbath."

This sounded promising. Doctor Jewett was an abolitionist, of course, and his cousin would surely lead the bounty hunter into strong arguments and resistance. Why was Solomon so concerned? His voice shook with fatigue and worry as he continued.

"But young Jewett broke an ankle on the ice late last night after I'd left to walk back here. I just had word that Henry Clinton, the bounty hunter, is planning to come here tonight instead, to seek my help in traveling to the town in the morning."

"No!" I scraped my chair back from the table to stand up. "Surely there's time to direct him elsewhere! Make him go away, don't let him come here."

My mother pulled me back down to sit, scolding. "Let your father speak, Alice."

"Wait a bit," my father said slowly. "Give me time to think."

We sat silent, our puddings cooling in front of us, while my mother poured the tea calmly and passed it around the table. Helen excused herself to check on the baby. My grandmother laid a hand on one of mine and pressed it compassionately.

"He's not looking for a child," my father mused aloud. "He wants the reward for the man, the rebellion leader." This was a stronger term for what Mr. Johnson had done before fleeing north. I leaned forward, eager for more.

Solomon McBride nodded. "But he'd take her if he found her, no doubt. He'd only have to sell her, and there are ships in Boston Harbor even now where he could do just that."

"Not for as much as the reward, though. Suppose we send the girls, young Sarah along with my Alice and the Clarks' Jerushah, on a visit to Miss Farrow in St. Johnsbury this evening as the Sabbath ends. Considering the season, I think it pardonable that they depart for their visit while the day is still light. They could deliver a gift of maple sugar, an early Easter visit," my father mused. "I daresay Miss Farrow and the Paddock household would welcome them to stay for the night, considering the season. And, in the morning, they might drive back here the long way around, through Upton Center. Your Clinton fellow would by then be on the road from here to St. Johnsbury and would never cross the girls' route at all. Will that suffice?"

"More than suffice, sir," Solomon agreed. "And if you could perhaps meet Henry Clinton in the morning here and send him along on that particular way, I myself would instead escort the young ladies to town and back again on the other road. I could stay at the St. Johnsbury House and gather some support and news this evening among the guests there, before bringing the carriage of young ladies home in the morning."

So it was agreed. We would borrow a carriage from the Reverend Alexander, since our wagon had gone north with William. And the old horse, Sam, with his gentle steady pace, would do nicely to draw us to town in the daylight, and back again the next day.

With barely enough time to wrap and pack three pie-shaped cakes of maple sugar and a basket of bread and eggs, to share with our as yet unaware hosts in town, Jerushah and Sarah and I found ourselves bundled under blankets and an immense bearskin in the minister's carriage, with Solomon McBride up on the front bench, clucking encouragement to old Sam, and my mother waving from the steps.

We were going to St. Johnsbury, a town I knew little of, aside from visiting once each year when my mother shopped for sewing notions and such in the stores there. And we were going to visit Miss Farrow, whom I'd seen just once, when she'd brought Sarah to Jerushah's home for safekeeping. I should have been nervous and concerned.

But I was instead excited by the adventure, as if spring itself had leaped into the carriage with us. Nor did this excitement suffer from being driven to town by Solomon McBride, whose presence in our lives now seemed a great good fortune, indeed.

CHAPTER 11

Inside the carriage, two seats faced each other: one forward, on which the three of us sat, and the other backward, now stacked with our bundled gifts. A light rain began entering through the carriage windows as Solomon McBride urged old Sam to a faster walk away from the village. Easing out from under the bearskin, I tugged at the window curtains and pulled them over the front windows, to keep the rain from our packages. Then I began to close the ones next to our seat. "We'll be cozy and dry," I pronounced.

Sarah made a small sound of distress.

"What is it?" Jerushah asked at once. "Are you worried about leaving the village? Alice and I will be with you all the time, and we'll go home again tomorrow. Don't be afraid."

"I'm not afraid of going to St. Johnsbury," Sarah replied. "But if you please, could Alice keep the curtains open, at least part of the way? Or it will be too dark."

The tremble in Sarah's voice persuaded me that a little dampness could be acceptable. "I'll only curtain the windows partway, and you may sit next to a window to see the day and the road if you like."

Agreed, we exchanged places. Jerushah smiled and laid one arm across my back, her hand reaching across to pat Sarah's nearest shoulder before returning to mine. "We're as snug as three bugs in a bearskin rug," she quipped. "Sarah, what can you tell us about Miss Farrow? She is such a heroine to us all, with her journeys and her assistance to the fugitives. Is she very grand in person?"

"Not at all! She is the kindest, sweetest woman, and even when I disliked traveling very much, she kept me comforted," our lamb explained. "And she gave me horehound drops to suck on so the wagon's movement wouldn't turn my stomach. And every night on the way north, she made peppermint tea for me, and bread with sugar on it, too."

"How kind, indeed!" Jerushah's bright face shone with merriment. She pressed my hand under the bearskin and tried another tack. "How many petticoats does she wear, I wonder? She dresses so well! Did she ask you to help with her corsets, to draw them in for her waist?"

"No, never. She told me she didn't want me to help her, that I'd already helped too many people too much." Sarah's voice dropped. "I don't mind helping people. It feels useful. When people are kind, it's a goodness to help them. But it's not such a goodness when they are not kind, because then a person's heart sometimes rebels." She stopped, staring out into the rain and snow-crusted fields around us.

Jerushah reached for my hand again, to press a different message, but I knew already what she meant. If we asked our friend to speak of her years in servitude, she'd suffer more sadness. So I suggested to Sarah, "You'll enjoy seeing Miss Farrow again, won't you? And helping to give her things, and having a cozy visit."

"Yes, and I've stitched her a handkerchief. Look!" She turned toward us, away from the window, and drew out from her skirt's deep pocket a square of linen, neatly hemmed and embroidered with an ornate letter "R." "Her Christian name is Rachel. Oh, it was so kind of your mother, Jerushah, to give me the fabric. Everyone in Vermont is kind, aren't they? I wonder whether the snowy winters make it so."

"Perhaps they do." I thought Sarah's point was well taken. "If we don't help each other, the winter's too long and hard for us all. Even now, it's cold enough and wet enough to make life hard."

The carriage lurched. I peered past Sarah and saw we'd entered a stretch of road with snow still upon it, unlike the mix of mud and ice in the village. Rolled hard and packed down, the surface suited sleigh runners best. The carriage wheels spun and slipped, as Sam pulled us forward.

Solomon McBride called from the upper seat, "Try to stay in place across the bench in there, to keep the carriage balanced."

Jerushah seized the strap to her right, to stay next to the right-hand window, and Sarah did the same for the left. I reached my arms backward to grasp the back of the seats, bracing in the middle.

Soon we reached the crest of a hill and a cluster of houses and barns amid generous fields. "It's the Four Corners," I told Sarah. I let go to point across her. "Look there, see that grand large house, the one that's perfectly square? That's William Arnold's house, and the upper floor is all a ballroom, where there are dances. Someday Jerushah and I will take you there to see. Such lovely floors, all pine, and furnishings from Connecticut. My father and our William have cut hay for Mr. Arnold from time to time, and I visited once with my mother."

A sudden glow of candles lit in the house's lower floor made me aware that the sky had darkened further, dimming the daylight greatly. The rain pounded more heavily on the carriage, and I helped Jerushah to fasten the right-hand curtain all the way down. I left Sarah's curtain half open, not wanting to upset her again, but I made sure the bearskin covered most of her.

"There are grand houses in Virginia, too," Sarah noted. "My mother takes care of the one where our . . . where the other Johnson family lives. Perhaps three or four times the size of the house over there. But I like Vermont houses better."

"So do I," Jerushah chimed in. "Liberty and justice make a house into a real home. Oh, Sarah," she added impulsively, "I'm sure your mother will come north soon. And your father and brothers and sisters, of course."

"Thank you." There was a silent moment in which, in the dimmed carriage interior, I could not read Sarah's face. Her thoughts must often be fearful—surely her phrase "the other Johnson family" referred to the masters who "owned" her family. She went on. "I am not as sure of their escape as I was, you know. I'm not a child any longer. But I am everlastingly sure that our prayers are heard, and that my family is comforted by heaven. As I am, also."

A tear ran down my cheek, like the one that must be on Sarah's own, I thought. I bent over her to kiss her, and Jerushah too leaned toward that side of the carriage. From above us came a shout, "Don't move about in there! Please, girls, stay settled. Sam's got all the work he needs just now."

The carriage jolted and tipped, and we rapidly spread ourselves properly across the seat again to correct it. Sarah put away her embroidered work, and Jerushah offered to start us singing.

It was a welcome suggestion. Over the next two miles, which brought us down the ridge, we sang "My Faith Looks Up to Thee," and all the verses of "Green Grow the Rushes, Ho," and then Sarah taught to us a song that she said everyone in the South sang, be their skins white or black: "I Am a Poor Wayfaring Stranger." It was sorrowful, especially the verses about seeing father, mother, and sisters again "in that bright world to which I go," but we gave it as much sweetness as we could, especially in each verse ending, "I'm going there no more to roam, I'm just going over Jordan, I'm just going over home."

We ended the tune and sat silent in the darkness inside the

rocking and lurching carriage, listening to Sam's feet clumping and splashing. Foreboding wrapped itself around my chest.

Jerushah's hand connected with mine again under the bearskin, startling me, but I squeezed hers firmly and determined to shake off the moment of disturbance. I began to talk about St. Johnsbury instead.

"My father says it's likely St. Johnsbury will become the shire town, now that the railroad is being built there. He says that Upton Center won't be nearly as important, not like a town where goods and people come and go each day. The rails are to be laid this spring, for the surveyors marked off the route last summer and autumn."

"There are railroads in the South already," Sarah piped. "I saw a locomotive once, with its smokestack and all. They make so much noise!"

"Then I shall never wish to live in St. Johnsbury, for I can't abide terrible noises. I won't even visit inside the mill if I can avoid it," Jerushah declared. "Honestly, Alice, I don't see how William and Matthew can abide the racket of the machines and the water."

"The mill is loud," I admitted. "They stuff their ears to mute the sound, you know. But don't you love to see how it all works, the belts bringing the water power to the turning of the saws and lathes?"

Jerushah pulled away, and I could tell she was staring at me, even in the carriage's dim interior. "No, not at all! Do you mean to say you like it?"

"I do! I'm sure it's not ladylike, but I like the certainty of it, the way every pull and turn leads into the next one."

Sarah saved me from embarrassment by adding, "It's an image of the heavenly kingdom, where every action is a right action. And work itself, you know, is Godly."

Laughing, Jerushah pointed out, "So is rest, on the Sabbath!"

The carriage tilted sharply downward, and for a few minutes we all worked to hold our places on the bench and not fall across to the other one. Then it leveled. A change in Sam's pace took our attention to Sarah's square of open window.

"We're here! We're at the Plain." I explained to Sarah, "Everyone calls it the Plain, the flat area where the finest houses of St. Johnsbury are built. Look, look at all the houses!"

A moment later, out the left-hand window, I saw the enormous brick house that was home to Judge Paddock and his family—and to Miss Farrow. I pointed it out and braced for the turn into the long drive.

But Solomon called down to us, "I'll drive the length of the main street first, so you can all see the Plain and the changes taking place. You won't know the town for the same place!"

We tied back all the curtains to see. Indeed, every patch of ground between the homes had something being built on it, and at the Bend, where the largest tavern stood, we saw an amazing sight: a building four stories tall, bright with lamplight and glowing windows, whose front bore the lettered description, "St. Johnsbury House." Merchants' shops, closed until the next morning, showed descriptions of their business on their shutters. In spite of the rain, carriages traveled along the muddy main street, some with lamps at their fronts. Windows around us glowed, bright and cheerful.

Solomon slowed the horse and turned the carriage with care in a long circular lane at the south end of the Plain. An imposing house stood high nearby, next to an inn, well kept, with young trees and outlines of flower beds notable under the last wet snow. "That's Dr. Lord's house," Solomon called down to us. "I visited there yesterday!"

I wondered whether there were even finer homes for the Gilman brothers, whose fortunes had grown as Dr. Arnold's family dwindled. The Gilman Mills made the best cookstoves, and their newly invented scales were sold all around the nation and even in foreign places. Surely the brothers were already wealthy! To our right now, I saw the pillars of the academy that the Gilman brothers had founded. Mr. Philemon Gilman, I knew, was bringing the railroad to town. But I had no time to speak of these people to Sarah and Jerushah, for we were again approaching the lane that led to the grand brick house that was our destination. All three of us braced for the turn this time and soon stood within the roofed portico at the back of the house, tapping at the kitchen door, our bundles in our arms.

Miss Farrow herself opened the door to us, and what a great commotion of embraces and greetings and delight filled that kitchen! At least, I supposed it was the kitchen, but it was so much larger than our own that after a moment I had to set down my basket and simply look around me. Two stoves stood by a brick chimney, a merry woodfire in one of them casting ample heat for the March evening. I counted ten candles lit, an extraordinary extravagance that made the room nearly as bright as day. The fragrance of tea and gingerbread made my stomach rumble with hunger and appreciation.

Miss Farrow at once insisted that we all sit at the table and have supper with her. "For Judge Paddock and his wife, Aunt Abba, are in Montpelier until mid-week, and I've been as lonesome as a lone dove would be," she explained as she brought dishes to the table.

The door swung wide as Solomon came in from stabling the horse, his garments wet as all outdoors from the journey. He stood dripping by the door, maneuvering to remove his capes and hat without splashing his shirt and breeches further. Jerushah jumped up to help and, at Miss Farrow's direction, hung the soaked garments near the stove to steam and eventually dry. Solomon joined us at the table.

Sarah glowed and chattered, more so than I'd ever heard her

do before. Leaning back in my seat, I watched and listened, glad that she felt at ease with this gracious woman whose skin color was so like her own, if a bit lighter. I tried to detect any accent of the South in our hostess's voice, but it was rare indeed—only in certain words that I recognized from Sarah's own speech, like the gentle elongation of the word "Lord" into something more like "Loh-ohrd." But otherwise, she spoke as a Vermonter born here in this town, if not exactly what we'd call "born and bred in the Green Mountains."

Our dilemma and our plan were soon exposed, and Miss Farrow approved them soundly. "No slave hunter will be encouraged to stay in these parts," she agreed. "And once Dr. Jewett gets hold of him and pounds him with a few hours of Abolition talk and tracts, this Henry Clinton will turn tail and run for Connecticut or Rhode Island, or further, and count himself lucky to escape. There's no need for you to fear at all," she assured Sarah, nodding to the rest of us. "This is a safe place, and a good one. Now, Mr. McBride, hot chocolate or tea for you?"

Soon Solomon headed "downstreet" to put into action his own plan to stay overnight at the new St. Johnsbury House. The taverns where the men gathered were closed for the Sabbath, but in the morning he would join the hotel's breakfast table and test out the news in town, talking with others and gathering word of how the anti-slavery groups in the region fared. He and Miss Farrow seemed to have another plan in common, exchanging a few cryptic words that hinted at more secretive doings.

In the warm kitchen, I caught my head drooping from fatigue, and Sarah actually fell asleep in her chair. Miss Farrow shooed Solomon out the door, decked in his mostly dried outer garments, and offered to show the house to Jerushah and me. We marveled at the French wallpaper with its scene of the Bay of Naples, wrapped right around the parlor walls. A library gleamed with polished wooden shelves, and I admired the rows of leather-bound volumes, many of them written on the law, and others on history, both of the region and of nature. Though there were no fires in them this night, there was a fireplace in each room, and upstairs, in Miss Farrow's bedchamber, a small coal fire warmed the room luxuriously.

We laid out a bed on the floor that Jerushah and I could share, and Miss Farrow descended the back stairs to gather up Sarah in her arms and bring her directly to bed. Sarah barely woke at all, and, tucked into Miss Farrow's featherbed, she smiled even as she curled against a soft pillow.

Candles out, the four of us safe and warm, I marveled at the room and what it said to me. Clearly, by her position in the fine bedchamber, Miss Farrow was no mere servant of the Paddock family, but a trusted and beloved member of their household. To Sarah, I thought, sleeping with this dark-skinned and tender woman must bring a sense of home and mother that the kindness of Jerushah's family could not quite match, through no fault of their own save their white skins. And to me, to sleep with Jerushah brought an assurance of what good friends we had always been.

In the darkness, she wrapped an arm across my shoulders, as she had in the carriage. Her soft lips brushed a friend's affection against my cheek. I smiled against her shoulder as she drew me close. Slowly, she stroked the length of my hair, released from its braids, and I felt her fingers gently smooth out the tangles of the day. She gave a deep sigh, and it seemed that she too appreciated this warm and trusted comfort.

A whisper tickled my ear as she pressed closer. "I am so happy," my friend murmured to me. "I am so happy to be here with you. And Sarah, of course," she added sleepily, as she curled her other arm snugly around my waist.

I listened to her even breathing, slowing into sleep. Accustomed to the full space of my own bed, I found the situation overly warm, and unexpectedly confining. After a few more minutes I loosened her arms so I could slip free, patted her shoulder gently, and turned to face the closed chamber door. Even as I drifted to sleep, Jerushah's warmth behind me, Sarah's safety assured across the chamber, still something from that day's moment of disturbance pricked at me. I dreamed of darkness and long roads, waking often to settle again. At last I thought to whisper a shred of prayer, "Heaven bless and keep us, and my family and William's, and watch over William and Matthew and Fred up north, please," into the darkness.

CHAPTER 12

Morning in a grand house in town matched mornings at home in some ways: the chamber pot to empty into the backhouse, fires to re-start, breakfast to prepare. Miss Farrow insisted on carrying out the chamber pot, as she knew the house and none of us did, but I followed along, in order to know where the little room with its three neat seats stood. At least, I would find my way here later, if the call of nature required, rather than put this gracious lady to any further such task on my behalf! Jerushah and Sarah watched the fire in the woodstove, and when Miss Farrow and I returned to the kitchen, I explained to them where the "necessary" was. Then I excused myself again, feeling responsible to my father, and sought the carriage house to check on old Sam.

By the time I had given him hay and grain and a fresh pail of water from the trough in the yard, breakfast was laid out. I wiped my hands on the towel and settled at the table.

"When do you think Mr. McBride will come to take us home?" asked Sarah.

Miss Farrow teased, "Are you in such a hurry to leave me, already?"

"No, of course not! I want to stay as long as we can!"

We all laughed, and Miss Farrow explained: "Your Mr. McBride is probably circulating around town this morning, after his breakfast at the St. Johnsbury House. I should think he'll come for you a little past noon. Give him a chance to eat a

108

good dinner with the men, so he can spread word, or gather words, if you grasp my meaning."

We did, indeed. Solomon McBride's efforts in the anti-slavery movement grew larger by the day. In spite of his pretty looks, he must be rugged and determined underneath. I promised myself I'd apologize in some way for having slighted him in the past.

Jerushah followed my thinking, but in a different direction. Stacking the dishes to be cleaned, she asked quietly, "Miss Farrow, do you always place children like our Sarah among the villages? Or do you take some of them to Canada, where the King's law makes them safe and free?"

"They are safe and free here, by Vermont's own laws," our hostess replied calmly. "We are all children of God's creation, and we have much to be grateful for in that status." Her look softened as she regarded Sarah. "I confess, I rarely escort children as young as your friend here, Jerushah. Most often I simply assist women and men to find their way to the ministers in Hardwick or St. Johnsbury, and I imagine those in Peacham, Barnet, and Upton would assist if called upon. And then we all help to find transport to a farm that can afford to pay for more labor, or perhaps toward Canada indeed. You know, there are many friends between here and the border."

We all moved close, eager to hear more. I wondered, "Are the friends mostly people from our villages who know that slavery is a sin? Or are they people who've escaped from the Slave Power to live here?" It felt strange to mouth the term "Slave Power" for the first time, as my grandmother had spoken it and as the ministers often did.

"Evil can only have power over us if we fail to invite Goodness to hold us and accompany us," Miss Farrow responded. "So I don't speak of the 'Slave Power' myself. But the question you've asked can be answered in the affirmative for both: There are many good people ready to help others reach their God-given freedom in Vermont. And there are more arriving each day. Although," she added, looking at Jerushah and me, "if you don't pay close attention, you may not realize how long some of them have lived here already!"

Sarah asked, "Who is it, Miss Farrow? Who is it from the . . . from the South that has lived here a long time?"

"Well, there is a dark-skinned man in Peacham whose grand-parents fought in the Revolutionary War, you see. He has lived in Vermont all his life, as did his parents before him. And," her merry eyes teased us, "there are young men, too. I am thinking in particular of four brothers named Hayes who live up near the border, in Coventry, whose parents have given my travelers fair lodging in the past. Their faces are dark as ebony, but they too were born in this state, albeit in its southernmost large town, Bennington."

"And women?" I had to ask it; were all the heroes of our time only men?

"Women, indeed," Miss Farrow confirmed. "Though it's said that we are the gentle sex, and mild, who else can make a hot meal so quickly, or bandage an injury, or convey welcome?" She nodded at me. "Courage is a French word rooted in the term for 'heart' in that land—*coeur*. Women often have deep and car-ing hearts, blessed by God toward service. So you must know that most women are ready to assist in seeing justice done. There's a place for you among us, Alice, if you'd care to put your hands and heart to labor for the sake of liberty." She added, "And of course for you also, Jerushah, if you like." But her gaze never left my face.

How should I reply? I knew my mother would understand if I said yes to this intriguing invitation, but should I betray my father's reserve and careful thoughtfulness?

Just as I was about to air this conflict, a knock came at the kitchen door, and Solomon McBride burst into the room.

"He's here in town! Henry Clinton—the slave hunter—he's here in St. Johnsbury! I just saw him, and he's at the St. Johnsbury House."

"No!" All of us girls cried out at once, but not Miss Farrow. She set down the plate she'd been cleaning, untied her apron, and clapped her hands together loudly for attention. We all turned to her at once.

"Fear and agitation are unnecessary," she said calmly. "It's a large town, and there's no reason that your paths must cross. Mr. McBride, hitch the horse to the carriage, while I help these young ladies to gather their belongings. They can be ready to ride out of town with you as soon as you are ready."

Solomon spun on his heel and retreated out the door, and Jerushah ran up the stairs to fetch our shawls. I gathered the capes and other garments from where they had hung near the cookstove and wrapped the warmest one around Sarah, whose teeth were chattering in apprehension. "You're safe with us," I told her, as I fastened the front of her shawl in a quick knot.

Unexpectedly, another knock sounded at the kitchen door, this time a measured one, polite and unhurried. We stared at each other. It could not be Solomon, could it? Miss Farrow said quietly, "Alice, take Sarah upstairs. Find Jerushah. The three of you must stay in my bedchamber until I come to fetch you. Go!"

I did, moving Sarah's unresisting form with me. As we reached the stairs, the cooler air seemed to bring her back to herself, and she scurried ahead of me, on tiptoe. We pressed Jerushah back into the chamber, quietly fastened the door shut, and leaned against it to hear. A man's voice spoke, but we couldn't make out the words.

A minute later, we heard voices in the dooryard. Jerushah placed a finger to her lips, gestured to Sarah and me to stand back against the wall, and eased toward the window. It was open an inch at the base, to air the room, and through the opening we all could hear the conversation.

"Yes, indeed, Mr. McBride came calling this morning. Here he is, about to travel back to North Upton, I believe. Mr. McBride, here is Mr. Henry Clinton, who has searched for you at the St. Johnsbury House and wishes to spend some time in your company!"

A smooth voice that I'd never heard before replied, "Indeed, I'd as soon spend it in the company of both of you. I'd no idea the fair town of St. Johnsbury numbered such gracious women among its inhabitants. Have you lived here long, Miss . . . er, Miss Farrow?"

Frozen, we listened, unable to guess what would take place.

I could tell the heavy footsteps of our horse emerging from the carriage house. Miss Farrow answered the slave hunter. "I would say I have lived here all my life, Mr. Clinton, but here in Vermont we share some humor around that phrase, for none of us has yet lived all his or her life! In fact, I was born just up this street, at the north end of the Plain. And you, sir, are you a New Englander yourself?"

"Not I," came the reply, "but from not far to her south, from Manhattan in the fair state of New York. So, Mr. McBride, as you see, I've caught your path at last! That old fellow who walks from village to village . . . what's his name—Old Joe? No, Old Mo; that's it. He showed his face in Upton Center and swore you'd headed here already, so I didn't bother to ride to North Upton after all. What brings you here with a carriage to draw? Have you brought company with you?"

Jerushah and Sarah and I stared at each other. Old Moses Cook had betrayed our plan. And the slave hunter's reasoning was obvious: If Solomon McBride had traveled alone from North Upton, he would have ridden a horse, not driven a carriage. What could he say to this evidence against him?

Surprising us all, Solomon laughed, and if it sounded false to us, perhaps we simply knew him better than the man from New York. "Clinton, you've caught me in the midst of doing a good deed. Don't hold it against me—I vow I can still wrestle you to the ground in a fair match, I'm not a whit soft! But I came to fetch Miss Farrow here, to assist in caring for a new mother in North Upton. Miss Farrow has quite a reputation for her strengthening care and medicinals."

Miss Farrow deftly added to this tale. "But I in turn have told Mr. McBride that I'm not free to leave town at present and have offered to equip him instead with appropriate herbs and remedies. And he is off to Dr. Jewett's home, to secure some assistance there, as well. When he comes back here in an hour or so, I'll have his basket ready."

The voice of the slave hunter betrayed a sour resentment as he growled, "I'll not go with you to Dr. Jewett's place, McBride, for he gave me a dose of his opinions last night at the Passumpsic House, and I've no need for a repeated administration."

We heard Solomon laugh at the New Yorker and say only, "Very well. And have you found your man? When do you head south again?"

"Oh, no, I've not found him yet. But I shall. And I've a strong desire to ride with you in your carriage of medicines and treatments, to this village of North Upton that I've yet to visit. Perhaps I'll find what I need along the way."

Jerushah whispered, "He thinks the medicines are for Fred! Solomon meant them to be for Helen, but the slave hunter thinks they are for the fugitive!"

Apparently, Solomon could not come up with an adequate response to this veiled and oily threat. Miss Farrow's voice interceded, fluid and graceful. "In the meanwhile, Mr. Clinton, perhaps since you are not visiting the good doctor, you might like to visit our stores and merchants. I can recommend Mr. Lovell Moore's shop for its dry goods and West India rum, which Judge Paddock recommends most highly. If the judge were at home, I would invite you inside, but as he is away, I fear you'll need to make do with the merchants whose custom he supports instead."

I thought this was a neat speech and expected Mr. Henry Clinton to admit he'd been outfoxed. Surely he must leave now!

Instead, he said slowly, "I think I'll wait here in the dooryard for Mr. McBride's return from his errand to the doctor. I would hate to miss my connection with him yet again, now that I've determined to ride with him to North Upton. Come to think of it, perhaps I'll ride along in the carriage to your opinionated doctor's after all. I can wait for you there and watch your horse."

Sarah had covered her face with both hands. I drew her against me, trying to calm her. "Miss Farrow will know what to do," I whispered.

But I was surprised when I heard Miss Farrow say to the men, "On this fine day, to ride in a carriage to the doctor's when he is only four houses down the street? Go, stretch those long legs of yours, pay him your call while I put together my parcel. Hitch the horse there by the water trough, Mr. McBride; he'll be fine enough while you do your errand, with Mr. Clinton to help you carry bundles back, if need be."

And this, oddly enough, seemed to satisfy the stranger, for we heard the two men's steps head out of the dooryard toward the street, and then the quiet latch of the kitchen door.

A moment later, Miss Farrow reached the chamber, entered, and urged us to the kitchen. "That fool won't be dissuaded. Now he suspects the house, as well as Mr. McBride. I want you to take the carriage on your own and head back toward North Upton. Then when the two men come back here, I'll say I've loaned the carriage to a neighbor. I'll encourage Mr. McBride to hire a single horse in order to get back to North Upton with his medicines, and, without a carriage, he will no longer be forced to carry that disgusting fellow along with him. He is sure to catch up with you along the way."

We all hurried down the stairs, and I had only a moment to say, "Are you quite sure Solomon will come after us? And we'll be safe?"

Miss Farrow bent to look directly into my face. "Can you drive that horse?"

"Yes, I suppose I can," I admitted. "Old Sam likes me well enough."

"Good. Then I'm sure. Come along, all of you."

But she escorted us first not to the carriage but to the carriage house. Swiftly, she pulled out three men's capes and hats and hastened us into them. On Sarah, the cloak hung to the ground, and the hat tipped down over her face. Miss Farrow seized a cloth to stuff inside the hat brim and replaced it. Jerushah and I stared at each other, almost unrecognizable in the male garments. Only our skirt hems protruding below the cloaks could give us away. Each of us rolled our waistbands slightly, so that just our boots showed under the stiff driving cloaks.

"Good! Now, Sarah and Jerushah into the carriage, and Alice to the driver's bench, and off you go!"

So, at ten o'clock of the morning on Monday, the twenty-fifth of March, I found myself garbed as would befit a young man, clucking my tongue uncertainly to my father's old horse, Sam, and flapping the reins to urge him ahead, north along the Plain, headed for the road up Mount Pleasant toward the Four Corners, hoping that before anything else went awry, Solomon McBride—without Mr. Clinton—would catch us up and resume his role as our hero of the day.

Courage, I told myself. Courage. And liberty and labor. Courage and liberty and labor and drive! Courage and liberty and labor and drive! I said it aloud and watched Sam's ears prick back toward me. It must have sounded like a command to him, for he picked up his pace and headed north and then northeast, toward the road to North Upton.

Two long miles later, it felt like a hundred hours had passed, and we arrived at the Four Corners. I stopped Sam and remembered to hold the reins as I climbed down from the driving bench to tap at the door of the carriage. The curtains were all pulled shut, but around one of them, Jerushah peered.

She had set aside her oversized borrowed hat but still wore the cloak. Sarah huddled against her.

"Is he here? Is Solomon here?"

"Not yet," I replied, worried about the hurried plan. "What if he can't get away from that Henry Clinton? What if he's being followed toward North Upton?"

The point seemed all too possible. Miss Farrow's plan had its virtues, but standing at the Four Corners, with nobody coming out of any of the houses, and a cold white sky promising spring snow, nothing sounded certain. How could we dare to go onward?

"We'll wait a bit," I decided. I climbed off the carriage step and led Sam, who drew the carriage. I turned up the north road—not the west one toward North Upton, but the one to the right. Leading Sam, I walked just beyond the bend in the road, then asked Jerushah to pull back her window curtain and keep an eye on the horse, whose head had already dropped into a position of rest.

"I'll walk back just far enough to see who's coming to the corner," I explained. "You stay here. That way, we won't get caught." Now that we'd left the town, a sense of adventure tugged at me, and I smiled at my friend. But Jerushah simply stared at me, then shook her head and looked at the horse. I gave him a pat on the neck and hoped he'd stand still.

Hands tucked for warmth under my swishing cloak, I trudged in the mud back toward the corner and crouched behind the wide trunk of a maple, one of a row not being tapped for sugar. In North Upton, that would be considered wasteful. But here they were, and wide enough to hide me, at least enough so that no casual eye would see me when driving or riding from the Plain of St. Johnsbury.

A few light snowflakes danced past on a breath of cold breeze, then ceased. I shifted from one foot to the other, trying to keep my feet from turning numb with cold. Men who drove horses wore proper boots, not ladies' ones with their thin soles. I wished I had William's cast-off boots.

The sound of a horse trotting pulled me to alertness. I stared and saw someone riding toward the Four Corners. Yes, it was Solomon McBride; he was swinging his head back and forth, looking for the carriage and the three of us. I almost stood to call to him—then hesitated. Surely, he would see the carriage tracks on his own and realize we had turned north?

He did. By his face the tracks puzzled him, but he took the turn onto the north-bound road, and a moment later, I could wave to him and urge him around the curve of the road. I also waved assurance to Jerushah, and as I explained my notion, Solomon dismounted and tied his hired horse to a fencepost. Sam snorted softly at the second horse but stood in place. Together Solomon and I walked quietly back toward the four corners of the road. To anyone watching from one of the nearby houses, we must look quite strange indeed, as we scuffed out the wheel tracks at the turn and then hid ourselves behind the row of maples.

We waited until I thought my feet would never feel or walk again. Solomon whispered, "Perhaps he's not coming." Then, just as we began to stand upright to go back to the carriage, we both heard the sound of another horse and crouched again behind the tree trunks.

A black horse with an oddly shaped saddle and a slender rider, leaning forward and urging the horse to trot, emerged from the St. Johnsbury road and hurried across the junction of the roads at the Four Corners. Its rider never looked at the crossroad or inspected the carriage tracks but slapped at the horse's flank instead, intent on following the signs that pointed toward North Upton.

There was no doubt who the rider was: the bounty hunter, Henry Clinton, headed for our village with his suspicions of Solomon McBride, determined to find and capture the fugitive, Fred. Most likely Fred already stood on Canada's land, so that my brother William and Jerushah's brother Matthew might soon return home. If we all—Solomon and Jerushah and Sarah and I—went to North Upton, Sarah would be the only colored person that the frustrated slave catcher could discover there.

I discovered that Solomon McBride and I had exactly the same idea of how to handle the situation. Bringing the hired horse to the back of the carriage, where he could follow along, we rejoined Jerushah and Sarah. Solomon climbed up on the driver's bench, and I gratefully entered the carriage, to tuck my frozen feet under the bearskin and inform my friends of the newest plan.

The carriage jerked as Sam began to move forward once again. We were headed north—toward the border.

CHAPTER 13

Within the carriage, the wintry cold of mid March bit sharply. There was little remainder of the day's earlier sunshine. I worried about how angry my father might be when he learned we'd extended the errand he'd given us, in this way. Jerushah and Sarah and I huddled close under the bearskin. I searched my thoughts for a mild story to tell, to distract Sarah from the perils of the day. But my mind seemed numb.

Jerushah asked, "Does Mr. McBride know the road all the way north?"

"No, I'm afraid not. But he can drive old Sam well enough to Lyndon Corner, and we'll find the road to Wheelock from there. Do you recall, Jerushah, that Helen's mother and father live in Wheelock? They have one of the big sheep farms there."

This direction gave me a start into talking about Helen and her family, and Jerushah, understanding the need for distraction, asked many questions. Though Sarah spoke little, she nodded as we conversed. I noted the gradual relaxing of her arms, which had been clenched about her chest. Warmed by the presence of Jerushah and me to either side of her, she breathed more deeply and her eyelids fluttered as though she might sleep between us. We lowered our voices and continued to speak of Helen and William and even of sheep farming, as best we could, making a lullaby of boring talk.

Sarah slid down against Jerushah's shoulder, nestling against her. I eased apart a little ways, so that they might have better leg room under the bearskin. My foot thumped against an obstacle under the rug, and I realized it was a basket; with slow quiet movements, I retrieved it and discovered it contained two loaves of bread and a paper of sweet biscuits. Miss Farrow must have tucked it there in the midst of our departure. I thought again of her invitation to me, but when I mentioned it to Jerushah, she said, "Oh, is that what Miss Farrow meant? I had no idea of it. I suppose it would be fitting for you to accept, as long as you didn't need to leave the village. As long as your father didn't object, of course."

This tied my tongue completely: Not only would my father surely object to a larger role for me in Miss Farrow's efforts, but the notion of not leaving the village defied the very sense of mission and exhilaration that I'd started to enjoy! Glumly, I turned the conversation back to the weather and recollections of last year's spring.

When this topic also petered out, Jerushah proposed that we sing. We began with a sweet old tune, then let our voices blend in "A Mighty Fortress Is Our God." The conviction that we were doing the right thing, for Sarah and for freedom, began to lift us and our voices. Soon a pleasant baritone mingled, as Solomon McBride caught the melody and joined us.

I wondered idly whether one might measure miles traveled in terms of verses of hymns completed. Before I had time to propose this, however, the carriage halted, and Solomon came to the door. Sarah stirred and woke abruptly with a small cry, but Jerushah comforted her while I answered Solomon's question about the town we were entering: Lyndon Corner, already.

"I don't know it well," I admitted. "I doubt that I've passed through more than twice, for Helen's marriage once and then with my father to bring home sheep, I think. But it's a busy center, with at least two taverns. I'm sure we can find someone who'll point us to the Wheelock road."

Solomon asked me to ride on the bench with him, so that I might confirm the names of Helen's parents and help him to inquire for our route. With Jerushah nodding agreement, I disentangled my skirt and emerged out of the cozy snuggle into the snap of the windy afternoon.

Up on the driving bench, I saw how much the sky had darkened. "Snow on its way," I speculated unhappily.

Solomon McBride tucked a woolen rug around my legs and clucked to old Sam. I realized he'd given up his own shelter to me. But modesty forbade me to share the cover with him.

A moment later, the road dipped downward into Lyndon Corner, and from a smooth packed snowy surface, it changed to ruts and mud and ice, as well as rivulets of dark water. Another carriage passed us, and up ahead I saw the cheerfully lit windows of the first tavern, at the stage inn on our right.

Several men stood outside the inn, and all looked at us as we pulled up near them. Solomon called down, "We're racing the weather, I'm afraid. Could you point us toward the Wheelock road? I'm looking for the Bradley farm up there."

"Horace Bradley?" One of the men stepped closer. "You'll have quite a pull ahead of you to get up there before dark. Might be you'd want to stay over for the night and head up in the morning?"

I spoke up. "I'm taking word to the Bradleys about my brother's wife Helen, their daughter. She's had a baby boy just born, and Mrs. Bradley may want to come down to North Upton to help with the care." Actually I doubted that Helen's mother would want to do anything of the sort—she must know that my own mother would care well for her daughter—but it made a good tale, and the men accepted it.

The tallest one, the one who'd already spoken, pointed out the turn and told Solomon it was five miles to South Wheelock, then another three to Wheelock village. "Might be best for you to leave your carriage here and borrow a sleigh to get up to there," he advised. "The innkeeper can fit you up, around at the carriage house."

This plan made good sense, even though the sleigh would be open, unlike the snug closed carriage. It took only a few minutes for old Sam to be settled into the innkeeper's stable, the carriage set aside, and the hired horse from St. Johnsbury Plain hitched to a wide sleigh. Though a few eyebrows were raised as our party of four was revealed, Sarah's small brown face evoked gentle smiles from the stable hands and an offer of an extra woolen blanket to tuck under the big bearskin.

Following Solomon's sharp look toward the inn, I saw a single unfriendly scowl, and a large man, limping slightly, spat noisily as he cleared his throat before entering the inn. The man's stare, and his scowl in Sarah's direction, convinced me there were dangers around us, beyond just the weather. Old Mo's betrayal of our movements had no doubt been accidental—but this man's dislike could lead to something worse. Without telling the other girls why, I urged them to sit down in the sleigh and tugged the covers quickly around all three of us. I wedged the basket of food back behind my foot and accepted two hot bricks to tuck there also, with gratitude, from the kind stable hand, all the while keeping my face turned away from the inn and hoping word of our destination would not spread. We must stay someplace for the night. How quickly could we take Sarah to true safety at the border the next day?

In front of our row of girls, Solomon wedged himself against the front of the bench with a courteous murmur toward us and slapped the reins. The young horse in front of us began a brisk walk toward the turn, passing several large houses along the way.

As soon as we made the corner, Solomon urged the horse to a trot. I dared not whisper anything about the unpleasant stranger, to either Jerushah or Solomon, for fear of upsetting Sarah. So I prattled about the road instead, and about Helen's family up ahead of us in Wheelock.

At least a dozen more houses lined the roadside, and then the road dipped through a covered bridge, where the wooden slats and sides echoed the horse's hoof-falls and the sharp whine of the sleigh runners on ice within it. Beyond the bridge, the houses spaced themselves out and soon were simply farmhouses, some dark and shuttered.

Our road followed the frozen course of a river. After the first mile, we saw no other carriages or horses. Jerushah broke apart a loaf of bread, and we each chewed our near-frozen mouthfuls, laboring to swallow. I wished there had been time to ask for tea at the inn.

Solomon leaned back slightly, toward the row of us, and I eased forward to catch his words. He asked, "How far did he say, to South Wheelock?"

"Five miles," I said. "About an hour for the horse?"

"About that," Solomon agreed. He glanced sideways, his face a dark red from the cold, with white areas around his eyes and mouth.

I thought abruptly of Uncle Martin and his furry beard and imagined its utility in the cold outdoors. Poor Solomon! I pulled my own muffler close around my face and, without thought, reached forward to tug up the collar of his driving coat. It startled him, and then he nodded his thanks. My own face heated with a blush, so I spoke quickly for the sake of distraction.

"When do you think the snow will start?"

"Before South Wheelock, I'm afraid. I've already seen some flakes. Look!"

He was right. I leaned backward and pointed out the start of the snowfall to Jerushah and Sarah, and we raised the edge of the bearskin to cover Sarah completely. Her bright eyes peered up at us from under its cover, and unexpectedly, we all three began to laugh. "Sarah, you're just a lamb hidden in a bearskin," Jerushah proclaimed merrily.

From where we sat behind him, Solomon's shoulders showed only his arms reaching forward to urge the horse along, but I thought I caught a short laugh from him also. Onward!

A slick-surfaced bridge back across the river brought us into South Wheelock, where at least the houses all stood occupied, with smoking chimneys and a few candle-lit windows. I saw no faces, neither outside nor at the windows, and the horse slowed and took a sharp turn to the right. Almost at once the road forked. "Left or right?" Solomon asked. I didn't know. But most of the sleigh and horse tracks on the snow led to the right, so we settled on that choice. A long smooth stretch of road proved us right.

The wind dropped, and snow fell heavily. Soon our shoulders and hats bore a thick white blanket of flakes, which also covered the bearskin. One at a time, Solomon warmed his gloved hands within his driving coat. I found myself leaning forward again, as if to urge the horse to pick up speed.

But crossing another bridge slowed us, and then an increase in the slope of the road brought the horse down to a walk. I asked Solomon, "Can the horse pull so many of us uphill? Should I get out and walk beside the sleigh?"

He reached behind to pat my arm clumsily with the hand he'd just warmed. "You're good to offer, but the sleigh slides well, and the horse can manage. Why don't you start the others singing again?"

A long stretch of straight road, rolled and packed to a good surface, lay before us. In the thickening snowfall, I could see no houses alongside. Soon even the road surface blurred under two inches or more of new snow. I noticed we were going more slowly. Rather than ask Solomon again, though, I tried to focus on finding other hymns to suggest, and Jerushah sang each one through at least four verses, as Sarah piped along under the cover. My cheeks ached with cold, and my face grew stiff. I brought my hands out from below the bearskin to rub my cheeks and sang as energetically as I could, trying to warm myself from the effort.

Between the heavy snow and the late hour—well past four o'clock, I guessed—the daylight vanished. A faint white glow hovered to the west of us. I sensed the horse picking its way, feeling for the road surface. Then it halted. Solomon shook snow off his coat as he climbed down, reins left behind and one arm reaching instead for the bridle at the horse's head.

"I'll lead," he said to us. "Alice, pick up the reins and hold them loose, so he won't feel any pull from them."

A step at a time, we went forward. My hands ached from the cold. I found a way to hold the reins with just one, so I could alternate warming one against me. Jerushah gave me an apologetic glance before slipping down under the bearskin to hold Sarah there, shielded from the weather.

Again we stopped. Solomon clucked to the horse and tugged forward, but it refused to move, planting its hooves in the snow and tossing its head in agitation. I sniffed the air, trying to guess what agitated the animal. Wood smoke! We must be nearly to the village. But why would that make the horse stop?

A deep growl in front of us froze us all in fear, except for the horse, which fought to back up, tipping the sleigh from side to side. Solomon yelled and held tight to the bridle, hanging from the horse himself, bounced with its movement. As the sleigh tilted sideways, I found my wits and scrambled out of my side of it, struggling to pull downward and keep it from completely capsizing. Sarah and Jerushah clung to the back of it, crying out.

So much noise and commotion—perhaps it helped to keep the invisible animal in front of us from coming closer. Its growl rose in volume, however, and the horse reared onto its hind legs. Solomon still clung to the bridle. I grabbed Sarah and pulled her free from the sleigh, and Jerushah scrambled out, just before it capsized fully into the snowbank at the left side of the road. The horse managed to come down in a half turn, dragging the capsized sleigh back the way we'd come. Solomon yelled and swore. One of his legs, caught in the leather straps of the reins and harness, jerked him so hard that he let go of the horse's head at last and fell, yelping with pain as his shoulders struck the roadway.

But I had eyes only for what stood revealed in front of us, a dead lamb dangling from its jaws, and the crescendo of its growl rising into a high-pitched threat: wild-eyed face suddenly visible in a gap in the snowfall, legs tensed to leap, body easily three feet long and muscular, and the long tail slashing back and forth behind it. A catamount. The fierce and powerful beast of the mountains stared at the three of us as we clung to each other, unable to think beyond the screams that erupted from all of us at once.

Unbelievably, Jerushah still had the bread basket's handle over one arm. I felt her pull back from me, and I dodged just in time as she hurled it into the storm, toward the beast that threatened us.

It leaped forward, so the basket never collided with its muscled, tawny body. But forward, for the catamount, meant across the road, over the snowbank, leaving behind the three of us and our terror as it carried its woolly and bloodied kill away.

I shook uncontrollably. So did Sarah, against me. So did Jerushah, now sobbing and saying "Mama, mama," over and over again.

"Help me!" came a hoarse cry behind us. "Alice! Help me!"

Solomon! I whirled and realized the horse stood shaking also, its harness tangled, the sleigh upside down, and Solomon himself on the snowy ground, one length of leather reins stubbornly wrapped around a wrist, and the other arm under him, his face pressed against his shoulder as he struggled to regain his footing.

"We're coming," I managed to say. "Jerushah, Sarah—we have to help Solomon. Come on."

CHAPTER 14

I wanted to fix everything at once. But it wasn't practical. Of the three of us, only I was willing to approach the horse. So that became my task: coax the frightened animal to let me hold its bridle, stroke its face, try to hold it from stepping into more confusion.

Sarah whispered, "What if that beast sets down the lamb and comes to eat us?"

Jerushah answered, as she knelt next to Solomon, "We're in heaven's hands, Sarah. Surely that's why the catamount already had its prey. Come help me, please. The catamount is gone now."

Sarah obeyed. Following Solomon's instructions, she worked a hand into one of his pockets to find a knife. Absent-mindedly, I wondered why someone who owned such a large and strong pocket knife would have needed to borrow my father's hoof knife. But I had too much to do to think about it long. I clucked to the horse and asked Solomon its name.

"Taffy," he groaned through gritted teeth. "Head shy, pat his neck instead."

I stopped reaching for the long nose and patted the sweating neck. Horses weren't supposed to be allowed to sweat in the cold, wasn't that true? What should I do about that? The animal responded to his name, stopped rolling his eyes, and let me grasp the bridle after all, as I continued to stroke his neck.

Sarah helped pull the leather straps tight enough for cutting, and Jerushah sawed at one determinedly, then at another. The harness separated from the sleigh. It tipped the rest of the way over into the snowbank.

A moment later, Solomon's leg came free of the straps. With Jerushah's help, he stood upright, his shoulders oddly contorted. One arm, the one that had been under him, hung awkwardly loose, and, as it moved, he cried out in pain. He grasped it with his other hand to hold it still. "Dislocated," he grunted. "I'll need help to replace it in the socket."

"What should I do?" asked Jerushah. Sarah closed the knife and tucked it into her sash as she buried her hands again under her cloak.

"You can't do it. I've had it done before, but it takes a strong man to press the bone back into the socket," Solomon explained. He asked me, "Do you think you can lead the horse?"

"Of course. How far do you think it is?"

"Not very."

All of us could catch the tang of smoke now. We must be at the edge of Wheelock's homes. I marveled that a catamount had been so close to the village.

"I can't see the road," I admitted. "Will the horse know where to step?"

"Most likely he will. Get on now, Taffy."

The horse eyed him skeptically, then stepped past him, in the direction from which the smoke seemed to come.

Sarah suggested, "Let's all hold hands, and we'll follow the horse."

Which is exactly what we did. I held the horse by one strap of the remaining harness, and Sarah held my other hand; Jerushah then linked to her and to the good left arm that Solomon offered. I thought my feet would freeze solid before we arrived, but knowing that Sarah and Jerushah must be suffering in the same way, I concentrated on not slipping or falling.

I counted to myself as we stepped. I could walk one hundred steps, surely. Maybe two hundred if I kept moving.

But it took only one hundred and twenty-three steps, with our four-footed guide, to reach the nearest house. A single window glowed, the most lovely sight I could imagine. Jerushah went to the door to knock.

One house further would be the home of Helen's parents, said the woman who came to answer the knock. She looked at Solomon with sympathy and offered to send her husband to walk with us, with a lantern. We accepted. I didn't think she noticed the darkness of Sarah's face in the shadows, and I was glad to be spared any question.

Though it seemed to take a long time, the truth of our passage to the next house might have been only a few minutes. This time, the neighbor rapped at the door, and, as Helen's father opened it, I called out from where I stood with the horse. "Mr. Bradley? I'm Alice Sanborn. I'm so sorry to trouble you so late, but I wonder whether we might come in. I have such good news for you about Helen and her baby."

"More good news?" The gray-bearded farmer peered out into the snowstorm. "It wasn't enough that William came here himself? What more is there?"

His wife crowded up to the door and said, "Don't ask questions when she's standing in the cold. Come in, my dear. Oh goodness, there are more of you!" She spotted Sarah's small frame and dashed out into the yard to gather her up and move her into the warm interior, with Jerushah and Solomon following.

My teeth chattered as I asked, "May I put the horse in your barn?"

"I'll take him," Mr. Bradley said, swinging a cloak over his shoulders. "Go in with the others, child. Your brother's already asleep, but I suppose he'll wake soon enough with all the company. Go right ahead in." He pressed me forward.

My brother? William? Dear merciful heaven, was William here, too, with Matthew? My knees buckled, and I sat abruptly on a wooden box inside the doorway as the warmth made my toes burn with feeling again. Oh, my. My mind must be frozen like my fingers, I reflected. I had no idea what to do next, or what to think. My brother?

From the kitchen beyond, I heard men's voices raised in surprise. Yes, sure enough: William, talking with Solomon. And then Matthew's voice as well.

Oh, my.

Mrs. Bradley came from the kitchen to tug me up from my doorway seat. "Come get warm, and tell us all about your journey and about Helen and the baby," she urged. "Your brother's not half talkative enough to suit me. How did the labor go? How is she healing? And the little one, is he suckling as he should? I've half a mind to see them myself, but I can't leave here until lambing's done and over," she rattled on. "And your father, how is the lambing going there? And sugaring, is he? My goodness!"

Little wonder that the evening seemed a jumble of voices and stories; of Fred's safe passage across the border at Derby; of William's decision to visit Helen's parents, so natural, but not a choice I'd thought of in our mad escape; of the fear we'd felt as Henry Clinton, the bounty hunter, had focused on North Upton; of the painful but quick adjustment of Solomon's dislocated shoulder so that his arm again could function. And at last, there was time to hope that Miss Farrow had found a way to send a message to Jerushah's family and mine, to assure everyone of our safety and let them know our mission.

The heat from the woodstove in front of me and a bowl of mutton stew inside me combined to soften my attention and sent me drowsing, in spite of all the talk around us. And when next I woke, it was in the darkness of an upstairs room, under a featherbed with Jerushah and Sarah and Mrs. Bradley's two younger daughters.

Deciding what to do next would have to wait until morning.

I slept, dreamless, until just after dawn, when a nightmare of wild beasts set me shaking under the covers, one side of me chilled where the Bradley daughters had slipped out to tend to kitchen tasks. I knew my duty and tucked the covers snugly over Sarah and Jerushah as I rose likewise, to ease my stiff and aching muscles into standing position and tiptoe down the kitchen stairs.

Breakfast became a merry gathering, with so many of us to crowd around the table. When, at last, the dishes were set aside and plans announced, it turned out William and Matthew and Solomon knew best—or so they said, having decided it all, while helping with chores in the two barns: one close to the house, where the horses were stabled, and the other, up the hill a short distance, for the hundred sheep and their increase of spring lambs. It appeared the chores had allowed plenty of breath for discussion.

"There's no point in my going further north," Solomon outlined. "I'm promised to a gathering in Hardwick tomorrow evening, and there's scarce enough time to get there as it is, with the horse to return to the Plain first. Matthew can convey Sarah to the Reverend Putnam in Albany—that's Albany, Vermont," he explained to Sarah, "not New York. And then you'll be sent to Barton, and then to the border, as soon as there's a rider to take you."

Jerushah and I exchanged looks, and she nodded to me to go ahead and explain how the plan went wrong. I sat up tall and straight and spoke firmly. "Sarah is not a parcel, and she won't be conveyed or sent," I asserted. "Jerushah and I are traveling with her until her destination." As the men stiffened in disagreement, I laid the ultimate argument out: "It's our Christian duty to see her secure in a good family," I announced.

A ring of pursed mouths and frowning foreheads told me the young men disagreed, although Mr. Bradley nodded from his position next to the stove. "That's good sense speaking there," he admitted. "She's very young to travel, and I'd want to see her comfortable where she goes. No telling when someone might take advantage of her youth and her position." By this he suggested that someone might turn our Sarah to servitude, although surely not slavery. He continued, "Why shouldn't the young ladies all travel together, then? With one of you fellows to drive, of course. But you're not taking the child to the border, are you? There's many a good family for her closer than Canada. Think of the Reverend Twilight, over to Brownington. He'd be sure to take her at his school, wouldn't he?"

Mrs. Bradley explained that the schoolmaster himself was a man of mixed race, but born free, of freeborn parents, in southern Vermont. Her phrasing reminded me of something that Miss Farrow had said.

"Coventry," I recalled. "How far is Coventry from here?"

"Twenty miles, more or less," Mr. Bradley guessed. "Brownington, now, that would be about sixteen or eighteen, I suppose. You can't get there all that directly, from here."

"Then we need to take Sarah to Coventry. That's where Miss Farrow would want her to go."

That statement perhaps spoke too firmly of something Miss Farrow had barely mentioned. But I saw Sarah's face light up as she too recalled the earlier conversation with her beloved Miss Farrow: a family of colored people, whom Miss Farrow knew and liked.

Jerushah saw the same thing that I did and spoke up for Sarah. "I believe Alice is correct. If we're not to take Sarah home to North Upton, then Coventry is where she should go.

There's a family there to welcome her, and she'd be close enough to the border if the need ever came for her to pass across, less than a dozen more miles. But it will be easier for her own mother and father to find her if she stays within the States."

Solomon pressed for details, and we told him all we knew. He took our side then and persuaded William and Matthew that the change of plans should follow. "The town's half French as well," he told them. "Matthew, I'll ask you to complete the next step of that task we've spoken of." Here he paused and looked meaningfully at Jerushah's brother, then at mine. They nodded slowly.

"What?" I asked. "What is it?"

"Just a small delivery to make," Solomon said, brushing his hands against the table to illustrate sweeping the subject aside. "Nothing to worry about. Lads, let's move our deliberations to the carriage barn, to sort out horses and directions. And we've a sleigh to rescue from a snowbank as well."

Even with the menfolk off to the barn, between the Bradley daughters and Mrs. Bradley and the three of us, the kitchen spared little space. After a few minutes I excused myself, saying I needed to remind William of something. Taking my adopted driving cloak from the peg by the door, I stepped outside.

Snow had fallen steadily through the night and still swirled lightly in the wind. The loose fluff on the ground reached the top buttons of my footwear—five or six inches, I guessed. I hitched up my skirt under the driving cloak, to keep the hem from becoming wet and frozen again. My mother would not like the condition of my clothing, I knew.

Already walking down the road with a horse and harness were Mr. Bradley and William and Matthew. What point was there in trying to talk with William when the others wanted him to help with the sleigh? Besides, truth be told, it was Solomon I wanted to ask about—so I'd ask my question of him directly. I trudged through the snow to the barn and pried open the nearest door.

Solomon saw me and paused for a moment in fastening the bridle onto Taffy, the hired horse. He started with "Why" and seemed to change his mind: "Alice, would you kindly help me lift the saddle? My shoulder's not what it should be, and I'd be grateful for your assistance."

His formality made me hesitate, but I needed to know the answer. I stepped close to take one side of the saddle and spoke directly. "Solomon, I doubt that you're a farmer, or taking on any other trade in the out of doors. And you're no teacher, and likely no lawyer. So how is it you earn your living, and why do you keep coming back to North Upton?"

Standing next to him, I watched his face work as he measured my question and his response. First his eyebrows lifted in surprise, then lowered in concern, then smoothed as he adjusted a faint smile and attempted a first diversion: "I'd be no sane gentleman if I didn't find you and your friends an attraction, young Miss Alice," he drawled. "But it's early in our acquaintance for me to say more than that, I'm afraid."

"Nonsense!" I stamped my foot, startling the horse. I stroked his neck in apology, remembering not to pat his face. "Gammon," I continued. "I'm a farmer's daughter, and I'm no fool. Are you running the Underground Railroad stations, Solomon McBride?"

"No, you're no fool," he agreed. He cinched the saddle girth snugly, then turned to face me and reached out a hand to touch my face. I brushed it aside and stood, arms akimbo, waiting for a proper answer.

He looked down at his feet, hiding his thoughts a moment, then looked back at me. "I'm no Underground Railroad man," he continued. "This far north, there's scarce need for more than a handful of right-minded men of the cloth and the good people of these towns and villages. You know that, I'm sure."

I nodded. "But no man can wander the countryside without pay or purpose and still have money to spend and meetings to attend. What purpose do you have here, Mr. McBride?"

A long sigh of decision came from him. He lifted a hand to rub his chin, a gesture that made me suspect he'd only give part of the truth. But even part would be better than none.

"Have you heard of William Seward?" he asked me at last.

"Seward? Of course. He's the one who countered Daniel Webster about whether a compromise on slavery can ever be just." The conversation held in our kitchen that Sunday before the sugaring off seemed ages ago, but I remembered. "What has Seward to do with you?"

"I'm Seward's man," Solomon said bluntly. "We're organizing the New England states for the debates in this session of Congress. The statehood of California and the territories nearby can't be left to chance. If Webster continues to betray the cause, the slave states are bound to take control of the Congress. Do you know what that would mean?"

My mind leapt to the obvious. "More slavery. More bounty hunters. More people like Sarah, hunted and captured and sold and tormented. Damnation for the Union."

The face that I was learning to read creased in a bitter smile. "Indeed, Alice Sanborn is no fool. Miss Sanborn, it's my task to follow Seward's lead and prevent that eventuality. No nation can call itself blessed or protected by heaven if it sinks further into the sin and inequity of slaveholding."

"And that's why you need to be in Hardwick for tomorrow's evening meeting?"

"It is." He stepped a bit closer and looked a long question into my face. "Would it interest you to know more, Miss Alice Sanborn of North Upton?"

His words, I saw, were a disguise for the intensity that blazed from the dark eyes looking into mine. The question echoed in my chest: Would it interest me to know more?

I lifted a hand to press back from the question—and the man.

"Not yet," I said carefully. "I have my own work to do. I'm taking Sarah to safety in Coventry. But . . . when I return home, if you pass again through North Upton, I may have time to listen."

His hand darted to brush against mine for the briefest contact, and he replied, "Until that day, then." He turned away and tugged at the horse, leading him toward the door. After a nod to me, he eased the door open and stepped outside, then drew the animal toward a nearby mounting block and climbed up into the saddle. He lifted his hat and, with a somber gaze, spoke again.

"Until that day," he repeated. He tapped the horse's flank with his hat and left at a rapid trot over the southbound road.

I, too, stepped out into the yard and closed the barn door behind me. Bemused, I looked down at my hand. Not a tremble, not a shake. And no mark from the touch that seemed still to be against my skin, with its unspoken possibilities.

The kitchen door opened, and Mrs. Bradley called to me. "Are the men back with the sleigh yet?"

"Not yet, I'm afraid."

"Good, then there's time for another pot of tea. And come see what I've packed for you all to carry north, and for William to take to my grandson."

I lifted my skirt a modest inch and moved from the dooryard into the house. I was glad to find Jerushah and Sarah busy brushing out their skirts and cloaks. For a little while, I preferred to avoid the questions they'd ask if they saw my face, which might give more than enough sign of excitement and anticipation.

Calm down, I said to myself. Calm down, and think about how best to go north, then home again. Surely no bounty hunter could have followed us this far. No strange old man like Moses Cook, either.

We fear what we've already seen, what we've heard. I had no clue of the real threat that lay just ahead of us.

CHAPTER 15

Mrs. Bradley's kitchen required constant attention. She had no cookstove, but one large open hearth, two smaller ones, and a brick bread oven. As we waited for the men to return with the sleigh, she encouraged us to join the morning's labor. She set Jerushah to kneading the bread dough, Sarah to stirring batter for gingerbread, and I managed the potatoes roasting at one hearth, while she stirred kettles in the other pair and managed her fires, especially the one heating the bread oven. Her fingers were wide and sturdy, like her figure, and I wondered whether Helen too would assume such a structure, now that she had borne William's first son.

Over my shoulder, I inquired about the other Bradley daughters.

"Lucy is sixteen now, and betrothed to Abram Hill, from Sheffield," our hostess announced proudly. "And Ilona is nearly fifteen, still too young for that, but Hez Davis walks her home from Sunday services often enough. I daresay we'll have one marriage after another at this rate."

"Are they at school today?"

"Heavens, no, child! At their age? They've been working here on the farm since they finished the sixth grade, each of them. Their father would never be able to manage so many sheep without the two of them, especially this time of year, for the lambing."

I'd never heard of young women taking so much of the farm

work, although milking and keeping chickens generally fell to the wives of North Upton. "Will this Abram Hill work with the sheep, too?"

"Oh, my, yes. He already has for the past few summers. That's how they met, you see, Abram and Lucy. But this time of year he's helping his father with sugaring."

"We've had a sugaring off already, down our way," I pointed out.

Jerushah added, "My father says our village will make close to a hundred and fifty thousand pounds of maple sugar this year, and we're about halfway to that, already."

"Imagine that! And up here on the ridge, we're only just starting to gather sap this week, and there's not a soul boiling it yet. Such a difference in season from here to there." Mrs. Bradley told Jerushah to let the dough rise again and asked her to help Sarah spoon the gingerbread batter into its pans. I backed up to give her room to cross again with an armful of split wood.

"The girls will be in for dinner at noon," Helen's mother went on, "and they'll be in a hurry, like as not, to eat and get back to their lambing. This time of March we'll have half a dozen lambs born on some days, with a hundred all told by the end of April. No, don't bother sweeping yet," she said to Sarah, whose helpful offer came as Mrs. Bradley seized the pans of batter and conveyed them to the oven. "Those girls of mine will track the barn in with them at dinner. I'll sweep the kitchen later, when they're back to the barn and you're all traveling again. But you could lay the table with bowls and such; there's a good girl."

So, Mrs. Bradley figured to feed us all dinner before we departed? A sense of time flying past chafed at me. Outside the steamy kitchen window, the sky had darkened again, and snow fell steadily. Only the absence of wind differentiated the weather from the previous evening.

Jerushah noted my gaze. "I wish it would stop snowing," she said quietly.

"Oh, my husband says it's most likely continuing for another day or two," Mrs. Bradley answered cheerfully. "It's sugar snow, you know, the kind that comes late and fluffy and will keep the sap running long and well. Cheer up; spring's around the corner when the sap is flowing."

How odd that seemed—spring surely came sooner in North Upton than in Wheelock, for I knew I'd tasted it already there!

Anxiety asserted itself in my throat again, and I asked, "Do you mind if I step out to the carriage house, to see whether the sleigh is here?"

"Go right ahead, and mind you tie a muffler around you before you add that long coat of yours. Wherever did you get such a coat?"

Sarah and Jerushah began to explain again the events at Miss Farrow's home, which Mrs. Bradley had missed hearing in the bustle of the previous evening. And I stepped out into the dooryard, wishing again for William's cast-off boots. My coat was warm and dry, but my shoes held the damp and cold.

Loud hammering from the carriage barn assured me that the men and sleigh had returned. I crossed the dooryard and opened the wide door just far enough to slip inside, closing it quickly to hold the heat in.

William looked up from his grip on the sleigh, which he held tipped up on one end as Mr. Bradley pounded its underparts. "Two more nails," he grunted.

At the other side of our host, Matthew crouched with a tin. He gave me a friendly smile as he passed two large nails to my brother and suggested, "We may want a brace against there, now that it's broken once."

"Right you are. Here, see if you can get the sense of the angle to cut, and there's a small crosscut saw over on the shelf."

I asked William, "How soon can we leave?"

"We'll be finished here in a few more minutes. Are you girls all set to go?"

"Now, don't be so hasty," Mr. Bradley scolded. "Take your dinner with us, so you've a hot meal inside you first."

But William's tense face assured me he'd noted the same things I had: the continued snow, the five-hour sleigh ride ahead. To be caught in the cold darkness could risk greater catastrophe than an upset sleigh. To my relief, he held his ground, and Matthew supported him. As they completed the repairs and turned to harnessing the horse—this time we would drive young Ely, William told me—I rushed back to the house to urge my friends into their cloaks.

Mrs. Bradley clucked and tutted over the notion of our leaving before her dinner was ready, then packed our basket with biscuits and ham and boiled eggs and pressed a last-minute cup of hot sweet tea into each of us. We embraced her fondly, grateful for the respite and warmth of her home and her concern, and left her to her hearths and oven.

Out in the damp and cold of the snow, Sarah gave a sigh that was almost a whimper. "I hope we won't be as cold as we were last night," she whispered to Jerushah. I saw how the tension drew her little face into deeper shadow under her hat and muffler. I left Jerushah to the comforting, while I walked quickly forward to meet the menfolk as they led two horses and two vehicles out of the barn: Ely pulling the sleigh, and old Sam hitched to our farm wagon, which was piled high with loose hay.

William explained: "Matthew can drive the wagon home to North Upton, but he can't go the way you came here—the road's too steep and snow-drifted for the wagon. So he'll come along with us down the Heights to Glover, then take the river road around to Lyndon Corner and home. Until we separate, you girls can ride in the wagon, with the hay for extra warmth. I'll tuck the rugs around you before I pile it up on you."

I saw the sense of this, so I resisted pointing out that once again, William and Matthew had decided our direction on their own. At least Jerushah and I had prevailed in our insistence on accompanying Sarah to the family in Coventry. One must choose one's arguments and only enter battle on the most important ones, I decided.

Besides, as the wagon rattled underneath us and we held each other snugly, cozy despite the falling snow, I could see what a difference that extra warmth meant to Sarah. Whether it was her younger age or some particular of her physique (I did not think it could be due alone to her dark skin, but perhaps to a family tendency), the cold cost her more dearly than it did Jerushah and me. Now a new topic of conversation, the sheep-farming life of the Bradley daughters and their romances, also warmed us in its way. The only drawback of our hay blanket was the way it made Jerushah cough, from the dust of it. But we tucked our mufflers around our faces and talked through them. And it hardly felt like the hour and a half that I knew must have passed before we turned off the steep hill road, onto the lowland road at the center of Glover.

I squirmed up from our hay-ride cocoon to see the town. Mill buildings, one after another, lined the river. A large inn, busy with wagons and sleighs, offered barely enough space for our two vehicles to pull in. Matthew uncovered his sister and Sarah and sent the three of us inside for tea and a chance to use the "necessary," for which I was thoroughly grateful after the bumps of the ride.

Around the smoky but deliciously warm hearth of the inn's parlor, a group of women and men welcomed us and pressed us to sit close to the fire. Cups of tea in our hands were followed by wedges of hot gingerbread richly scented with maple.

"Where might you young folks be headed?" The question came from one of the men, a round-faced grandfatherly sort with spiky white beard. "Is it Mr. Twilight's boarding school you're going to? It does seem late in the term for enrolling, but maybe you've been enrolled there already and are returning?"

I shook my head, smiling. I knew it was Sarah's dark skin that made them think we'd be on our way to that school. "We're headed to Coventry," I replied. "My brother's driving us there."

"Ah, for a visit with family, then? Would you be an Ide or a Cleveland—or maybe a Labelle or Gagnon?"

The man's way of speaking the French names made them almost sound English after all, but I recognized the implication of these last. He thought we might be French-Canadian, and Catholic! I quickly denied any such connection.

"I'm a Sanborn," I announced, aware that everyone must know the name and family. "And my friends—my friends are a Clark and a J—J—Johnson." I stuttered over the name Johnson, which was also the surname of the fugitive, Fred. It seemed maybe I shouldn't even speak it. But nobody in the room took alarm, as far as I could see.

"Oh, a Sanborn. Then you'll be related to Ralph at the grain mill, eh? But I don't know any Sanborns in Coventry."

"No, we're visiting friends there." I thought I'd better cut off this avenue of exploration. What if someone here mentioned where we'd gone, and word got back to Henry Clinton? Even though that seemed a world away, the past two days had convinced me that the bounty hunter could be persistent. "No, thank you, we won't stay for dinner; we've got to drive north. Thank you so much for your hospitality." Not only had the tea and fire eased us, but the sweet hot drink had quieted Jerushah's cough, and Sarah fairly glowed with warmth.

My friends added their thanks, and we hastened back to the dooryard, with our insides heated and braced for the colder ride of the open sleigh. God willing, my brother might have added hot bricks for our feet, as well as watering the horse and obtaining directions. This latter, I realized, was still in process, as William listened attentively to a young man in a broad-brimmed hat quite out of place for the season.

"And if thee reaches the second pond, thee will have just passed the turn and must turn back to it. No, thee doesn't want to go to Albany; thee wants to take the shorter road directly to Irasburg, and, from there, thee will be but an hour at most from Coventry itself. Mind now, don't thee try to cut through the Gore. Local folks do call it 'bear ridge' for good reason. Keep to the main road; thee shall see it well enough."

Matthew stood next to the wagon and beckoned to Jerushah. Sarah and I went with her.

"Jerushah, I'd be obliged if you'd come directly back home with me in the wagon now. Surely William and Alice can conduct Sarah to this family in Coventry. Mother would want you home, and then you could assure Alice's mother also that she'll soon be there. You've a duty to Mother, too, you know."

"But Matthew, I know Mother would want me to watch over Sarah and be sure she's in good hands," Jerushah protested. She lifted her head bravely to meet her brother's gaze, then was taken by another coughing spell.

"You see," Matthew added, "you should come home for the sake of getting out of this weather, too. Mother won't forgive me if I let you traipse around the north country with some sort of cough or cold. Come with me," he pleaded, gentling his voice.

Jerushah shook her head even as she coughed. When she could speak again, she said, "It's the hay that's made me cough. Riding under it again will only make it worse. Give my love to Mother, and tell her we'll only be another two days longer than you, at the most."

William joined us. "At the most," he agreed. "Most likely sooner. The sleigh's a better way to travel in this weather. Matthew, tell Helen I'm hurrying to be back to her and the child, would you? And . . . you have the parcel?"

"Of course. I'll give the parcel to your father, and I'll make sure Helen has enough help with wood and such."

So it was agreed: Matthew drove off with old Sam and the farm wagon, while we three girls curled ourselves up under the bearskin and woolen blankets, where indeed a handful of hot bricks radiated their comfort. I had a moment to wonder about the parcel being sent to my father—more papers? What did they signify? Then William climbed in front of us and clucked to Ely to get under way, from Glover up the ridge road toward West Glover and its ponds, and onward through the northern county seat of Irasburg, toward our destination in Coventry. We would be following the directions of the man from the inn's yard—a man who must, said Jerushah, be a Quaker, judging by his wide-brimmed hat and curious manner of speech.

This was of great interest to both Sarah and me, as I'd never met one of the Quakers before, and Sarah knew of the group's reputation in fighting for immediate emancipation of all people of her race. Bread and ham under the bearskin fueled our conversation, and if every mile brought us closer to having to separate from Sarah, it also brought us closer to meeting the friends of Miss Farrow. If I couldn't go West, at least I was having an adventure here in Vermont.

William leaned into his driving and left us to our talking. We didn't stop in West Glover at all, and in Irasburg we only paused to let Ely take water and grain at a stable next to the courthouse and its massive brick-walled jail.

So it wasn't until we were once again under way toward our final northern village that I realized why the cold and snowy afternoon seemed so much warmer than its predecessor: it was

Jerushah—she was burning hot with fever. At once, I swiped my hands over the outside of our lap robes to gather handfuls of snow to cool her face and made her suck on some for water to ease her cough, to little avail.

As Jerushah's cough increased in sound and frequency, William turned at one point to look at the three of us. Mirrored in his face was the concern that I knew must be on my own: Jerushah was truly ill. This was not the kind of adventure I wanted. We must reach Coventry quickly and trust that the family there would take her into shelter for the care that she might need.

Dear heaven, I prayed silently, please don't let it be the spotted fever.

CHAPTER 16

The last mile into Coventry village sloped sharply downhill toward the Black River. It should be called the White River in this season, I thought wildly, as we crossed it on a rattling covered bridge. Two general stores and a shoemaker lined the small common, along with a steepled church, a brick meeting-house, and several large homes. William pulled up by the first store, thrust the reins into my hands, and jumped down to inquire the name and direction of the colored family with its four sons, to whom we must introduce ourselves.

Sarah woke beside me; her quiet sleep in the corner of the sleigh had reassured me that she had not fallen prey to the miasma that must have struck Jerushah's chest, and even the most terrible coughing had not woken her. Now, she readily gathered the situation and sat up, examining her surroundings with both curiosity and trepidation. "There are so many build-ings here," she noted, "that it's almost like Upton Center! Do you think we'll be visiting at one of these whitewashed houses?"

William's re-appearance answered her question: "It's a farm family named Hayes," he reported. "But the farm is close to the village." He urged Ely out of a tired stance and into a slow pace up a small hill.

"It's not at that 'bear ridge,' is it?" I worried.

"No, although I believe that's another two or three miles down the same way. But this farm is at a bend of the river."

We passed through another covered bridge, and I saw a well-laid-out farm on a wide plain. Wood smoke rose from a chimney at the main house and darker smoke from a second, smaller building. When we pulled into the dooryard, a tall and broad-shouldered man stepped out of this smaller structure, setting a sharp-looking hay fork against the building before stepping toward us. He wore a brown leather cap and over his blue clothing a brown apron, also of leather, on which he rubbed his massive fists. They, like his face, were black as grease, and the acrid tang of coal smoke came with him as he approached our sleigh. He was a blacksmith. In the tension of the moment, I swallowed a sob of confusion: a black-skinned man who was a smith. The size and strength of him frightened me—he was nothing like Sarah, or even Fred the fugitive. I dared not rise from my seat.

Fortunately, William suffered none of my discomposure. As he stepped out of the sleigh to introduce himself and our errand, I struggled to pull myself together. Lowering my gaze, embarrassed for having stared at the man, I wiped another handful of snow across Jerushah's sweated forehead.

Without such a task to occupy her, Sarah grew restless as the men conversed. Abruptly, she cast aside her part of the coverings and slid down from the sleigh's leather bench, standing and straightening her clothing. In the dim light of late afternoon, she peered around the yard and must have found the gaze of someone watching from within the house. The kitchen door opened, and a tiny woman with a pockmarked brown face, yet gentle in appearance, came toward us, wiping her hands briskly on her apron.

"Don't mind the menfolk," she told us with a smile. "Come into the house and warm yourselves. Have you traveled far? I'm Belle Hayes."

Sarah gasped, "Oh!"

Manners demanded better of me, and I stood at last, stepping into the snowy dooryard, and spoke. "This is Sarah Johnson, and I'm Alice Sanborn. We've come from North Upton. Sarah's been living with my friend's family—this is my friend, Jerushah Clark. Miss Farrow mentioned you and your family to us, and we felt we needed to come."

"Ah, Rachel Farrow—any friend of Rachel's is a friend of mine," Mrs. Hayes answered. "Come in, come in."

Jerushah's shoulders convulsed in another paroxysm of coughing, and she held a handkerchief to her mouth. Mrs. Hayes already had an arm across Sarah's shoulders. Upon hearing Jerushah's cough, she pressed Sarah toward the house and bustled forward to help me, saying crisply, "Bring her inside, right away. There's still some daylight left; we'll send one of the boys to fetch the doctor. Andrew! Edward! Where are you?"

I gave Jerushah my shoulder to lean on as she climbed down. The flowered scent of her hair barely remained through the smoky fragrance that the Bradley kitchen had bestowed upon us all, and below that, I caught an odor of illness in her breath. It shocked me, and I did my best to move her with all possible swiftness out of the falling snow and into Mrs. Hayes's kitchen, where an aroma of supper hovered and a kettle steamed at the hearth.

So, in a matter of minutes, two burdens eased from my shoulders: concern for Sarah and whether there would be a safe and welcoming place for her to reside, in her separation from her own distant family and from North Upton; and uncertainty about Jerushah's illness and how best to meet her needs. A pair of sturdy young men, with complexions wondrously mingled of their father's extreme darkness and their mother's elfin look, undertook the tasks of riding out to fetch the doctor and bringing extra wood from a nearby shed. Sarah accepted directions to fetch cups and pour hot water into a teapot.

At last, I sat, overwhelmed by both relief and fatigue, on a comfortable chair near the hearth, letting the heat penetrate my frame, dry my shoes, and induce me to remove my awkward long driving coat and regain some sense of recognition of my own self once again.

Upon the arrival of Doctor Kendall, I learned that part of my relief was premature: the doctor looked grave as he listened to Jerushah coughing, and felt her fever and tested the pulses of her wrist and throat.

"What sort of damp has she been exposed to?" he inquired of me, resting his long fingers again gently on Jerushah's wrist and regarding his stopwatch. "Cellars, other cold, wet places?"

"Only the ride from North Upton," I replied, and seeing his questioning look, added, "a few miles from St. Johnsbury. We've been more or less on our way here for three days now."

"In a closed carriage?"

"Part of the way. But mostly in a sleigh. And for a little while, in a wagon of hay."

He brushed his other hand in the air. "The wagon of hay is nothing. But the open sleigh, with the cold vapors, may have done some harm. She has a spasmodic cough, with a cold upon her chest."

He turned to Mrs. Hayes, and the two began to discuss what remedies to apply. A mustard plaster, of course, to the chest, and a tea of slippery elm, alternating with coltsfoot. "I would add thyme as well if you have it," the doctor recommended. "And here are some lozenges of anise and honey. One every hour at least, until the cough is relieved. For the fever, administer the mustard plaster and plenty of warm covers, so as to sweat the fever out."

William and the man from the smithy, who must be Mr. Hayes, came in, accompanied by the two boys I had seen earlier. The doctor greeted them all, then excused himself from the newly crowded kitchen. Mrs. Hayes saw him to the door—and it was only because I stepped to hang up my cloak that I overheard what the doctor said as he left: "We must hope that pneumonia does not set in."

Mrs. Hayes's swift sideways glance at me told me that she realized I'd heard, but she said only a quiet thanks to the doctor and turned back toward the others. I stood for a moment, facing the frightening possibility, then determining to do all I could to make sure pneumonia did not, in fact, settle into my friend's chest. That such peril could arrive now, after bounty hunter and storm and catamount, gave me grave doubts that Nature's course was a kind one. I glared at William's back and thought of his certainty that Nature would reveal heaven's beauty and purpose.

Mrs. Hayes lit an oil lamp and a pair of candles to brighten the room. Supper came soon, hearty and good: frizzled beef over biscuits, and an orange vegetable that I did not recognize but that delighted Sarah. "Sweet potato," she called it, though it resembled no potato I'd ever seen or tasted. Corn bread with stewed fruit followed, turning the repast into a true feast.

By the time I crawled under a featherbed with Sarah, Jerushah had cheered, and Mrs. Hayes's teas and plaster and rubs, along with the doctor's lozenges, promised a turn for the better, even as her fever crested and broke. I hoped for the best—and dreaded the worst.

That night I dreamed of an endless sleigh ride through dark and icy woodlands, interrupted by the cries of wild animals that ran close behind me. Driving the sleigh was a silent man in black raiment, who edged closer each moment to me as I sat back to grip the bench in clenched hands. In the dream, his coat flew off him and landed on my face, blinding me and wrapping me in an oppressive heat.

When I struggled awake from the dream, I realized Sarah too

had developed a fever, and a sudden tearing cough that sounded uncannily like the sound of the wild beast of my nightmare.

CHAPTER 17

All the plans we'd made in Glover shattered under the weight of illness.

Some decisions came quickly: Mrs. Hayes ordered her sons to improvise beds in the kitchen for both Jerushah and Sarah, so she could keep the air around them warm and steamy and administer mustard plasters, teas, and broth. I insisted on being between them, rubbing their hands with cool wet flannel, laying chilled compresses on their foreheads, and giving each a familiar face to regard. If need be, I could sleep later in a chair between their beds. Mrs. Hayes also made an immediate decision to keep her boys and husband apart from her coughing guests. She fed William with them in the other room, when they came in from early-morning chores.

"Doctors talk about miasmas that carry illness, but I've seen the cough and worse go leaping from one bed or chair to the next," she explained to me as she laid out a hearty breakfast on four plates for the sons, then a fifth one for her husband and a sixth for William. I offered to help carry them, but she told me instead to fill my own and keep the girls company.

I had no appetite, so I simply returned to my seat, bending close to Sarah first to see that she was sleeping, then to Jerushah, smoothing her hair with my hands. She rested her hot face against me as the fever rose again, coughed in a long spasm, then whispered, "You won't leave me here, will you?"

"Never," I swore. "I won't leave your side, and you're going to get well, you are, you know you are. Drink some more of this so you won't cough so much."

But the return of her fever, after the previous evening's easing of it, frightened me. And for Sarah—she was such a tiny thing to start with. I knew that small children often gave way to more serious illness.

As Jerushah drifted back toward sleep, I held her hand, then eased back to the chair so that I could hold Sarah's also, as they both lay there. It was all my fault, for driving the carriage away from Miss Farrow, into the March weather. What if pneumonia did set into Jerushah's chest—or Sarah's? Fear and grief wrestled in my throat, and salty tears leaked down my face.

The door from the other room began to open, and I let go of Sarah's hand for a moment to sweep a palm across my cheeks, brushing aside the evidence. I would be strong for my friends. I took Sarah's small dark hand again and realized she was sweating heavily. Hope returned. A rustle of skirts and apron next to me confirmed that Mrs. Hayes had come back to provide more tea.

I nodded toward Sarah and the beads of sweat on her face, without letting go. "Is her fever breaking?"

Mrs. Hayes drew back the featherbed a little from Sarah's shoulders and rested a palm on her brow. "Not yet. But the more she sweats, the better. I think she's too small for a second plaster to her chest, but we'll keep her bundled up." She tucked the featherbed back into place. "You didn't eat anything," she observed quietly.

"I can't."

"It would be better if you did. Keep yourself strong, and it might be the sickness won't touch you. You and I, we'll remind each other." She nodded encouragingly, and placed a dish with a slice of bread and ham next to my chair. To my surprise, she added, "You know that your brother must leave today, to carry word home. And he has a newborn son, he tells us. He needs to leave very soon."

I let go of the hot hands of my friends and stood up, confused. "But we can't leave yet. Jerushah is too sick to travel. Doesn't he know that?"

"He knows."

"Then how can he leave? He can't leave us here!"

Mrs. Hayes tipped her birdlike face with those bright, dark eyes to one side and replied, "You can go with him, you know. I'll take care of Miss Jerushah and send her safely back to you when she's well again."

"No!" Abandon Jerushah, leave her among this family that none of us really knew, this family who could in no way be related to us, even as the most distant cousins, these people whose skin and eyes and hair were all so different? I lowered my voice to be calm and ladylike. "You're very kind. But I promised her I'd stay with her."

"I thought maybe you would. So your brother will head home on his own, and we'll write to him when it's safe for you two girls to ride again, and he can fetch you. Might be that will work best after all. I'll bring him now, so you can tell him yourself, Miss Alice, shall I?"

"I—I guess so. I mean, yes, please, ma'am. Yes, I'll tell him."

The front room of the house was noticeably cooler than the kitchen. The Hayes boys and their father must have gone out to work through the front door, so as not to disturb the patients in the kitchen. I felt awkward, and relieved at their absence. William stood next to the small window, hands clenched behind his back. He heard the door and turned to face me.

"Have you packed? We should leave. It's a long way home. And we'll need to stop at Lyndon Corner to return the sleigh and retrieve the carriage. But if we start right away, and the weather holds, we could make it all the way by tonight."

156

I hadn't even noticed before, but now I saw the sky outside, bright blue with "horses' tails" of white clouds streaking across it, moving northeastward with the wind. A cold whistle of air around the door assured me the sunshine brought no real warmth as yet.

"William, I can't go with you. I can't leave Jerushah here with strangers, no matter how kind they are. And she can't go out—she'd surely catch her death of pneumonia if we took her into such weather. Don't you see?" I pleaded, watching the emotions race across my brother's face like weather. "I can write to you when she's well again. The post can carry my letter, and then you—or Matthew—could come up to get us. Please, William, please understand."

"I do understand," he said at last. "But it's presuming on strangers, as you've said. It's not right."

"Then I'll work to make it right," I announced with determination. "I'll mend and cook and clean and help. It can't be easy for one woman to feed five men, day in, day out." Rashly I promised, "I'll do the spring cleaning here, too, while Jerushah gets well. And Sarah. Only let me stay, William. I know you can see your way to it."

Once the decision became clear, William's urgency took him out the door after the briefest of thanks and farewell to Mrs. Hayes, around the edge of the door to the kitchen. Through the little window of the front room, I watched my brother hurry toward the barn, calling out to one of the Hayes boys along the way. A moment later, the young boy—he must have been about ten years old—helped William hitch the sleigh, and with a quick wave toward the house, William took off southward. From the spring of the horse, I knew Ely had been well fed and rested and must be as eager as my brother to return home.

Now the reality of my situation tumbled upon me: here I stood, in the home of strangers of another race, knowing nothing of their background or ways, with two friends in danger from grave illness, depending on me. And if I failed, not only would I lose these two who meant so much to me—I would do so without help or comfort from my own distant family, who could not even know my situation until days after I might write to them. I wished I had thought to send a note with William. I missed my mother terribly, and tears again slipped down my cheeks.

But the very salty heat of my tears reminded me that I had no time to lose in self-pity. I tugged out my handkerchief, grateful to feel the cool cleanliness of it as I mopped my face. No more weeping. As my mother would say, hands to work, and let God hold your heart. Liberty and labor, I reminded myself. Onward!

My return to the kitchen came just in time: Mrs. Hayes struggled to support Sarah while positioning a chamber pot for her. More hands clearly were needed. I knelt next to them and with a nod, took on the guidance of the sturdy white bowl, making sure it would not tip as Sarah crouched unsteadily over it, with our hostess's arms around her shaking body. A spasm of coughs seized her, so I had all I could do to keep the bowl in place—but I did it, and Mrs. Hayes did her part, lifting Sarah back onto her bed and covering her snugly.

I stood with the bowl, clutching its thick handle. It should be emptied in the "necessary" but I didn't know where the outhouse was—the night before, and early that morning, I'd only used the bedroom chamber pot myself.

Mrs. Hayes looked up. "I'll take it," she said quickly. "Just let me tighten the covers."

My promise to William returned to me. "No," I said, "I'll take it myself. I should find the place, anyway. Is it nearby?"

"Out the door and turn to your right, and you'll not miss it."

"I'll find it."

I went out without adding a cloak or boots, knowing I'd just be out there a moment, taking care of the task. The blue wind-swept sky and the clear air, free of steam or illness, woke me in a new way. There was work to do, and I knew how to work.

That first day in the little house outside Coventry, I did more than work: I labored to prove that neither I nor my friends would be a burden on Mrs. Hayes. That meant helping with the noon dinner, as well as learning to prepare sweetened tea according to direction, with whichever herb was selected by the small, bent hands of my hostess. I tried to jump for tasks without being asked, and twice more, I carried the contents of the chamber pot outside. If I had been home, my mother would have tested my own forehead for fever, assuming only illness could make me so willing to undertake the humblest tasks. As it was, though, each moment out in the crisp air with brightly burning sun strengthened me and gave me a certainty that I barely understood.

I found myself whispering a prayer in the fading light of late afternoon: "Dear Lord in heaven, please let Jerushah get better, and Sarah. Guide Mrs. Hayes, please, and help me be strong in helping her."

Afternoons raised fevers to their highest, Mrs. Hayes warned me. And her prediction held valid that day, as Sarah began to sob between spasms of coughing, and Jerushah's gaze turned to a glaze of unhealthy exhaustion.

Frightened especially by Sarah's heat, I asked Mrs. Hayes, "Should we not try to cool her now? To reduce the fever?"

"Not yet," came the reply, while without complaint she carried another pair of heavy heated bricks wrapped in flannel to place at the feet of our two patients. "If the fever rises further after sundown, then that must be our choice, but for now, we must try to sweat the illness out of each of them. Here, see if you can coax Miss Jerushah to sip on this tisane, while I do the same for our little one."

I noticed "our" and for a moment felt envy, that this woman's affection for Sarah would soon replace mine and Jerushah's in the life of our lamb. But I corrected myself firmly, trying to accept instead the rightness and peace of Sarah being embraced by people of her own race. If her parents never escaped the Southern tyranny, she would need as close a replacement family as she could find.

I rubbed Jerushah's hands again with minted water and held a cup of tea to her lips, supporting her head and neck that she might swallow a little without choking.

A cold gust of air announced the arrival of two of the Hayes sons. Though I'd heard all their names the first evening, I had little recollection of them. Listening to their quiet conversation with their mother about the lambing at a neighbor's sheep farm, I placed the youngest boy, the ten-year-old, as Sylvester, the next older one as Edward. Each helped himself to a bowl of soup and tiptoed into the front room.

When the other two sons, Charles and Andrew, arrived, they had little to say, and their father gave only a weary sigh as he filled his mug and bowl. Their size and strength still shook me and made me glad they sat in the other room. Why had I thought all colored people were small and weak? And if these men were so strong, how could they have been among the enslaved people I'd read about and imagined?

A few minutes later, Mrs. Hayes said to me, "I think Sarah's less heated. Touch her cheek and tell me if you think the same."

I turned away from Jerushah to face our dark lamb, and laid the back of my hand against the small face. Yes, she was less hot, less fevered. I smiled at Mrs. Hayes, and we shared a moment of relief.

"Still," she said quietly, "I think I'll just ask Charles to lay his hands upon her, to seek a good healing."

Baffled at this statement, I sat silently between our two patients as Mrs. Hayes went to the front room. She returned with Charles; I saw that he had a wide dark face, much more like his blacksmithing father than like his tiny mother. His gaze was steady, and he gave a small nod to me as he said quietly, "My mother says you've been a right hard worker. We're pleased to have you."

Relief coursed down my backbone, letting it sag at last from the stiffness I'd tried to maintain for the day's labor. My promise of earning our way in this household could yet see success. I let go of Sarah's hand as the young man—I guessed that despite his height he might be only about fourteen years of age—approached her bed. He knelt on the floor next to her. I edged backward to make space, pressed back against Jerushah, whose unsteady breathing suggested no relief yet from the day's fever for her.

Charles spoke gently over his folded hands: "Our Father in heaven, bless this child and her spirit, we pray, and lift from her the burden of illness. Make her whole, and allow her to stay among us on this side of the Valley of the Shadow of Death. Bring her into your wholeness and your holiness, for the sake of the Lord Jesus, who gives liberty to every soul." Then he blew for a moment on his own palms, curiously pink and veined with a dark tracery, and placed his hands on Sarah's shoulders, his head still bowed in prayer.

I held my breath, wondering. Who could dare to pray so directly? Who could place hands upon the sick and expect them to rise, as in the Holy Book? I thought of Lazarus, and then of the small girl called back from death's shadows. I could not see Sarah's face, in the dimness of the room. I whispered, "Amen."

Charles lifted his face, then his hands, and opened his eyes. He turned toward me, and I tugged at my skirt to make room again.

161

"Would you want me to lay hands on this young lady, now?" he asked quietly. "The spirit is sweet as honey among us this night."

I shook my head—to tell him "No." I stared, and again shook my head. My voice cracked as I said, "I don't know if she'd want it. I don't mean any offense. But I can't speak for her. May I ask you instead to pray for her? She's been like a sister to Sarah." Without meaning to, I found those forbidden tears again coursing down my cheeks.

"For our Sister Jerushah, I will pray, with hope," the dark young man replied and rose, ducking his head under the low ceiling, to return to the front room and the other men there.

Mrs. Hayes bent close to Jerushah. "May I check her fever?" she asked as she reached out a hand.

"Of course." I scrambled out of the way and stood awkwardly.

Concern creased the older woman's face. She looked up at me as she changed hands, using each one to feel the heat of Jerushah's forehead.

"We'll try cool cloths now," was all she said.

The next morning, Sarah woke asking for something to eat. Her hollow cheeks gave evidence of how violent the fever and cough had been, but clearly she had turned a corner and would rise up. Mrs. Hayes spoon-fed her cornmeal pudding and honey, and offered some also to Jerushah.

But my patient—for so it now seemed she was, as I had declined the laying on of hands and taken responsibility, in spite of myself, for speaking for Jerushah—my patient was not yet through the fevers and chills that had set in more violently during the night. Alternating cool cloths and hot ones, depending on which she needed, I'd been awake most of those hours to tend her. My head ached. Cautiously I cleared my throat—was I coming down with the sickness also? No, I seemed well enough other than my aching head, just so very tired.

Mrs. Hayes soon sent me to the attic bedroom for a nap, saying she'd tend Jerushah and Sarah both for a while. I lurched to my feet and climbed the steep stairs. Her boys must be coming in soon for their breakfast, I thought as I laid my head down. I did not wake again until past noon, as the light from the window showed clearly. In haste, I returned to the kitchen, knowing I'd neglected both my nursing duties and my obligation to be of help.

Fear held its hands to my throat so that my breath refused to properly inflate my chest. How could I have slept so long, leaving Jerushah alone among this house full of black and brown faces? Friends of friends they were indeed—Miss Farrow's friends—but that wasn't the same as family. And for Jerushah, I must be the closest to family in this home.

I rubbed my palms against my face, trying to wake properly. I needed to wash my face, and I longed for a bath—no, whatever I needed, it would have to wait. I stumbled toward the two beds. To my right, Sarah sat up against pillows, spooning her own dinner. To my left, only Jerushah's white face showed within a cocoon of covers, and her eyes were closed. Please let her be sleeping without fever, I thought as I tiptoed close to make sure her chest was rising and falling. But over my shoulder I saw Mrs. Hayes at the door, opening the latch to allow someone into the room: the doctor.

I knew at once that Jerushah must be even more ill than before, for Mrs. Hayes to summon Doctor Kendall again. At that moment, Jerushah's white calmness shattered in a burst of coughing that threatened to choke her, and I struggled to lift her toward a sitting position. Mrs. Hayes, quick as ever, pressed the featherbed into a support behind Jerushah's back, her hands and mine touching as we supported Jerushah's already thin frame. The rattle of the deep coughs and the pain on my friend's face tore my own chest in sympathy.

The doctor's directions were quiet and clear. I helped Jerushah to submit to his examination, putting forth her tongue, which was brightly reddened, and allowing the doctor to listen at her chest between ragged seizures of coughing. When he asked me, I lifted Jerushah's blouse from where it met the waist of her cotton petticoat. At the sight of the dry red rash covering her skin, I gasped.

"Spotted fever?" I croaked.

"No, no," the doctor briskly contradicted, with a quick glare at me and an instantly reassuring arm around Jerushah's shoulder. "Not at all. No, quite a different illness. Not spotted, but scarlet. Scarlet fever," he assured me as he gently ran his one hand across the sweat-damp and roughened skin revealed at her midsection. "Or scarlatina, if you will. In the hands of a skilled nurse, a far less dangerous illness." He turned to Mrs. Hayes, squinting in emphasis, lifting his hands to punctuate his words. "But you must do exactly as I outline for you. You must begin at once to lower her temperature with wet cloths and, if necessary, a tepid bath. The sooner the fever drops, the less harm it will do in the long run."

He began to measure out a light sleeping dose for the afternoon and another one for the night, as well as a draught of opium to quiet the racking cough that continued to shake Jerushah and weaken her. I listened to his instructions and wondered whether this was also punishment from Providence for having refused the laying on of hands that Charles Hayes had offered.

But there was no time to dwell on the guilt rising up within me: All my strength must go to being the best nurse possible, and I strained to remember each instruction of the doctor's. If so much depended on skilled nursing—well then, I would become a skilled nurse, and bring Jerushah through.

★ ★ ★ ★ ★

It was another long week and a half before the joint efforts of
Mrs. Hayes, her newly bonded assistant Sarah, and my own
hands and heart could assure a recovery for Jerushah. Somewhere in the midst of that time, Good Friday and Easter came
and went, marked only by evening readings from the Bible and
a fresh roast of lamb from one of the neighbor's flock. At last,
on the second Tuesday after Easter, I begged a sheet of paper
and wrote my letter home, asking that William be sent to fetch
us. "Jerushah is well enough to travel and surely will complete
her recuperation best at home. And please tell Mrs. Clark that
Sarah is staying safe and happy here, in all praise to heaven's
kindness and the kindness of this family." I signed the letter and
offered Jerushah the other side of the page to write a note of
her own, a sentence, a little wobbly but perhaps reassuring to
her mother that she had come through the scarlet fever and was
recovering her own strength, bit by bit.

As Andrew Hayes, the oldest son, tipped his hat and headed
out the door into a warm and melting spring morning, to take
my letter to town to meet the post carrier, I counted the likely
time left to wait: a day and a half, perhaps two days, for my letter to reach North Upton. And another day for William to drive
north. And then the next morning, we would ride in the carriage, all the way home, by the end of the fourth or at most fifth
day from now.

Assured that Sarah was reading to Jerushah, and that Mrs.
Hayes wanted no assistance with her bread making for the moment, I pulled on the long driving cloak that had disguised me
on the journey north, the journey that now seemed so long ago.
I stepped out into the dooryard, unencumbered by a chamber
pot or any other burden, and allowed myself to stand in the
sunlight and savor the new season.

Above me, a pair of crows flapped noisily across the half-open sky. From the edge of the field, where some small trees formed a marker, other birds trilled. The land rolled in soft, brown swells around, with a long vista that must have been miles across—why, I could even see the rooftops and steeples of the village from here, and it was at least two miles away, I knew! No mountains closed in the farm or the town. How could that be? Had we come north of the Green Mountains themselves?

Far to the east, a blue haze assured me there must be forests and hillsides in that direction. But otherwise, I might have stepped into a different place entirely, so far from my familiar shapes and enclosures.

I heard a river and recalled crossing a covered bridge just before arriving at the Hayes homestead. Circling the barn, I saw the bridge and decided to walk the road to its wooden frame, for a stretch and a change. Seeing the snowbanks pulled back from the edges of the muddy road gladdened my heart, and I didn't even mind the puddles, though I drew up my skirt to keep it from becoming soiled and wet.

The sturdy bridge, free of ice and snow, held an aroma of sun-warmed wood even at this early morning hour. I peered through its side to watch the wild abandon of the spring river, capped with white foam and dancing with light and scraps of tree bark and twigs. A splash below drew my attention, and, at the second splash, I gasped to see the shining iridescence of a large fish leap upward, then vanish in the froth. Another one followed, then others, to either side.

So, I lingered for longer than I meant to, and when I came to my senses I hurried back to the farmhouse that had become so familiar. I scraped the mud from my shoes as best I could and rushed to return to the kitchen. My promise to work hard must be kept, so my friends would be blessed with recovery. I was sure that was the exchange I owed to Providence.

And they were indeed blessed, for the first laughter in a long time met my ears. "Read it again," Jerushah insisted, as Sarah dissolved in giggles at the foot of her bed. "I want to hear it all again. Now!"

Mrs. Hayes met my gaze and nodded. We shared the satisfaction of having provided the "skilled nursing" that the scarlet fever required. I hung up my cloak, set aside my shoes to dry, and padded across the kitchen to take a turn at adding wood to the stove.

Even in that action, the presence of spring came to my attention, for it took much less wood to keep the baking heat of the oven now. I offered to finish shaping the loaves and setting them to rise, and my companion, the woman who now loved Sarah as much as Jerushah and I did, gave me a pat on the shoulder as though we had always been friends.

"Thank you, Miss Alice, that would be just fine. I'd like to get outside for a few minutes myself, to see if there's any green showing yet."

"Go right ahead," I confirmed. "But it's still mud season out there, I do believe." I hesitated, then said, "Mrs. Hayes, I'd be glad if you'd just call me Alice, instead of Miss Alice. It seems as though we've worked together long enough for that, doesn't it?"

"Yes, it does," she replied with a smile. "And you may call me Belle."

We nodded contentedly at each other, and I rolled the dough firmly with the heels of my hands, to stretch it for a tidy loaf of bread.

As Mrs. Hayes—that is, Belle—took her turn out the door for a taste of spring, I listened to the merriment of my friends, and counted again to myself: two days, three days, four days, home.

CHAPTER 18

Acknowledging both the healing of our patients and our shared efforts opened a door to a different kind of conversation in the kitchen that afternoon, while Belle Hayes and I scraped and wiped bowls and plates and set the kettle of soup heating for supper. It began in a common enough fashion, although in whispers—for Sarah and Jerushah both were napping—with Belle asking me about my brother's wife and baby.

I explained that Helen was a Bradley, but saw from Belle's expression that she didn't know the family. "They're neighbors to our Sanborn cousins in Wheelock," I explained. "That's how William and Helen met, at a sugaring-off in Wheelock."

Belle nodded and passed the short stack of plates to me to set on the sideboard. "And the baby? It's their first?"

"Yes, a boy. William Junior." I paused, realizing I didn't know Mr. Hayes's given name. "Is one of your boys named for their father?"

"No, that's not our way," Belle said.

I was curious. "Do you name them for grandparents, then?"

"Ben—that's Mr. Hayes—he chooses the names for the boys, from Bible names or from good men he's known."

"Oh, yes, lots of people choose names from the Bible," I agreed. Cautiously, aware there might be painful history, I asked, "Then would it be you to choose the names for any daughters? Did you have a favorite name waiting?"

"I had a daughter before the boys," Belle whispered. "We lost

her young. She was Mary. I didn't have a second one. But"—
her whisper dropped even lower as she marveled—"the name
waiting was Sarah."

"Ahh."

Dishes set aside, we began cutting up potatoes to add to the
soup. I thought about family and how it connects people. I said,
"I have two more brothers, who are older than William. One of
them is named Charles, like your son. The other is John."

"And they also have wives and children? Did they meet them
nearby?"

"No, they don't have wives at all. At least, not so far as I
know. They're both in California, and they don't write very
often." I remembered that my mother had a letter from "the
boys" that had arrived just before word of the slave hunter coming to North Upton. Was Henry Clinton gone now? And what
news of California was there in that letter? Perhaps another letter had even come by now.

Belle said softly, "I don't know how my sons will find wives.
I'm thinking they may have to go to Canada to find them."

I marveled at the notion: no family ties, no cousins, and, even
when the Hayes boys went to church or to help with barn rais-
ing or haying, there would be no black- and brown-skinned
young women for them to court.

"Are there many colored people in Canada?"

"More than in Vermont!" She smiled and pushed the pie pan
of peeled and quartered potatoes toward me. "Would you add
these to the kettle and stir it a bit?"

"Of course."

As I stirred, she swept carefully, trying not to wake the others. In the peacefulness of the moment, I realized she was holding the broom with only one hand, with her other hand pressed
in a fist against the broomstick. I set the spoon to one side of
the stove and bent to help her gather the pile of peelings for the

scrap bucket.

"Does it hurt?" I asked without thinking.

Belle's eyebrows flew up in surprise. "Does what hurt? Oh, my hand?" She held up the small fist for a moment, then shrugged and placed the fist against the broomstick again. "Sometimes. But mostly I don't notice it now. It happened years ago." She tipped her head in that birdlike fashion that I liked seeing and told me, "Worse things, much worse, have happened to slaves in the South. But I was never sold south of Rhode Island myself. I was fortunate. And I was freed before somebody else chose a husband for me, which was a mighty good thing. Ben came sailing into my life, on a merchant ship from Bermuda. He'd already earned his papers on board, and he was ready for a change."

I hesitated, then decided to risk asking. "Does that mean you came to Vermont without anyone helping? Without the Underground Railroad, I mean?" I flushed, knowing I'd said it wrong, unsure what to add.

Mrs. Hayes laughed. "Child, every soul on this earth needs a helping hand, and Ben and I have had plenty of them, colored and white. But if you're asking how we reached this place, well, we drove here with a wagon, like anyone else might do. Your Underground Railroad never sold us a ticket of any kind. Though I suppose," she reflected, "you might say our home is something of a station in itself, for those who come this far. Most of them go on to Canada, although not all of them."

We both looked across at Sarah.

Belle added, "Yes, I don't doubt she's seen terrible things. But she may forget some of them. She can stay here and make herself at home. And you and your friend Jerushah have given her a good start in being a girl again."

Part of me was silenced by thinking about Belle as someone who'd been enslaved. How could anyone have known her intelligence and care and still thought she could be "owned"? And the other part of me was silenced by thinking about Sarah being hurt. I knew some of the horrors of slaveholding, and I knew we were keeping Sarah safe, and that her parents were not at all safe—but to picture someone you love being threatened and wounded—that's a heart-rending thing. My tongue froze stiff in my mouth as I tasted the idea.

Three polite knocks at the kitchen door startled us and woke our resting patients. I jumped up and looked for a stick or a flatiron for defense. What if Henry Clinton had tracked us north, after all? I remembered the scowling man at the inn at Lyndon Corner and didn't doubt he'd betray us to anyone hunting Sarah.

Belle motioned for me to stay back. With her broomstick held forward in her good hand, she moved toward the door. "Who's there?"

"Mrs. Hayes? It's Solomon, Solomon McBride. I'm a friend of Alice Sanborn and Jerushah Clark. I've brought a letter, and the carriage to carry them home."

Solomon! But my letter could barely have started on its way to North Upton as yet. How could he be here? And why would he come north, rather than my brother William or my father?

At my nod, Belle lowered her broomstick, and I set down the iron poker that I'd seized from the woodbox. She stepped to the door and opened it, as Sarah raced past her, calling out, "Solomon, Solomon, I'm all well! And so is Jerushah!"

"Good news indeed," Solomon agreed as he patted Sarah on her shoulder and gave a courteous half bow to Belle. "Mrs. Hayes? I'm pleased to meet you, and Mr. and Mrs. Sanborn and the Clark family send you their thanks. In fact, they've sent you maple sugar and a tub of butter, too, which I'll unload from the carriage now that I know I've found the right place." He looked across the room and added, "And Miss Alice Sanborn is also 'all well'?"

"Y—yes, of course I am," I replied, wanting to say a dozen other things but compelled to keep them for another time. "Solomon, what are you doing here? My letter can't have reached home this soon. What has brought you north?"

"For that, I'm afraid you'd better read the letter I've brought you. But the short answer is, I've come to take you home. And perhaps to do some business on the way, if time allows."

Jerushah struggled to stand up, and Sarah raced back across the room to help her, then threw her arms around Jerushah's waist. "Oh, Jerushah, you can go home now, but I don't want you to go away!"

At that moment, Andrew Hayes called from the dooryard, "What's all the commotion? More guests, Mother?"

I saw the spade in his hand and realized that he, like his mother and me, was prepared to defend his home and safety if need be. As explanations were shared, he set his spade aside and helped Solomon to carry an array of baskets and bundles into the kitchen.

While the men did this, I opened the letter, which proved to be from my father. It was brief:

Dearest Alice, I write with much sadness to tell you that William and Helen's babe has gone too soon to meet his Maker, and we are all in sorrow, for, despite the baby's young age he was greatly loved. Helen has taken to her bed. Your mother says would you please come home as soon as this letter reaches you, and bring Jerushah with you, and Sarah if need be. The Lord giveth, and the Lord taketh away. May He keep you safe as you return to us.

Oh, poor William! And Helen. I wept for them, and Jerushah and Sarah came to enfold me in their arms and to share the news and the sadness.

The room filled with more men, as the Hayes sons and Mr. Hayes arrived for supper. We three "girls" went up to the attic chamber to fold and pack what little we had brought, and to hold each other, preparing to separate. Sarah would of course stay here in Coventry. Jerushah and I might wait many months or even years before seeing her again, although we all pledged that we would write letters endlessly.

"Must you go after supper?" Sarah asked.

"No, not until morning," I told her. "Solomon and the horse must both have a night's rest." I realized that Belle must be struggling to expand the supper we'd planned, and working on her own in the kitchen. So I urged the others to come down with me, that we might all prepare the table and gather one more time with the family that had embraced us so kindly.

Jerushah sat at the table with us. Her cheeks still lacked the roses that should bloom on them, and her face showed hollows where it had been plump and rounded. I thought her breathing came too shallow, but she had no cough, and she ate all of her supper, even accepting butter on her cornbread. Belle and I looked at each other, and I asked, without saying it aloud, my worried question: could my friend travel safely in the carriage on the long ride home?

I saw Belle's hesitation, although after a moment she gave me a small nod. It failed to convince me. I began to list in my thoughts the items we'd need in the morning: hot bricks, blankets, a camphor salve in case Jerushah began to cough in the outdoor air. The responsibility and concern helped me to avoid some of the sorrow that I felt waiting to pour into my heart, for the moment of leaving Sarah behind us.

Had I known what lay ahead, I would have seen how small a sorrow indeed that was. Yet through it all, a spring birdsong of happiness and possibility teased me with a promise, each time I looked up to see Solomon's eyes on me, a half smile interrupting his conversation with the other men at the table.

CHAPTER 19

That last night in Coventry, I slept between Jerushah and Sarah in the kitchen, aware of each minute passing as I listened to them breathe. Sarah slept the ready sleep of childhood still, and Jerushah sank into the exhaustion that still gathered her each evening. I wondered whether her exertion in joining the family for supper had been wise. But it was done and over, and all I could do was hope for safety and speed on the next day's journey. In the darkness, with only a faint ruddy glow from the coals in the stove's firebox, I let my thoughts range at last to my family in North Upton. It hardly seemed possible that I'd been away so long—April ninth already, and tomorrow the tenth.

I ached for William and Helen. Such joy there had been between them with the birth of their son—and the measure of joy must also be the measure of loss and sorrow. I thought about my father, who clearly shared their loss. And my mother? And what word had there been from my older brothers? I thought of the rest of the village also—the twins with the spotted fever, and school surely closed for the season now, and whether the snow still lingered. How long had I been away? It felt like an entire season.

Jerushah's breathing came in fits and starts, small gasps caught among the threads of sound. Overwhelmed by concern, I repeated the Twenty-third Psalm as I cupped my hands together: "Yea, though I walk through the valley of the shadow of death, I will fear no evil: for Thou art with me; thy rod and thy staff they comfort me." Seeing a flock of sheep in my mind, a kind shepherd guiding them with his strong staff, I settled among the covers and drifted into uneasy dreams, of lambs and ewes, of open fields and sheltered villages, and of the wet sound of spring dripping from the edges of the roof above. And if the shepherd's face looked like Solomon's, that was only the folly of sleep and dreams, and my waking self knew better than to trust even the kindest dream.

Morning erupted in a flurry of activity, as I helped Belle prepare a hearty meal of hotcakes and sausages and fried potatoes and dark strong tea. We travelers needed sustenance, and so did the young men and their father, preparing for a day of fence-building and more lambing. Sylvester, the youngest Hayes boy, had taken the night hours in the neighbor's barn with the sheep; he announced three more lambs when he joined us.

"How many sheep are on that farm?" Solomon asked.

"About seventy-five," Mr. Hayes replied. "Which means near to a hundred lambs. We only have half a dozen here, with the smithing to manage and all."

"And you're sugaring, too?"

"Just enough for ourselves." The brothers began sorting out the day's tasks, and I rose to help Belle. I notice that Solomon and Mr. Hayes had their heads together at the far end of the table, but I was too busy stacking plates to grasp their conversation.

"Just set the dishes to the side," Belle directed me. "I'll take care of them. You and Jerushah and Mr. McBride here should be off. You'll make better time while the roads are still frozen."

Sure enough, the cold of the night would wear off in a few hours, and the roads would turn to mud and water. Solomon excused himself from Mr. Hayes and went to hitch up the carriage, and I saw through the window that he'd brought our

175

young horse Ely with him. It made the thought of home more real to me.

I turned to Belle. She held Sarah and Jerushah in her arms already, then gently drew Sarah to one side. As I joined them, I saw the gap forming between us: a sturdy brown-skinned woman and girl, arm in arm, and a fragile white woman and her friend about to depart. Impulsively, I reached to embrace Belle for the first time, catching the scent of her that was so different from my own mother, but now so familiar to me from our labors together. "I'll miss you," I told her.

"Write to me, then," Belle answered as she returned my embrace and set me next to Jerushah again. "Write to me about those brothers of yours, and about your choices ahead. I'll write back when I find time. And who knows, maybe we'll see each other again some day." She held my gaze a moment, then looked down at Sarah. "Now then," she said briskly, "let's help carry the baskets and blankets and such, Miss Sarah. And we'll see your friends off with a smile, won't we?"

So we all did our best to smile and say our last farewells brightly in the dooryard. Solomon and I tucked so many blankets around Jerushah that she laughed in protest. I heard the way the laughter almost set her to coughing, so I made an end to the fuss by climbing into the carriage next to her and allowing Solomon to shut the door.

With a cluck and a flourish, we were on our way, waving one last time, then shutting the side curtains for warmth, as Ely and Solomon took us away from Coventry, away from Sarah, and back to the southward road.

Chapter 20

This time our route took us along the Black River, not just from Coventry to Irasburg, but on toward Albany, Craftsbury, and the long post road to Hardwick. I recalled there was a minister in Albany who helped fugitives determined to cross into Canada—was it the Reverend Putnam? I thought that was the name—but also in Hardwick was a "secret place" where Solomon had hidden with Fred Johnson for two days. When had I heard these things? It seemed a lifetime ago. I wished I could ride up on the top bench of the carriage with Solomon and ask him about all of the route and the people and places along it. But this time, duty kept me inside, snug against Jerushah to make sure she stayed warm. At least the upright position might be good for her chest, I considered.

At Craftsbury Common, we stopped at the stage inn, so that Ely could be watered, fed, and rested. Although I missed Sarah already, I noticed the relief of not worrying whether danger lurked in each public place. I took Jerushah inside to tidy up and have a cup of lukewarm tea by a stingy and sooty fireside. "We'll be home tonight," I encouraged her.

"I know. And I don't mean to vex you, Alice, but I am so tired already."

"Eat a little more," I urged her, breaking off a piece of Belle's fresh sweet biscuit spread with butter and honey. "It will strengthen you."

"I'll try."

And she did, but I doubted that more than a quarter of a biscuit found its way into her. More than ever, I wanted to bring her home to her mother, to the warmth and comfort she needed.

Solomon looked into the parlor. "We should start again," he urged. "It rained up in the hills last night, and I don't know how the crossings will be, past Hardwick. And it's two hours of driving still to Hardwick."

Actually, it was three hours. A lake between Craftsbury and Hardwick, swollen from the snowmelt, lay partway over the road for at least a mile. Two farm wagons accompanied us across the flooded stretch, and Solomon walked in the water next to Ely, encouraging the horse to step even when the water hid the corduroy log surface underneath. I pulled back the smallest curtain on the carriage door to watch.

A mill pond at Hardwick threatened the road also, but an alternate wagon route took us around on firm ground. Again, we stopped for the horse's sake.

This time the stage stable was at a tavern, mostly empty since it was as yet barely three o'clock, and the able men of the town were still laboring, whether in shops or on farms or in the woods. But it was a coarse place and had no ladies' parlor. Jerushah refused to enter, so I brought tea out to her.

"I don't like it. It's bitter, and it's almost cold," she said to me, a hint of petulance in her voice. "I want to be home, Alice. When will we reach North Upton?"

"Soon," I soothed. But I was not confident. I tucked the blankets snugly around Jerushah again, and ducked back out of the carriage to find Solomon. He was striding toward us, a furrow of concern across his forehead.

Speaking quietly, he told me, "There are still nearly twenty miles ahead of us. That's at least four hours for the horse, maybe five. And that's if the roads and crossings are good. It may be that we should stay over for the night here and start again in the morning."

I shook my head. "We can't. Jerushah won't even go inside this place. She needs to be home, Solomon."

"I thought that was what you'd say. So I asked the stable-hand to let me have a pair of torches. We'll be driving in the dark for the last hour, although the road should be frozen up by then, even if it's rough in between. It's the dark of the moon tonight, but I've driven by starlight before. If the sky is clear." He looked up, but neither of us commented on the bank of clouds scudding eastward over the sky.

"Let's go, then," I agreed. I took the two torches from his hand, set them securely inside the carriage, and climbed back in, to brace myself against Jerushah and keep the jolts and lurches of the carriage from toppling her sideways, as off we went.

A covered bridge took us across the noisy and wild waters of a river that ran east of Hardwick, and then we were on the stage road itself. One yellow stagecoach raced past us, pulled by a team of four horses. I wondered how well Ely could manage, just one horse drawing three people in a carriage. It seemed that Solomon had slowed the horse for the long uphill road. I added another hour to my guess of when we'd reach North Upton.

Next to me, Jerushah slept uneasily, crying out sometimes from uneasy dreams. I heard her cough once, and then a bit later a spasm of coughing struck her. I rubbed the camphor balm into the tender skin of her throat and held the jar under her nostrils for a bit, and it quieted the cough. She barely woke even as I did this, and I felt her cheek repeatedly for fever. But no extra heat rose in her as yet.

My head began to ache. I tried to think of a hymn to sing, or a folk song or love tune. But the sway and thump of the carriage drove the tunes out of my mind. So I began to line out Psalm One Hundred as best I could, singing it to myself: "Serve the Lord with gladness: come before his presence with singing. Know ye that the Lord he is God: it is he that hath made us, and not we ourselves; we are his people, and the sheep of his pasture."

With no listening ears except my own, I mused over the presence of sheep in so many of the Psalms; then I reflected on my brother William's assertion that the beauty and harmony of Nature proved the goodness of God's works. So far, I thought bitterly, this journey had little harmony of Nature with which to make such a claim. Saying the words of the Psalm again, however, I drew comfort from the notion that the Lord would watch over us.

The carriage slowed further. I pulled back the door curtain and put my face out into the crisp air. The sun must have settled behind the mountains; I could feel the difference now, as the road continued to rise. I heard Solomon softly talking to Ely, urging him forward. Up ahead, a cluster of houses and a large inn waited.

"Walden," Solomon told me briefly in the inn's dooryard as he took Ely out of the harness and walked him toward the stable. "Take Jerushah inside. It's Nate Farrington's stage tavern. We'd best all eat a hot meal and give the horse a rest."

A generous fire blazed in the ladies' parlor, and I settled Jerushah into a bench beside the hearth, then inquired about the evening meal.

The young woman tending the public room offered to bring a meat pie and a loaf of bread into the parlor for us, and when I inquired for hot water to make a tisane for Jerushah, she was more than agreeable. Perhaps it would ease my headache, too, I thought. I returned to the parlor and assured Jerushah that supper would soon arrive. She asked to tidy up, so I walked with her back into the inn's yard, and we found the "necessary." But on the walk back to the parlor, I knew her strength was about gone for the day. She coughed repeatedly, yet would not let me apply the camphorated balm again, saying it must wait until after the meal, back in the carriage.

Solomon joined us, and we made good use of the meat pie, which was salty and rich and well sauced. Even Jerushah ate some of it, and I kept coaxing her to take a bit more. Seeing her sup gave me some comfort, and I said to Solomon with good cheer, "What do we have left before us? Six miles or so?"

He winced, and shook his head. "More like twelve." At the shock on my face, he explained, "The horse is worn clear out, Alice. He pulled that long stretch, but he's lost his speed from the morning. I don't think he can take us further tonight."

Jerushah caught this last news and began to weep. "I want to go home, Alice. I must go home. I can't stay here. You must take me home, tonight."

I apologized to Solomon. "She's exhausted, and she doesn't know what she's saying. If the horse can't, he can't. Poor Ely." And poor Jerushah. I patted her hands and tried to comfort her, saying, "We'll make much better time in the morning, think of that. And how happy your mother will be to see you in the daylight. You don't want to wake her in the middle of the night, arriving so long after dark, do you?"

Solomon reached out toward Jerushah also, but she pushed his hand aside. "You'll take colored girls through the darkness, won't you? But you won't take me home because I'm not a slave. Is that it? You've no pity for a white woman, have you?"

I was horrified at her words. Solomon stood at once, his face as pale as if he'd been struck. Jaw set, he turned on his heel and left the parlor.

"Jerushah, Jerushah," I begged, "you mustn't say such things. You know that's not true, and it's not kind, either. Solomon

181

came all the way to Coventry to fetch us, and he's driven all day, and walked in the water, and taken care of the horse—"

"Yes, he's taken care of your stupid horse, but not of me, and I'm the one who's been ill for so long," Jerushah sobbed. "I belong at home, Alice. Make him take me there."

"In the morning," I argued.

But she wouldn't hear of it.

In a few minutes, Solomon, his face grim and shuttered, re-appeared in the parlor. "I've hired another horse," he announced. "I'll come back for Ely tomorrow. Come now, the carriage is hitched and ready."

I protested. "But you're tired, and it's dark, and the hire of a horse is costly."

"It surely is. There'll be at least two 'colored girls' short of a ride north, for having the driver spend his coins tonight instead," Solomon responded angrily. "But it's spent and done, and I'd appreciate Miss Jerushah's speed into the waiting carriage."

Ashamed and upset, I helped Jerushah from her seat and fastened her cloak around her, without much to say. I bundled the blankets around her in the carriage, then realized Solomon had not mounted to the driver's perch. I climbed back out to see why he was waiting.

"I'll need you to ride outside the carriage with me," he said tersely. "I can't hold a torch and drive. And I'll need extra eyes to be sure of the road."

So I fastened my own cloak securely, explained the plan to Jerushah, and took the torches out of the carriage. We would not light them until we had to; it might be that the stars would give us enough light to travel by on the wide stage road, if we went slowly and carefully. Solomon propped them to one side of the high bench and gave me a hand to take the long step upward, then joined me. A single rug of heavy wool, damp but not wet through, he shared across our laps. Though the bench was not long, I edged as far as I could away from Solomon, sure that he must hate me as well as Jerushah by now.

He took the reins, spoke calmly to the hired horse, and eased us out of the inn's yard. "There now, Jim, there's a good fellow. Slow and steady, and we'll make it by midnight."

I said nothing in reply. What words could heal what had just taken place? Instead, I sat as straight as my own sore muscles would allow and strained to see the road ahead. If I could help in keeping us on it, I would do so.

Twelve miles. I shivered at the thought.

Beside me, Solomon relented enough to tug the woolen rug further around me with one hand, as he guided the horse with the other and stared directly ahead.

CHAPTER 21

Whether it was luck or Providence, the sky did clear as the April night settled around us. But it was cold—cold as a winter night, I thought. I drew my collar up and buttoned the highest button, to hold more warmth within the heavy cloak. And I adjusted the strings of my hat, to pull it snug around my face. Then I placed my hands back under the driving blanket, careful not to disturb Solomon as he focused on the road ahead.

I could hear water splashing through the empty pastures around us. Though the farms to either side of the stage road raised sheep, it was too early in the year to turn them out across the hills. Lambing was barely underway, and the ewes needed shelter for birthing and for the first few weeks. Besides, the fields huddled as if still dead under the last unmelted snow. The water trickling all around us flowed down the hills, under the snowpack, until it reached bare ground, like the road where we traveled. And here the water hesitated, forming a top surface of mud as much as a foot deep over the frozen heart of the land.

If the night were cold enough, the mud would set up into icy ridges. The carriage would jolt over them, but at least the wheels could roll free of the soft suction that had dragged us to such a slow pace earlier in the day. Thinking about this, I wished for more cold, more frost, in this night, although I worried that Jerushah, without my added heat, was feeling the plunge in temperature to some ill effect.

I could do nothing about the inside of the carriage. I hoped, even prayed, that Jerushah could hold herself well bundled within. Then, unable to change my circumstances or hers, I resolved to see clearly at least what unfolded before me.

Because sheep pastures lined the sides of the road, few trees marked its edges. Stone fences bordered each pasture; their heights could rise with bundles of brush added to them. A faint glimmer of light occasionally came from the wet stones where water gurgled and flowed. We must not run the carriage up against the walls or we could damage the wheels. I began to describe the walls in a low voice, hoping the narrative might assist Solomon as he drove.

After a few minutes, he spoke. "I appreciate your effort, but the horse is probably seeing more than we are. At any rate, he is picking our way down the center very well thus far. So there's no need for you to call out the stone walls just now."

I nodded, then realized Solomon couldn't see me, as he stared directly ahead. So I said quietly, "I rarely see the stars this bright. I suppose it's because I don't stay outside after dark very much. Do you know the names of the constellations?"

"A few. The one to our left, in the shape of a saucepan, is Ursa Major, the Great Bear. In some places, it is called the Big Dipper, which I think better suits its outline. You've heard that it's also called the 'drinking gourd' by the runaway slaves? They know it hangs to their north, and it's a bright steady guide to the route toward freedom."

"I didn't know. I like that. But what can they do if the sky is cloudy?"

Solomon choked down a chuckle. "Be grateful. It's harder to chase runaways in a darker night. Or when it rains. So you see, whatever the weather, it's in favor of freedom."

"Or against it." I didn't mean to contradict, but I saw clearly the paradox. A night that protected by darkness was a night without bright guidance. And vice versa.

Again came the low laugh. "You're a sharp one. Yes, I'm afraid the best help is not Nature, but kind souls, willing to help. Like Vermont's native son Thaddeus Stevens, who keeps fighting for emancipation for the entire nation, territories and all."

"But you're not from Vermont the way Senator Stevens is— did I hear you're from Connecticut?"

"No. I sometimes ride from there to here, but my family is from Boston. My father owns ships, and my mother keeps the accounts."

I fumbled for what I knew about Boston and ships. "Codfish? Is that what the ships are for?"

"Not ours. Trade, mostly. But less now, since my father refuses to carry human cargo. He'll not be a slaver, no matter what the money." Pride resonated in his voice.

"I'm glad," I replied simply. "He must be a good man."

"He is."

We rode in silence for a while. Relief eased my stiffness; the conversation didn't seem hateful.

I remembered something that I should have asked about. "Your meeting in Hardwick, was it a week ago? No, more than that, ten days at least. Were you successful?"

Without turning, Solomon began to describe it. "I wasn't needed there, except to tell them what the other regions are doing. More than a hundred people, men and women, gather there each month to choose how best to push for emancipation and free states. Webster's disastrous speech in early March turned all of New England against him, I vow, for it's come clear that he has no spine at all. He'd allow slavery in half the new territories, for the sake of peace within the Union. But he's misjudged his own people. Once you waken a people to what's right, they'll not sleep again until they see justice."

"Was it your father who woke you in that way?"

The question came oddly, but he grasped its intent. "No, my

mother. She was a schoolteacher before she married and is a Sabbath teacher now. She's always taught the natural equality of mankind, and I believe she chose her husband such that she could teach him, likewise!" I could hear the smile in his voice. "They work well together. She leads in the thinking, and he takes action."

"And you? Are you for action, like your father?"

"I hope I can be the best from both of them. Now then, Miss Alice Sanborn of North Upton, don't you think this questioning has been a bit one-sided? Tell me about your own father and mother, as you see them."

I thought for a moment and began, "My father takes care of what he loves. And he loves my mother, and us, and the farm. And especially his horses and sheep—"

The horse in front of us, not Ely any longer but the hired horse, Jim, abruptly stopped and blew noisily from his nose.

Solomon shook the reins and clicked his tongue. "What's the matter, old fellow? Come on, let's keep going."

But the horse stamped a foot, then edged backward, making the carriage wobble. Beneath me I heard Jerushah call out, "Stop! What is it?"

I looked at Solomon. "I need to get down and speak with her—and see that she's still well bundled in the blankets."

"Not yet. Wait, hold the reins while I step down to see if there's something in the road. It may be partly washed out, so that the horse won't step there." He steadied the carriage and gave a low command to the horse to halt, which it did, but with ears pricked up and a nervous repeat of the lifted front foot.

The cold air around us shook with a small slide of air and brought a sudden sour tang toward my face. I grasped Solomon's sleeve. "Don't step down."

When he too realized what the scent was, he laughed and agreed. "Skunk! Animal, not human. But it hasn't shot out a direct spray yet, or we'd all smell much worse. Perhaps we should light a torch and see whether I can chase the animal out of our way with it."

I twisted around to grasp one of the thick limbs, each with an end wrapped round with tarred cloth. But I thought out loud, "If you light it, then you'll have to quench it, and it won't light well a second time, will it? We may need it more for something else."

"You may be right. Hold off, then, I'll just step down and make some noise."

The horse backed against the wooden shafts again. I called down to Jerushah: "It's only a skunk in the road. I'll come down to you as soon as Solomon dispatches it." He was already down onto the road, one hand at the horse's flank, the other reaching for the bridle.

"Ho, Jim, there's a good fellow, ho, now, let me see if I can clear the road. Alice," he called up to me, "pick up the leads and hold them with just a little pull, not enough for Jim here to think you want him to back up any further, just enough to say halt."

I lifted the braided leather straps and tried to guess what Solomon's instructions meant as I pulled back slightly.

"Good, that's quite right, hold it there. There now, Jim, let me pass you and see what I can do."

The darkness at the road level gathered itself thickly beyond the horse's head. I followed the activity by sound: a scrape along the road, a pause, a booted kick and another scrape. Then a stone tossed, and another. The skunk odor flared.

Footsteps hurried back toward the carriage. "I don't think I've suffered a direct spray, but I caught him with one of my stones, and he's moving down along the stone fence now. We'll give him a few minutes to get along. Do you want to come down while we wait here, to talk with—your friend?"

Oh, dear. The warmth of conversation vanished in that tense phrase. I must encourage Jerushah to pour oil on the troubled waters she'd engaged with her petulant demand earlier in the evening. But it would have to wait until she had rested on the morrow, I knew.

I passed the reins to Solomon as I scrambled down from the perch, trying to hold my skirt out of the way at the same time. He moved toward the horse, and I opened the carriage door.

Jerushah sat, not on the leather-covered seat but on the floor, a tumble of wraps and blankets around her. Her face was so white that it shone in the faint starlight. And her eyes, although open, seemed simple dark gems, lit without color. She whispered, "Is it gone?"

"Yes, gone from the road." I crawled into the heap of blankets and wrapped my arms around her, willing her to be warm—not hot, not chilled. I rested my cheek against her cold one and cooed as if to a small child, "We're almost there, Jerushah. Just a little longer. We must be close to the loon ponds by now, and the road will level out." I stroked her hair. It felt thickened and damp.

"I want my mother," she whimpered against my shoulder.

"I know, I know, dear one," I crooned. "We're taking you home."

Though each moment I stayed with her meant a delay in resuming the journey, I thought it best to soothe her and be sure she was as comforted as possible. Moving her back onto the seat, I wrapped her in the smoothed out woolen blankets and tucked them snugly into place. She seemed aware of what I was doing, and whispered, "Thank you." The fragile whisper sliced my heart, and I promised again that we'd soon have her home.

Solomon bent to give me a foothold, and I resumed my perch, holding the reins for him as he, too, climbed up. This time, his cluck of encouragement moved the horse forward.

My guess of being close to the loon ponds soon showed itself to be correct, as a wide expanse of ice to our right confirmed.

"Three and a half miles, more or less, to Upton Center and the North Upton road," Solomon said. "I've ridden this stretch often, though rarely driving it myself. The stage makes better time. Tell me about your father. You were just starting to do so."

"He takes care of us." The words lacked detail so I tried to explain more. "Whatever need there is, for the farm, the house, the people around him, he notices and he labors to meet the needs. He'll even know when a horse is about to go lame, or if a lamb doesn't breathe the right way, or when my mother will need heavy things carried, and he's there."

"That's a gift indeed."

"Yes," I agreed, wishing I could see Solomon's face. Between the darkness and the way he looked straight over the horse's back and ears, seeking the road, I could only get a sense of his profile. I depended on hearing the subtleties of his voice. And his reply had been reserved. I thought I could guess the reason. "He takes care of us," I repeated, "and he's kind to others. But he sees when there is risk, and he won't step toward such dangers unless he's forced to. Solomon, it's not that he doesn't see the need for emancipation, for human dignity, for the end of slaveholding. But he sees also what it will cost to bend the Southern states to such a choice."

"So, he favors gradual emancipation, or colonization, then," Solomon concluded in a matter-of-fact fashion.

Did a bitterness underlie his words? I struggled again to defend my father's choice. "Yes, that's true. But he does more than just favor it, he gives to it. He tithes to the church and to the Colonization Society. He would protect Sarah, you know, and that's why he sent us to Miss Farrow's that day, even though it was the Sabbath." So long ago!

"Yes, I see. Well, Seward says we'll all run out of softer choices as we wrestle for the territories to be free states. Sooner or later, each man will have to take a side for free or slave."

"Will the Southern states give way?" I thought of Uncle Martin, out in Illinois, printing the arguments for abolition of slavery and for free states to emerge from the western territories. "Will it be agreed, sooner or later?"

Solomon sighed. "I've no way to see far into the future, and nor can Seward himself guarantee the course of events. Your father's right about the risk: to force a view on an independent state is to provoke a violent response, and already the slave states have bonded together, both in Congress and in public opinion. But Alice, we can't hold back on this. You know it as well as I do, that to treat another human as an animal is to make a mockery of Creation itself. The heavens will forsake us if we forsake the paths of righteousness and mercy."

"You sound like a minister."

"Some days and nights, I feel like one. A Methodist preacher, riding a wide circuit of churches in a wilderness!"

We laughed together, and the night felt warmer. And lighter, but in a rosy way. No, that was no mere feeling—the night was indeed filling with a red light that hovered in the sky, toward North Upton. I grasped Solomon's arm and with my other hand pointed to the glow. I asked anxiously, "Is it fire?"

A quick turn of his head gave him a view. He said, "I mustn't watch it, for it will spoil my eyes for the shadows of the road. But you shall see it, and tell me what you think. It's not fire. It's the Aurora Borealis, the Northern Lights. Have you never seen them before, in the north sky?"

"Never! Are they always there, at this time of night? I never knew!" A curtain of red rose against the starry sky, and green lines danced through it. I gasped at the loveliness and strangeness of it all. The sky itself moved, a curtain of color rippling.

Soon a deeper green rose up from the horizon and pressed the rose portion aside. Flares of color shot upward in graceful curves. Then vertical lines of black against the green intensified the sense of a curtain. Who could draw such a drapery aside? I recognized the hand of the Creator in action. I wondered aloud, "Will Sarah see this, too, from Coventry?"

"I doubt she's awake or out of doors," Solomon said dryly. "But if she were, no doubt she could. They rise far from here, near the polar ice caps."

"And we can see them from here? Then they must be miles and miles across."

"Miles and miles," he confirmed. "And speaking of miles—" he slowed the horse slightly—"that glimmer ahead of us is the inn at Upton Center. We'll reach the turn in just a few minutes."

Houses and their inhabitants slumbered to either side of the road. At the four corners, by the general store and hardware, several lit windows at the big inn proclaimed some others awake in the middle of the night—or at least the remnants of hearth fires, for the ground-floor light was more ruddy than golden.

The buildings, including the two churches, blocked much of the view of the sky. By the time the horse had taken the turn onto the North Upton road, the heavenly lights had dimmed. I watched the last of them with regret.

"Will they rise again tonight?"

"Perhaps not." Solomon's smile came through his voice. "Will you rise each night now, to seek them?"

"I doubt it. Our village doesn't shape itself for a northern vista like this," I admitted. "Or any vista at all. I'd have to go elsewhere."

The words hung between us. I pondered them, realizing it was the first time I'd ever considered leaving North Upton for the sake of anything other than a trip to town to purchase cloth or needles or other supplies. I asked what came to mind: "How could you leave Boston, and your parents? Do you see them often?"

"Often enough. My road for Seward is a long one that takes me over most of New England, and sometimes to Pennsylvania too. If you enjoy wonders, I venture you'd enjoy Philadelphia. It's still the seat of freedom, you know, with the Liberty Bell and the sense of Ben Franklin in its streets and buildings." His voice turned bitter. "I'll never understand how Madison could have allowed the Capitol to be built in a Southern state. It's gone to their heads down there."

I sat silent a moment, unsure what to reply. A sudden change in the horse's movements saved me the trouble.

"Easy, fellow, what's in your road now? Another skunk?"

But the horse didn't stop this time. Instead, he veered sharply to the right and changed from a measured slow trot to a rapid one, then attempted to run at full speed. Solomon pulled sharply at the reins with one hand, his other clinging to the perch bench, as I did with both of mine.

"Ho, whoa, slow down!"

A barking cough from my left, from a rise of land still forested, made the hairs on my neck flutter in fear. The cough cleared itself into a growl, then ended in a short and plaintive howl. Wolf! No wonder the horse was bolting!

The carriage bounced on the frozen ruts of the road, threatening to wrench itself free from the running horse. Beneath me I heard Jerushah scream in fear and pain. I called out to her, "Hold on! Hold on!" But could she hear me over the racket of the wheels, the hooves, the clatter and groan of the strained carriage?

The torches dislodged from their corner and fell loose into the road. I strained to grasp the bench more securely, found a leather strap and clutched it, and scrabbled with my cold, half-numb feet for a foothold.

Just as I doubted I could hang on any longer, Solomon's commands drew a response from the horse, which slowed and then stopped, shaking and heaving, its hoarse breath almost a human sob. It edged sideways, head twisting toward where the sound of the wolf had echoed in the woods now well behind us. I could hear no other sounds above the gasping of the horse itself, and the near-hysterical weeping inside the carriage.

"I must go to her," I told Solomon, and he dropped down to the ground, reins firmly grasped, easing his way forward along the horse's sweated flank.

"I can't help you step down," he explained, in a crooning tone that I realized must be for the sake of the horse. "Jim needs me up here, don't you Jim? There's a good fellow, it's safe now. Easy, boy, easy."

Grasping the iron bar at the edge of the perch seat, I dropped down, ignoring my skirts. I wrenched open the door to the carriage and ducked inside, arms outstretched, to enfold Jerushah. "Are you hurt? Tell me, tell me where you're hurt!"

I held her until her sobbing ceased. She said at last, "I'm only bruised, I think. What was it, Alice? Why did the horse bolt like that?"

"A wolf," I said shortly. I blamed myself for not having told my father that I'd heard one—how long ago was that?

Solomon came up beside the carriage. "I think we can go on from here. He's pulled something in one leg, but he seems able to walk. Do you want to stay inside with your friend? Is she hurt?"

"She's not hurt much," I replied, unsure whether it was true but hoping so. "I think I should stay here, though, if you can drive well enough without me for the last of it."

"I'll manage. Or more to the point, old Jim and I will. I think I'll walk beside him for a ways. Watch your skirts, I'm closing the door."

As best I could, I held Jerushah and tried to sing to her, a lullaby over and over again. My arms ached. In the warmth that our bodies generated under the blankets, I realized for the first time that I, too, was exhausted. I thought of my bed in my own home and longed to reach it.

I might have drifted to sleep next to Jerushah, had I not noticed the clutch and heave of her chest as we sat there. I asked, "Jerushah, are you crying?"

"No, not crying," she said with a gasp. "But—can't get enough air. Open the curtain. Please!"

I seized two of the window curtains and drew them back, letting the cold night air rush into our faces. It served no good purpose, for her ragged breathing continued. I counted her breaths, then, instead of singing, and each time one faltered, I held her more snugly against me.

The rush of the Sleepers River reached me, and I knew we must be almost to William and Helen's house at the edge of the village. Minutes later, the carriage stopped at last, in front of the inn. Solomon opened the carriage, took in the situation with a glance, and ran to pound at the door of the inn.

"The other door," I called to him. "The house door. It will wake them sooner!"

Jerushah's father, in hastily assembled clothing, opened the door with a lit candle in one hand. He, too, was quick to grasp what was needed and called over his shoulder to his wife.

"Jerushah's home! But she's ill. Come quickly!"

Minutes later, Solomon walked me across to my own dear home, but not yet for any moments of rest: we woke my mother, to help tend Jerushah. Solomon walked back with her to the Clark house, saying he'd bed down over the tavern, after stabling the horse.

When I found William's wife Helen asleep in my bedchamber, I gave up entirely on my hope of comfort for the night. I fed the kitchen stove with a few splits of wood to wake its flames. I moved the tea kettle over onto the heat.

Before it could come to a boil, however, I fell asleep sitting up, in the big chair next to the stove, unable to absorb this latest disaster of the night.

CHAPTER 22

It was called rheumatic fever.

My mother and Jerushah's had been sure of it, but Doctor Jewett came from St. Johnsbury in the afternoon, after Mr. Clark had ridden our old Sam in the morning to tell the doctor he was needed.

My mother told me about it, as she assembled our supper. I had set aside my travel-soiled garments and wore my second skirt with an apron over it—the one I'd worn on our adventure for two weeks sat soaking, in hopes of lifting some of the stains—but fatigue made me a poor assistant in the kitchen, and at last I sat half numb and watched her capable movements from stove to shelf to table and back.

"It's no fault of yours or Mrs. Hayes's, for you nursed her well through the scarlatina. But it settled in her heart, and now it's rheumatic fever," she explained. "That's why she can't get her breath. It's not the lungs now, but the heart itself."

"And Doctor Jewett? Did he bring medicines for her?"

Bending to place a pan of biscuits into the oven, my mother waited to reply. Even when she stood up again, she spoke slowly, reluctantly. "There's no medicine to be had for it, he says. Only to try to bring back her strength and hope for some relief."

"No! There must be medicines for her!"

"Not everything has a cure from a bottle," said my mother firmly. "Let Nature take its course, and see what Providence may provide."

I was so tired. I knew that I should resolve immediately to provide more care for Jerushah myself, but a wave of despair leaked into me. Everything in my life seemed to go wrong. A sudden rap at the outer door caused me to rub a fist across my dry eyes and step to open it.

Solomon stood on the step, one arm braced on the doorframe. He nodded wearily and said, "Tell your father I've brought Ely back and stabled him; he'll need some attention to his legs, most likely his feet, but otherwise I think he's well and feeling his oats."

"What about the hired horse? Was Mr. Farrington angry about his leg?"

Solomon rubbed his own eyes. "I looked at the leg again this morning, but the horse seemed better after he'd rested. I rode him slowly. He spooked a bit when I took him past where the wolf was last night, but I don't think he's lame after all."

"Thank heaven."

We nodded to each other, both knowing that two horses settled into their proper stables could not balance the worry of Jerushah's illness. But at least we didn't have to feel guilty about the horses now.

My mother called from the kitchen, "You don't have to stand at the door, Mr. McBride. Come in, there's hot tea and more. Supper's nearly ready."

"Thank you kindly, Mrs. Sanborn, but I've promised to sup at the tavern this evening, and even for that, I'm afraid I'll need an hour of sleep first. I had a short night of it." He added in a lower voice to me, "I'm off in the morning on the east-bound stage. There's no time to talk about it. But I'll be here again in ten days. Can you hold some papers for me?"

"Of course."

He handed me a small leather satchel, and I placed it on a shelf just above the doorway, making sure he saw the location in case he needed it again when I wasn't at hand.

"How else can I help?" I wanted to say more than that, and at the same time, I wanted to wait.

"Get some rest yourself," he said softly. "Think of the Northern Lights as the opening for a new season. When I come back, we'll plan some of it together, if you like."

"I'd like that."

We shared a long look, and that familiar half smile rose to Solomon's face, despite the fatigue that creased his cheeks and darkened the hollows around his eyes. An urge to brush a lock of his dark hair back from his forehead came to me, but I let it pass and stood holding the door, smiling back at him.

He turned and walked down our lane toward the road, careful to skirt the largest puddles. I marveled that I'd once thought him too short, for I admired his well-balanced frame, and his way of walking that conveyed confidence and strength. He reached the road and half turned, lifting an arm to wave, and I lifted mine. Across the length of the lane, I could have sworn for a moment that our hands had touched, for mine was as warm as could be.

My mother called out, "Close the door; you're letting in the whole of the outdoors, Alice."

Meeting the clatter of supper dishes and the aroma of a maple pie just out of the oven, I turned back toward the kitchen. Everything was the same as when I'd left—and everything had changed.

"Lay out the tray for Helen, would you please? Let's see if we can tempt her to eat something this evening. And I've started a basket for you to take across to Jerushah in the morning. Thank you, Alice, it's good to have you home. I don't know how I managed it all while you were gone. Take that tray up the stairs, and then come tell me about the people who've taken Sarah in with them, while I finish dishing up."

My mother's calm directions and a good night's sleep fitted together to bring me a better morning on Friday. I woke early, with the calling of birds saluting the sunshine, and I left my improvised bed in the front room to draw water, wash up, and stir up the coals to start the kitchen fire.

As I stood up from adjusting the draft for the fire, my father came down the stairs, buttoning a jacket over his woolen shirt. He raised an eyebrow to see me up so soon.

"Early to bed, early to rise? Come to the barn with me if you like."

I caught up an old jacket that would not suffer in the barn and followed him out into the blue brightness of the day. Besides the songs of robins in the leafless branches, I heard a rooster crow, and the morning scuffle of sheep in the pen attached to the barn.

"Solomon said you might want to check Ely's hooves. Father, I'm sorry I missed so much of the lambing," I said as we went inside to grain the horses and sheep. "How many are born now?"

"Fourteen so far," my father replied, "and we only lost one. There are twelve more ewes still to lamb."

That meant fifteen lambs born from eight ewes. All twins but one. A good number. "And will we keep them all for wool, or send some to market young?"

"Wool. Ha!" my father snorted. "The price is down so low, we'd steal from ourselves if we kept them all. I've a buyer for two dozen lambs when they're six weeks old. Part cash, part cow."

"Part cow? But we already have one, and William another. Why?"

"The train." At my puzzled expression, he continued: "Once

the railroad reaches St. Johnsbury, we'll ship butter and cheese, maybe even milk, to Boston and Portsmouth. Most likely half the state will go to dairy." He lifted Ely's front left hoof, poked at the center flesh with a finger, and then scraped it lightly with his pocket knife, then proceeded to do the same for the other three. "Nothing much wrong here, but your young man was right to mention it."

I blushed. "He's not my young man. He just drove us, first halfway north, then back from Coventry. But he's nice, isn't he?"

"Seems to be. Seemed eager enough to go fetch you back, too." For a moment his bright eyes teased me, then turned serious again. "Helen and William need you here. So does your mother. She doesn't show it, but the baby's death is hard on her. She needs another grandchild to help her past the grieving, but that will take a while. You'll see what you can do to keep her talking, would you? No more running east or west or north?"

"Yes, of course. And what should I do about Helen and William?"

"Just keep them talking, too. Too much silence around here while you were gone." He emptied grain into the feed boxes for Ely and Sam and then filled two pails to take out to the sheep in the paddock that lay half under the barn, half in the weather. "I'll finish this up. Go help your mother with breakfast, there's a good girl."

Again, Helen declined to join us, so I took another tray up to her. But as she had the previous evening, William's sorrowful young wife barely lifted her head from the pillow to thank me, then turned again toward the wall.

I touched her shoulder. "I'll come back up later, Helen, and maybe we can talk." There was no reply.

After breakfast, I cut out and folded a paper flower to decorate the basket of bread and honey for Jerushah, and told my mother I'd be back shortly. Going down the lane, in the warmth of the sunshine, I dared to hope that Jerushah might be feeling better. And perhaps Solomon would be in the house, too, visiting before he left on the day's stage.

What a long time had passed since I'd stepped into the Clarks' large kitchen! The three small children sat at the table, spooning up their oatmeal and sugar. I sat down to keep them company, asking, "Is your mother home?"

"With J'rushah," the oldest child confirmed. "J'rushah gets to have bread and milk for breakfast. In bed!"

"Fortunate Jerushah," I agreed. "If you'll finish your porridge, I'll tell you a story."

Just as I reached the end of a stirring rendition of "Goldilocks," Mrs. Clark came into the room.

"Oh, Alice, how kind of you to tell them a story," she said immediately. "Now, all of you, go wash your faces and find something to keep you busy. You've a Bible verse to learn, haven't you? Shoo!"

She turned to me, a drawn look on her face. "I won't invite you to visit Jerushah, Alice. She's just drifting back to sleep, and that's best for her now." She reached to stack the bowls from the table, and I gathered up the cups for her. "Thank you. You're often thoughtful, aren't you?" Her voice tightened to match her face. "That's what I don't understand, I must say. You can be so thoughtful, but you dragged Jerushah through that cold night, when she'd not yet recovered from scarlatina. And now look what you've done. How could you?"

I stared, shocked. "But we tried to stop for the night at the inn in Walden, Solomon and I, we tried! It was Jerushah who wouldn't stay. She said—" Oh, dear, I mustn't repeat the terrible things she'd said; she wasn't well. "She said she needed to come home, that we must bring her."

"And you should have known better," Mrs. Clark snapped,

her voice rising even higher. "You were strong and healthy, and she wasn't. You should have kept her warm and safe, not taken her out in some wild ride through the wilderness. Look what you've done!"

From the top of the stairs, a faint voice called, "Mama? Mama, don't!"

"And now you've woken her up when she needs her sleep, as well!" The accusation was so unfair that I stood speechless, as Mrs. Clark continued her tirade, even as she rushed to the stairs. "You're thoughtless, and I want you out of my house. Go!" I heard Jerushah still protesting, as her mother gathered her up and took her back to her room.

What should I do? I took the bread and honey out of my mother's basket, and the folded paper flower. Tears ran down my face, and splashed the paper, spoiling the folds. I picked it up and crumpled it in one hand, and, with the basket in my other, I stumbled down the hallway and out into the dooryard— where a strong arm caught me and suddenly two hands seized my shoulders. Solomon's concerned face looked directly into mine.

"What is it? What's happened? Is it Jerushah? Is she worse?"

I shook my head, brushed at the tears, tried to catch enough breath to speak. "Her mother," I forced out. "Her mother thinks we did this to her. She told me to leave."

"Ah, Alice! Alice, Alice, you know she's only overwrought. Give her time. She's frightened for her daughter, and most likely near as tired as the rest of us. Don't fret, Alice." He pulled a handkerchief out of a pocket, dusty but dry, and mopped my cheeks. I reached up to take the cloth, to do it myself. A door slammed behind him, and he quickly stepped back from me, leaving the handkerchief in my hand.

It was Matthew, coming out of the tavern, a pair of driving cloaks over one arm. "Alice, just the person I needed to see." If he noticed my red eyes and wet nose, he was too polite to say so. "It's good to have you both back. And tell me about Sarah: is this family up in Coventry a good one for her?"

"The very best for her, until her own parents catch up with her," I responded, glad for the distraction. "And Matthew, the father is a blacksmith. So there are plenty of visitors each day, and Sarah will enjoy that, too."

"Yes, she will, you're right about that. Sweet little Sarah, always happy to help out. Well, I'm glad for her, though we all miss her something fierce. Now, Alice, I'm sending these cloaks back to Miss Farrow, with Solomon on the stage. Isn't there a third one that you wore?"

I agreed and ran to fetch it from home. I knew Solomon watched me, but there was little we could say to each other in front of Jerushah's brother.

Just as I returned with the dry, brushed cloak over my arm, the stage, early for once, pulled up in front of the tavern, its horses fresh and stamping, the yellow paintwork of the carriage gleaming near the top but otherwise well splashed with mud. "Stayed the night in Upton Center," Young Sam said cheerfully. "Off schedule thanks to all the mud, and the bridge at Richmond was torn away last week . . . what a mess . . ." he rattled on.

Matthew and Solomon slapped each other's shoulders, and Solomon climbed up to share the driver's perch, while Matthew strapped a satchel—a larger one than the one Solomon had left with me—onto the back with the other luggage. Two men in town suits sat inside, lifting their hats politely in hello and farewell as the driver tugged the horses' dripping noses away from the water trough.

"I'll see you in ten days," Solomon called as the driver slapped the reins and shouted for the horses to move.

"Ten days. I'll see you then," Matthew called back.

I only lifted the handkerchief to wave. But I was sure that Solomon's reminder was as much meant for me as for Matthew. So, as I walked back up the lane to my own home, at least I had something warm with which to balance the angry words of Jerushah's mother. Before going into the kitchen, I took Solomon's handkerchief, dust and tears and all, and folded it carefully, to tuck into the pocket of my skirt.

CHAPTER 23

Although I did my part in tasks in the kitchen that long Friday, and carried noon meals to both Helen in the upstairs room and my father in the lambing pen, my hands and feet performed without my heart. How could Jerushah's mother blame me for this deepening shadow of illness? And what could I do to restore my friend—her health and her love for me? Helen's refusal to talk with me and my mother's false cheer took me further into a gray world of despair and discouragement. Even the weather turned dismal. A small rain began in late morning, increased in the afternoon, and then, as the temperature dropped sharply, a glaze of ice formed on every surface. Heading to the barn to see my father again, to ask him whether he could come in for supper, I inched across the dooryard, afraid to slip and capsize in my Sunday skirt. My daily one hung damply in the kitchen, clean now but considerably worn from our journey.

The barn reeked of a winter's worth of manure and the discards from the day's lambing, the fluids of birth turning sour. I leaned across the rail of the pen, watching my father inspect the four ewes captured within it. The glimmer of a birth sac showed between one set of legs. The other three ewes, not so far along, simply bleated and groaned.

"Mama wants to know, can you come in to eat?"

My father shrugged wearily. "For just a few minutes. Tell her I'll need something hot and sweet later, to keep awake into the evening. Has William come yet?"

206

"Yes, he's up with Helen." Rain hammered the barn roof. I looked up into the half-empty hay loft, but it was too dark to see much. "Is he sleeping in the barn for you tonight?"

"Yes, if these lambs don't come soon, he'll have to. I doubt he'll go up to the loft, though."

Stained and limp, my father's clothing looked as exhausted as he did. Were none of us able to hold up in this shadowed spring?

I turned to take his message back to the house, then paused and asked, "I've heard no mention of that Henry Clinton, the slave hunter. What happened when he came back to North Upton that day?" It had been nearly two weeks, I realized.

"A nasty piece of work, that young fellow." My father spat eloquently into the waste pail. "He wouldn't believe anyone and said that the runaway, that Fred Johnson fellow, must be hidden in someone's cellar or attic. Climbed up and down in every house in the village, and twice in your brother's mill. It took until the next stage, four days later, for us to get rid of him. Back to Boston, or New York, or wherever he hangs his hat."

A weight I hadn't realized I'd carried dropped away. "Then he's gone for good?"

"As best we know. Still, a bad penny often turns up again."

"Why would he come again? Wouldn't he know that both of them, Fred and Sarah, have gone north now?"

"We'll pray it's so." He lifted the latch of the pen's gate and came out to wash his hands. "You and your mother ought to see from all this, there's no good place for the colored people here. Send them all on ships back to Africa; that's the best way for them to be safe. When an animal smells a strange breed, it almost always attacks. At least the males do." My face must have spoken my shock and disagreement, for my father gave a low growl and finished, "Go tell your mother I'm coming in a few minutes."

In the kitchen, William sat at the table, spreading bacon

grease on a thick slice of hot bread. I inhaled the scent of it all, trying to cast off the sourness of the barn. "How's Helen tonight? Will she come down to sup with us?"

"Not tonight. Maybe tomorrow." William too wore a cloak of weariness. "This rain is a confounded nuisance. The water's up so high, I've got to let it all run over the dam and through the sluice, wide open. There's no sense even trying to operate the mill."

"But doesn't it always run high this time of year?"

My mother put in, "Just let it go. Water over a dam is no use to anyone. You'll have better days ahead."

William shook his head. "It shouldn't stay so high for so long. I'm losing some of the river bank on the far side. It's never been this bad before."

That seemed to sum up the day for everyone: never this bad before. My father came in, scraping his boots at the doorway but keeping them on his feet, with an apologetic look toward my mother. "Can't stay but a few minutes, Abigail. That bag's about to bust, and there's maybe twins, maybe a threesome of lambs in this one."

William hurried his own supper and left with my father. I offered to tidy up and sent my mother up to read to Helen. As she climbed the stairs, I remembered I had a question for her, too: "Charles and John—have they written?"

"Not since the letter that came before you ran off."

Ran off? I protested. "Father sent us to Miss Farrow's; I didn't run off."

"Yes, I know. I'm sorry. I'm tired, too. If you want to read the letter, it's in my workbasket in the front room."

When the plates were clean and stacked, I took a candle into the front room to read the letter from California. John said the two of them had taken places at a general store, to save for a bit before staking another claim. He said they were starting to see a return on their labor. Charles had penned a postscript that crossed John's writing, and I squinted to make out the words: "Met up with the Thrasher family from Peacham Corners. Miss Emma is grown and keeping company with me. If all goes well, I'll bring her home with me in another two years."

At least something good was happening to somebody in my family. I wondered why my mother hadn't urged me to read this letter sooner. Well, she had her hands full, I could see that, but still, I felt neglected in the absence of any word from her about this.

I carried the candle back to the kitchen, then realized I might as well quench its light and go back to my narrow bed in the front room and sleep. There was no good coming from this day for me.

Saturday passed in much the same way, warming long enough to turn the weather to outright rain without ice. My mother said she thought Helen might join us for Sunday dinner, if I asked her to do so. In the evening, I did, and though she still had no life in her voice, she said she might as well get up the next day, if her head didn't hurt much.

And that was the lone bit of light that Saturday, a "perhaps" from Helen. I ached to visit Jerushah but didn't dare knock at the door for fear of her mother's anger. William arrived late, well past supper, and went directly to the barn, but my father sent him home again to rest and came inside himself at darkness.

"I doubt the next lambs will come for another day yet. Maybe we'll get a Sabbath rest after all."

Rising on Sunday to a third day in a row of rain, I wished the Sabbath rest could apply to staying home. But I knew half the village would be waiting to see me at services, whether or not they said anything. Brushing my hair and then my skirt, I tried to prepare for their curiosity.

I had estimated wrongly, however. With Jerushah's mother and father darkly glowering in their pew, and my own parents placing themselves between me and the aisle to block the glances and questions, I sat silent through both the sermon, which was on faith the size of a mustard seed, and the second service of lessons on the Prodigal Son. Only for the hymns did I rise and try to sing. But my heart seemed lodged in my throat. Did the other people of the village agree with Jerushah's mother, that her terrible illness was my doing?

On the way out at lunch, I heard a comment behind me: "It's a harsh bargain, one girl's freedom exchanged for another girl's health." Someone hushed the speaker. I refused to turn but held up my head, determined not to weep in public. My mother took my arm in hers, and we walked down the road in a darker silence.

I longed for Monday, and the solace of labor. I even offered to take the evening shift in the barn for lambing, but my father told me that it was time I behaved like a young lady and stayed out of the barn. So I spent the afternoon darning the worn parts of my workaday skirt, adding a fresh strip of wool to the hemline, and regretting even Helen's emotional arrival at the supper table, interrupted as it was by her tears and retreat.

Monday dawned clear and cold. It occurred to me that the westbound stage would arrive at some point. But Solomon was unlikely to be on it—he had said ten days, which must mean he'd be gone until the next Monday. I wondered what he was doing and how far he had gone—to Portsmouth? Or all the way to Boston?

William arrived at the house at mid morning. I told him Father was in the barn, of course, but it was me he wanted.

"I've got to go down along the mill pond," he told me. "There's a pair of logs jammed by the sluice and more limbs catching on them. It's backing up the water too high. Come and hold a rope for me as I go in."

"Wouldn't it be better to have the men hold it? I'm not that strong."

"I know. Matthew's coming, too. He'll hold the rope attached to my belt, but I need someone to pull as I loop another around the logs. Between the two of you, I can do this."

My mother told me only, "Wear William's old boots. And a barn coat. And look for some of your father's gloves. It will be cold work. Come back for dinner, all three of you, so I know you're safely done with it."

I doubted Matthew would be able to come to dinner at our home. But I didn't argue. And it was a relief to see him smile at me as William and I joined him by the mill. At least someone in Jerushah's family didn't hate me.

"Stage just arrived," Matthew mentioned with a gesture back toward the heart of the village. "I heard the bells behind me as I came down here."

My heart gave an extra thump, but my mind knew well that Solomon wouldn't be on the stage this time, so what point was there in thinking about it? I bent to tie the bootlaces more snugly, stood up and nodded, and asked, "Where should I stand, William?"

We allotted ourselves as points of a triangle: Matthew at the near bank of the mill pond, me at the far bank, and William to edge along the beam over the dam, toward the sluice gate, where a tangle of tree limbs had already amounted to an ominous bulk of blockage. The water pounded against the mill footings, shaking it as I walked through and out the other side.

Three throws of the knotted end of the rope from Matthew's side failed to reach me, each time falling short into the raging waters. More branches piled up in each minute. William shouted over the noise. "Change sides, so you're throwing the same way the wind is blowing."

I tramped back through the mill's narrow extension over the river, cold and dark despite the sunlight beyond the windows. Matthew patted my shoulder reassuringly as he passed me. This time, from his far side toward my near one, the knot arrived in a heavy thump against my leg and I caught it. Matthew came back to the near side of the pond to help me fasten it to a wooden piling, so that I needed only to brace my weight against it to adjust the length of the line. He returned to the far side, where he'd secured his own rope accordingly, and William held the loose ends of both ropes. Matthew's rope he secured to the heavy leather harness around his chest, made for just this task. Mine he formed into a loop, to slip over the most obstructive tree trunk in the pile-up at the sluice.

Step by step, William edged out over the waters. The wooden dam trembled under his feet, and water surged against him, up to his knees. I watched Matthew tighten the line of rope as William moved further into the flooded current.

He looped my rope over the closest limb and nodded to me, shouting something I couldn't hear but assumed was "Pull!" I pulled. The weight of the limb and the force of the water battled against me. William leaned forward to add his own weight to move the limb. It lurched abruptly, changing position. I strained to hear him: "Good! Pull it again!"

Matthew's gaze was on the limb, then on me, and then back on William. We maneuvered further, and suddenly a tangle of branches broke loose, sailing off down the surging river. All three of us cheered, unable to hear each other but sharing wide smiles.

My feet ached from bracing against the low wall, and my arms from pulling the rope. It was good to let go a moment and flex my arms while William moved the loop at the end of the tree-hauling line. He snagged it around a wickedly rooted old stump and waved for me to pull again.

This time, even with William pushing at the stump, I could not pull it loose. William waved to Matthew and shouted something that Matthew seemed to hear, for he nodded, and took an extra turn in his rope around the piling, then stepped away from it and re-entered the mill bridge, to cross to my side of the pond. He grasped the line with me, and we both heaved at it. The stump began to ease back. William pushed at it with both arms, then a booted foot, his other leg braced on a massive trunk wedged against the dam.

Just as the stump began to move backward against the current, a shout came from an upstairs window of the mill. Because it was high above the waters, we all heard the words. A man shouted out, "You're no better than thieves! I've found his jacket right here. I know you've got him. Where's that blasted runaway? Tell me!"

William jerked upright, staring up at the window, and in the movement, he lost his footing with the braced boot and capsized into the water around his knees. Instantly the safety rope tightened, pulling with a sharp crack against the piling on the far side of the mill race. Matthew dropped the log line and ran back toward William's safety line. I followed him. Already, William had vanished from view.

Together, Matthew and I strained at the safety rope, desperate to pull my brother from the river. But it was caught on a limb and tangled, and we made no progress. Matthew dropped his coat at my feet and rapidly tied his suspenders in a loop around the safety line.

"I'm going out there," he yelled over the noise. "Pull when I tell you to."

"I can't!" I screamed in panic. "I don't have the strength!"

Matthew turned toward the upstairs window. "Clinton, you bastard, get down here and help the girl. Now!"

Clinton? The slave hunter? My heart thumped, and my chest seized without breath, though my hands never let go of the rope. "William!" I screamed into the waters. "William!"

Matthew looped one arm through the leather straps of his suspenders and leaped into the waters, pulling himself along the safety rope toward the sluice gate, where William must be caught among the branches. The extra weight on the line bit into my palms. I pulled as best I could. Again I screamed out my brother's name. "William!"

"Better drowned than a live pair of thieves," came a coarse shout at my shoulder. Henry Clinton, his elegance vanished into road-worn clothing and a fierce scowl, stood next to me, hands stuffed in his pockets.

"Pull with me," I demanded. "Pull!"

"First tell me, where's the runaway? Where is he hiding? What have they done with him?"

"Canada!" I yelled at the bounty hunter. "He's gone to Canada! Take hold and pull!"

"I'm damned if I will! They've cost me five hundred dollars and more. Let 'em drown," the man snarled.

A white-hot rage took me, and I lost all thought but burned only to hate this man who chased and sold humans, and who wouldn't lift a hand to save my brother from the river. "It's you that's damned, for sure," I screamed. "Pull, or I'll hunt you down myself after! Pull!"

Out in the waters, I saw Matthew's head and shoulders bob dark and wet next to the tangle of limbs. Had he found William? I screamed again: "William! William!"

What changed the bounty hunter's mind, I'll never know. Perhaps it was the sudden sight of the body clutched in Matthew's arms. But suddenly two stronger hands reached past mine and seized the rope, pulling with me. Even so, I dreaded that we might not have the strength between us to draw the weight of two men out of the river's grasp, and every inch gained seemed too slow, too late. Was William breathing? Had the logs crushed him? I couldn't see enough to know.

The weight of the two men came closer. I saw that Matthew had thrust one of William's arms into the leather loop of his suspenders, and he pushed as if against a pulley, maneuvering William toward the edge of the waters. When they were close enough, Henry Clinton helped me loop our rope around the piling so we could both let go and bend down to tug at William's limp arms and legs. Matthew pushed from below, and we heaved from above. With a sucking wrench, the waters released my brother, and we pulled him up onto the wet and slippery ground.

I knelt next to William's body, tilting his face to let the water run from his mouth, pressing down on his chest regardless of whether ribs had snapped or not, desperate to see breath move in him again. I heard a cry from behind me and looked toward the river again. Now Matthew hung from the leather loop, and there was no extra person to push from below for him. At the water's edge, the slave hunter struggled to tug Matthew loose from the river, and I strained to hear what he was yelling: "I can't pull him out alone. Come help!"

William's frame convulsed in a sudden choking cough, and I let go and ran to the river's edge. With the slave hunter, I grasped at Matthew's arms and locked my fingers into one of his hands. We pulled as mightily as any two people could, and desperation or Providence itself fueled our strength, for as Matthew scrabbled in his water-logged boots against the edge, we tugged him upward, and he slid forward onto the solid ground, a muddy and wet figure gasping for breath.

Now anger again swept over Henry Clinton's face, and he drew back a booted foot and kicked at Matthew's chest. "You lied to me, you whitewashed son of a gun. You deceived me!

Me, and the law! I'll have you thrown in jail for it, too!"

Horrified, I screamed, "Stop!" But he kicked again, as Matthew scrambled to get away, heaving water and vomit and rolling over, so that the boot failed to reach its target.

And with that violent movement that connected only with the noisesome air, the bounty hunter slipped on the wet mud. He tumbled, unable to grasp the rope, into the terrible rush of waters.

A moment later, he was gone.

CHAPTER 24

There could be no question of what must be done: Though my father could not leave the lambing long, for fear of harm to the birthing animals and their progeny, he must report the presumed death of Henry Clinton, as well as launching a search downriver for the body or, in perhaps some miracle, the possibility of a living survivor. He saddled Ely and made haste, first to the minister, who could gather men for a search, and then on to Upton Center, to find Judge McMillan and recount the events of the day.

I sat in the furthest corner of the kitchen, being the least chilled of our group, hands cupped around a mug of honeyed tea. Helen, risen from her bed to tend her husband, bustled around the stove as though she'd never suffered the loss of her babe—she had responded instantly to the demand to restore the heat of his blood, and the need for relief of his bruised ribs as she wrapped a length of bandage around his chest. Her crooning over William sounded to me as though she had taken him on as a replacement for a child in her arms.

Matthew had stayed only long enough to drain a mug of hot broth and to allow my mother and father to thank him for ensuring William's survival. Red-faced, he pushed aside their attention, saying only, "What else could I do? You'd have done the same." My father insisted on providing a dry shirt and coat for Matthew, who then apologetically rose and said he'd leave us to our nursing tasks. I followed him out of the kitchen toward the outer door, unsure what to say. As he reached the door, I saw his gaze catch on the leather satchel of Solomon's papers that I had left on the shelf there. He hesitated, then seemed to decide something, opened the door, and nodded to me as he went out into the cold. I watched from the dooryard to be sure he did not stumble as he walked down the lane and crossed the road to his home.

Would Jerushah and her parents blame me for this, too? Or blame William? I tried to track the tangled causes of the day's disaster. First and foremost came the flooding waters, of course—the force of Nature that overwhelmed our plans. Second, I faulted the bounty hunter himself for his greed and anger. It seemed clear to me that had he not attempted to kick Matthew with such violence, he would never have fallen into the river. I wondered whether his drowned body might even be entangled with the very trees that blocked the sluice gate. Would the searchers find him there?

I tried to turn the net of reasons in my mind, to see another side. Henry Clinton might have family who loved him. Would they say his death resulted from my brother and Jerushah's brother having assisted in the escape of Fred Johnson? Would they, like Clinton, consider William and Matthew to be thieves of valued property, destined for jail themselves?

My mother, when I asked her this, told me to stop thinking. "Go comb out your hair," she instructed crisply. "The judge is sure to arrive here to listen to your account. He'll receive it better if you look like a lady, instead of a half-drowned doxy."

Once again, I smoothed my Sunday skirt over an old set of outgrown petticoats, as my workday garments hung to dry by the stove. In the front room, without the aid of any looking glass, I struggled to comb the long, wet tangles of my hair and pin them into a semblance of neatness. At once, my mind filled with the tangles of the trees at the dam, and a rushing like wild water took me close to fainting. I bent over and let the blood flow down into my head, determined not to collapse. Too much was at stake.

I watched and listened, and when I heard hooves and wheels, I hurried to the window. Behind my father, a carriage followed him up the lane, drawn by two horses. When it stopped by the horse barn, Judge McMillan descended from it, and so did another man. My father dismounted from Ely, said something to the men, and began to unhitch their horses. Ah: They expected to stay quite a while, then. I went to greet them and invite them into the kitchen.

Judge McMillan was my mother's second cousin, and his greeting to her was gentle but firm. "I've brought Doctor Jewett with me," he explained, "as he was sharing my noon dinner. He'll examine your son and then visit the other young man as well, and bring him here. We will both listen to their accounts of what has taken place."

My father entered and said, "The Reverend Alexander sent word: they've found Clinton downriver at the next dam."

"Hrrmph. Dead, I presume?"

"Dead." With lowered head, my father murmured, "God rest his soul."

"Amen," said all of us in response.

The doctor confirmed that William had three or four cracked ribs and assured me I'd done no further harm in compressing his chest to make him breathe. "On the contrary, you may have saved both his life and his mind that way," the doctor said calmly. "Too long without air and the brain withers. I'll step across to the Clark home now and return as soon as I can. Thank you; I know my way. I'll spend a moment to see my other patient while I'm there, but I won't be long."

Helen stood behind William, her hands on his shoulders, and refused to take a seat, even once the judge had taken his. She

219

spoke out: "My husband needs rest. I want this over and done with."

Judge McMillan nodded his white-haired head and patted the table gently with one hand. "So do we all, my dear. That is why I've come here myself and have not yet asked William to report to the courthouse." The edge of warning in his voice reached Helen, and she gripped William's shoulders so tightly that he gave a small cry of pain. The judge did not comment on this but asked Helen, "Would you be so kind as to make me a cup of tea? I imagine your husband might want one, also."

My mother, seeing the sense of the judge's request to Helen as a way to calm her, stepped away from the woodstove and waved Helen toward the steaming kettle.

"I think I'll step into the front room and write some letters," my mother offered graciously. "If you want me, you need only call." My father also excused himself, to the barn.

So, as Helen poured tea and passed a plate of sweet biscuits, we exchanged awkward comments about weather and sugaring, horses and sheep and the price of wool. In about a quarter of an hour, the doctor returned with Matthew at his side, and our accounting began.

With both patience and courtesy, the two older men listened to William and Matthew. Matthew gave the sequence of events, and William only added a few details. I stayed silent, except to repeat what I'd heard Henry Clinton shout from the mill window, and to confirm the vicious things he had said at the edge of the river.

Doctor Jewett inquired, "How did he happen to be at the mill?"

William looked baffled. I had no notion. But Matthew after a moment said, "I'm afraid he may have been looking for me. He'd come back to town on the stage a few minutes earlier, and I didn't meet it, but most likely he'd seen me walking down to the mill. Last time he was in the village, he followed me through every room of the tavern, but he may have thought we had a hidey-hole somewhere."

"A hidey-hole?" Judge McMillan raised his bristling white eyebrows. "Not for fugitives, I take it."

"No, sir. And we don't have one. But there is a pair of cupboards behind the stairs, which he may have suspected held something, even though they are locked from the outside. My father does a brisk business at the inn, and we sometimes set aside the week's monies there, until one of us can go to the bank."

I thought this was especially wise of Matthew to mention, since the judge's brother-in-law owned the bank.

"I'm afraid you fellows will have to tell us about this man Fred Johnson. Is there indeed a warrant for his arrest?"

William spoke up. "No, sir. I looked at the paper that Clinton had, and it was only a letter from a plantation owner in Virginia, accusing Mr. Johnson of violating the law by teaching his children to read."

A silence lingered in the kitchen, heavy with opinion: how could a man be considered a criminal for teaching his children to read? In that moment, I regained my confidence in what we all had done.

"He kicked Matthew," I said now, returning to the account of what had taken place by the river. "Henry Clinton kicked him when he was lying on the ground, still vomiting up water and more. It was the second kick that missed, that threw him off balance and sent him into the water."

Dr, Jewett and Judge McMillan exchanged glances. Dr. Jewett waited for the judge to speak first. It seemed to me to be a very long wait.

" 'But the fruit of the Spirit is love, joy, peace, longsuffering, gentleness, goodness, faith, meekness, temperance: against such there is no law.' This is what Scripture teaches us, and the law of Man is intended to amplify the law of God," the judge said slowly. "It would seem that you two young men, Mr. Sanborn and Mr. Clark, have suffered from an abundance of the fruit of the spirit. And with regret, I observe that Mr. Clinton appears to have suffered from its lack."

As the doctor nodded agreement, Judge McMillan placed both hands on the table to push himself to his feet. "I will bring your accounting to the High Sheriff on the morrow," he continued. "Dr. Jewett, would you kindly write for me a document that captures the salient facts as we have heard them this day? I believe there will be no need to convene the grand jury for this. Providence appears to have arranged matters to an end that may have its losses but is otherwise satisfactory."

The doctor stood also and called into the front room his thanks. "I'll come back again at mid-week to examine all my North Upton patients. God keep you all. Enoch," he said to the judge, "I believe it is my turn to drive that fine team of yours."

As the two men departed, Helen drew William up the stairs to rest until supper, and my mother emerged with my father, each determined upon tasks to accomplish for the afternoon. I walked Matthew to the door again, and again I saw him note the leather satchel.

"It belongs to Solomon McBride," I whispered to him.

"I thought as much," he replied. "Keep it safe. Better put it where it's not so easily noticed."

"I will," I promised.

And I did, moving it to the pantry and placing it in a corner behind the flour barrel, with a cloth napkin laid over it so that my mother might not be struck by its presence.

I wished I knew some portion of Scripture that would justify opening it to see what papers it contained. But the sensible half of me was quite sure there was no such portion, and I nudged the flour barrel snugly back against the hidden satchel.

CHAPTER 25

Tuesday morning, to my great relief, Helen took William home.

"I need to go to the mill," he protested when she announced her decision at breakfast. "I never finished clearing the sluice yesterday, and the water will tear out the entire cribbing of the dam."

My father intervened. "You're not the only one in this village who knows how to haul off a tree or two," he said dryly. "Gerald Hopkins, Steve Cobb, and I took a look at the mess last night. Water's down a bit, by the way. At any rate, Cobb is bringing a team of work horses from Upton Center, and we'll clear the jam today."

William stood, struggling to button his vest over his bandaged ribs. "Then I'll get right down there and clear more room for them to pull. There's a pile of boards that will have to be uncovered and moved."

"You'll do nothing of the sort." That was Helen, loudly. "You'll come up to our house and stay warm and dry and watch from the window, and I'll take care of you."

I thought the pair of them would overturn the table as they hollered. I looked to my father to stop them, but he had pulled back his chair and simply grinned, well entertained, waiting for a break in the noise. When it came, he said, "Helen, do you suppose you might allow William to sit and rest inside the mill, upstairs, where he can check the angles of the ropes and supervise us old-timers? And I don't suppose you might be able to set out some kind of noon meal for us there? I imagine one or two other fellows may join us, and untangling that mess is like to take much of the day."

It was a clever diversion. Helen at once sought my mother's help in supplying a share of the bread and ham she envisioned, even as she announced which of her preserves she'd pull out of the cupboards, and asked whether anyone had churned the cream from William's cow during her time of convalescence. I heard the tremble in her voice as she mentioned this, but she went right on into more plans and instructions, showing a courage that I hadn't guessed she owned.

My mother beckoned me aside. "Run to William's house and pick up any of the babe's clothes and such, and set them aside in the bedroom," she suggested. "Don't let those be the first thing that strikes Helen when she gets home. I'll slow her down at this end, as we pack the foodstuffs."

Relieved to have a reason to slip outside, I hurried down our lane. Gray clouds massed over the western hills threatened more rain, although a patch of blue danced over the village. I came closer to Jerushah's house and looked for signs at the windows, especially at her bedchamber upstairs, but saw no face or waving hand. I longed to hear her say that her illness wasn't my fault—or better yet, to hear that she'd recovered.

I saw no sign of the Clark family, though, besides wood smoke from the house chimney and the tavern one. So I turned left onto the village road, stepping along the edges where the mud was less soft. A group of schoolchildren threw a ball among them in the schoolyard. No smoke rose from the school chimney, nor movements inside the schoolhouse; I should have asked my mother whether the term had ended early, what with the spotted fever and such, but it seemed likely. I called out to young Isaac Parker, who came to the road's edge and replied that there would be a convocation at the end of the month but no classes until then.

Three men stood outside the store, and all nodded a greeting to me as I hurried past. I overhead one say to another, once I'd gone by, "And she was there when he landed in the river. What I hear, somebody should have helped him into it a lot sooner."

The relief of the morning slipped into misery once again, as I thought of how the previous day's events had cascaded—the wrestling against the river, and the disastrous end to Henry Clinton's life. Thank heavens, the searchers had found the man's body and sent it off to Upton Center, thence to be driven by wagon to Woodsville to meet the train south to Hartford, where they said the Clinton family lived.

From the road, a wagon, piles of lumber, tree trunks, and a steam-powered saw blocked the view of the mill pond. I wanted to see whether the waters were still rising, and whether the tangle at the sluice gate had grown. But who knew how long my mother could delay Helen, now that she had the bit in her teeth, so to speak? I'd best get to the little house beyond the mill.

Folding the baby's clothing and blankets washed me with sorrow, and pity for Helen. My mother had been wise to send me ahead—if this task drew me to the verge of tears, how much more painful would it have been for Helen? I piled the small items, then carried them to the back room and set them on the top of the dresser there. Poor Helen. At least she would have the privacy of her bedroom to weep over the small garments and the heartbreak of the baby's death. How soon would she and William try for another child? I felt a prayer in my chest and breathed it outward, that they might be blessed soon with expectation, and with a healthy second babe.

Back in the damp, chilled kitchen, I scrambled to start a fire in the stove and set a kettle of water to heating. My mother and Helen entered as the water in the kettle began to boil, and Helen swept me aside so that she might clean her kitchenware to her own satisfaction. Seeing my mother lay out the contents of two large baskets, I assured her I would go mind the fire in our own stove and excused myself from Helen's home.

Should I stop at the mill first, to watch the men and horses at work there? I remembered the sight of Matthew retching in the mud, and the feel of William's cold face before I was sure he'd draw breath. I decided that home was a better place to be. I hurried down the road, careful not to stare at Jerushah's house as I passed it again. A drizzle of rain began, turning the day gray and misty.

Our kitchen held a silence that didn't speak to me of peace. What had Judge McMillan said about the fruits of the spirit? Love, joy, peace, long-suffering: that was Jerushah. Thinking of her struggle to breathe, of my mother's explanation of rheumatic fever and its damage to the heart, I sat down next to the stove and wept a torrent. The words spoke to me of Sarah, too, and I missed the delicious pleasure of taking care of her and seeing her adapt so eagerly to schooling and stories. I wept even harder.

When I could find no more tears or sobs, I reached in my pocket for a handkerchief. I had none with me. Going up to my bedchamber would mean facing the tasks of reclaiming the room from Helen's occupation: airing the sheets and covers, at least by the stove—not outside in the rain. Instead, I opened the chest of linens in the front room, hoping to borrow one of my father's large handkerchiefs that would be stacked there after ironing.

The piece of linen that I lifted, though, was unlike those made by my mother. The hem stitching included a periodic ornate twist, and at one corner of the smoothly ironed square was the letter S, embroidered in white silk.

Solomon! It was Solomon's, the one he'd dabbed at my cheeks on Friday morning. Rather than crumple it against my cheeks again, I mopped the salt wetness off with my sleeve and stroked the linen square and its sinuous embroidery work. I realized how little I knew of Solomon's life: Would his mother have made this? Or a sister? Or perhaps—and I sighed at the thought—some young lady of Boston with whom he had an understanding?

Since I could find no answer to this bothersome question, I folded the handkerchief neatly and placed it in the pocket of my skirt. Then, in the silent empty house, I tiptoed as if someone might hear my steps, all the way to the pantry corner where I'd set aside the satchel of papers that Solomon asked me to keep.

Holding to what I knew was right, I resolutely left the clasps closed. But I brushed my fingertips against the leather, remembering the strong arms that had driven me home from Coventry, and the hands that had seized my shoulders in concern.

CHAPTER 26

The week crept by. Although some sunny hours came each day, so did showers of rain. I helped with some of the latest arriving lambs, including a difficult birth of twins so intertwined that their legs had to be pulled one at a time from the mother's birthing passage. My father brought all the sugaring buckets from the maple woods, and we washed and stacked them, to set aside until next March. Pruning the apple trees and moving the hay forward in the loft also took my father's attention, and each time I saw an open hour arriving, my mother seized my labor for some aspect of spring cleaning: scouring the kitchen floorboards, oiling the ironware, even patching sheets. Word came from the store, when my mother or father would stop there for some small item, that Jerushah lingered still at the edge of disaster. Helen kept William tied to her apron strings, although he escaped to the mill to check his dam and sluiceway once or twice each day, watching for any need of intervention by the other men of the village. One afternoon as I crossed the dooryard from the barn to the house, I heard wild geese calling overhead, arriving from the South.

When the stage pulled into the village on Friday afternoon, I begged a few minutes to see whether there were any letters for us, and also to discover whether anyone had arrived to visit or do business in the village.

"Don't go bothering Mrs. Clark," my mother warned. "Wait until she invites you again. She has her hands full, between nursing Jerusah and taking care of those young ones, and cooking for the tavern as well."

Soiled snow hung on in the yard in heaps to either side of the lane, but patches of ground stood open all around, brown and yellow with last year's grasses. A red-winged blackbird perched behind the barn and trilled, then flew off as I shut the door behind me. I turned to see his red shoulder patches with their gold edges. The scent of wet earth hung in the air.

From the road ahead, I could hear people talking but couldn't see who was standing between the inn and the bulky yellow body of the coach. Although I longed for a letter, whether it be from Charles and John or, oh dearest hope, from Sarah, to stumble into another round of Mrs. Clark's anger would not be wise. I edged along the roadside by our fence, trying to reach the point where I could see around the coach, and straining to place the voices. One, I was sure, was indeed Mrs. Clark.

The others turned out to be the coachman, a white-haired lady in a neatly tailored green velvet traveling skirt and matching jacket, and Matthew—who appeared to suffer from a heavy cold as he mopped at his nose. Mrs. Clark was holding a valise, in dark green leather, that must belong to the woman talking with her. Matthew's arms strained under a large covered basket, a canvas sack, and a wooden crate.

The coachman noticed me, waved cheerfully, and said, "Young Clark there has the letters. Make sure he gives you yours. Got to get on through St. Johnsbury to the coast, and," he nodded toward Matthew, "I'll make sure your message is delivered. Back again on Monday next." With a lunge upward, he reached his seat and urged the horses to leave behind the water trough and be on their way.

Mrs. Clark stiffly introduced me to the woman standing next to me. "Mother, this is Miss Alice Sanborn, who lives across the way. Alice, this is Mrs. Proctor. She is here for a long visit, to help with the children and Jerushah."

I offered a polite nod from the waist, almost a bow, and said how pleased I was to meet Mrs. Proctor. "And may I ask, Mrs. Clark, how Jerushah is recovering?"

"Hmmph. I'm sure you'd like to hear that she's well again," Mrs. Clark said in an acidic tone. "But she's not. No fever, but even to take a few steps across the room is too much for her most days. I see you're well enough yourself. Although," and her tone softened a bit, "I understand your brother took some damage on Monday last. Give my regards to his wife, would you please? I'll pay a call on her, after Mother is settled in."

"Yes, ma'am."

Matthew turned toward the house and said over his shoulder, "I'll bring your letters by in a few minutes, Alice."

I didn't dare press him to yield them right away, so I said thank you and wished Mrs. Proctor a pleasant stay, then turned toward home. My mother stood at the door in her cloak and bonnet.

"I want to take some yarn around to Helen, and see whether she and William have butter to spare. Your father's up in the orchard. Mind the stove, please, Alice. I shan't be long."

"Matthew's bringing letters for us soon."

"They'll keep until I return. You may read them if they happen to be from your brothers." With a swoosh of skirts and a quick smile, she headed out.

A long hour stretched for me, stirring a stew that needed little attention and peering into the oven at potatoes slowly roasting, until I heard Matthew knock rapidly and come straight in. Two letters! I thanked him and asked again, "How is Jerushah?"

"She doesn't get enough air into her," Matthew confirmed. "Makes her tired. But I think it's also from missing Sarah, and you. There was a letter for her from Sarah today, so maybe she'll pick up some when she reads it. I can't stay, Alice, I've got to go back. They have me fetching and carrying, and moving things for my grandmother. She's taken Jerushah's room upstairs, you see."

"Then where's Jerushah?"

"Oh, she's been in the back bedroom behind the kitchen since the day after you both came back. The stairs are too much for her."

Oh! That was why there'd been no face or waving hand from the upper window all week! I caught a bit of hope that my friend might not have given up on me.

"Tell her I'm thinking of her, Matthew."

"I will." He lunged out the door.

In my hand, the letters shook. I steadied myself and examined them. One was from Charles and John. The other, the one I'd hoped might be from Sarah, had an unfamiliar hand on it. How strange—it was addressed to me: Miss Alice Sanborn, North Upton, Vermont. Like the first one, it bore a ten-cent stamp, indicating it had traveled more than three hundred miles to reach me.

I set down the letter to my mother from my older brothers and fumbled to open the one addressed to me. It was the first one I'd received, and my heart pounded in anticipation. Could it be from Solomon?

Yes! But how odd! It said nearly nothing:

Much Esteemed Friend, Miss Sanborn,
Two letters when merged may become a single whole of meaning. I write to you from New York, trusting that you may hold safe that which is in your custody, while to any who should know enough to seek it, you give free access and the names of Luther and Joseph, and the urgent state-

ment that the need has grown to seven or more.

Your humble servant and admiring friend,

Solomon Duncan McBride

Two letters when merged? Surely Solomon could not have known about the letter from Charles and John. The phrase "that which is in your custody" was clearer, for it must refer to the satchel of papers. Luther and Joseph? There were two Josephs in our village, one an old farmer, the other the blacksmith's very young son. And nobody named Luther. The only Luther I could even recall was Dr. Jewett. Yes, Solomon was acquainted with Dr. Jewett; I recalled the stand-off at Miss Farrow's home, at the Paddock House in St. Johnsbury Plain. Henry Clinton had argued with Dr. Jewett and spoken of his abolitionist views, had he not?

I read through it all twice more and came to no firmer conclusion. At last it occurred to me that Solomon might have sent a second letter to me. Could it have gone astray? Perhaps Matthew still had it, in the canvas post bag.

Clearly, I needed to confer with Matthew. But when?

To keep my hands occupied as I turned this matter in my thoughts, I opened the other letter, the one from Charles and John. Seated at the kitchen table where the late afternoon light glowed warmest, I smoothed the creases of the page and studied the crossed lines of writing.

Because Charles wrote with flourishes on his capitals, it was easy to pick out his words first. He said they had both recovered well from winter colds—Mama would be relieved to read that—and taken a new river lease, where others were already finding significant gold. He also wrote that he and John had invested in a general store where they had worked all winter. Hmm. It sounded as though they were not yet rich, and not yet coming home.

John's words crossed Charles's at a right angle, using the

page a second time. His letters, tight and narrow, came better for me if I held the page a few inches away and looked for words rather than letters. With a start, I saw the word "Gilman"—that was the name of the family that owned the mills and scale company in St. Johnsbury. I puzzled over the phrasing and finally made out:

> The agent here for Gilman & Co. is one of the Paddock lads from St. Johnsbury, and he tells me that town is bound to be your new shire town, when the railroad is completed along the river. His sister Claire is with him to keep his house, and she brings me a feel of the home state. She is as smart as our Alice, and I dare say you would like to know her.

Aha! For John to mention a girl's name at all, I was sure, meant that she had caught his serious interest. I would have to let Miss Farrow know that Claire Paddock and her brother had met mine. What a powerful magnetism might come of Vermont roots, such that both of my distant brothers could find girls from home to spend time with in the California Territory.

Behind me came a light tap, as of someone knocking for entrance, but not at the door to the yard—rather, it came from the door down to the cellar. Startled, I stood up. The door creaked open.

"Matthew! What are you doing here? And how—oh, you must have come through the tunnel!" I couldn't believe I had forgotten all about it. "Why? Is there something wrong? Is it Jerushah?" My throat clenched, my stomach lurched.

"You girls! No, there's nothing wrong. But I didn't want anyone to see me come over here." He coughed into a handkerchief, blew his nose loudly on it, then looked around quickly. "We have to hurry. I saw your mother go down the road. And your father is out, too, isn't he?"

"Up in the orchard, but I don't know when he'll come down. Why do we have to hurry?"

"So nobody will know I came here, and we don't want anyone to think about the tunnel, either." He propped the cellar door open with a muddy boot and tiptoed across to the table in his stockings. "I have a letter from Solomon. You have one also, right? We need to put them together."

Ah! Two letters when merged . . . I pulled mine out of my pocket and unfolded it. Matthew did the same with his.

He pointed. "Look! See where it tells me he's put the names and numbers elsewhere—that's your letter he meant. He was afraid someone might open one or the other letter and it wouldn't be safe. See, here we are: I'm to go to Luther—that's the doctor—and he'll have papers for me from Joseph. And Solomon needs seven or more of them this time. You know he's coming through on Monday's stage, don't you?"

"Yes, but I don't understand! What papers? And who is Joseph?"

"Joseph Gilman, of course. Hasn't Solomon told you anything? I thought he was going to, before he left. We all agreed he should."

I was baffled. "The stage was early," I reminded Matthew. "Maybe he meant to, but couldn't."

"Yes, that's probably it." Matthew looked around again, and out the window to check that my father and mother weren't near the house. "Listen, Alice, I must not be seen here today; it would raise havoc with my mother and also put Solomon at risk. Your father knows some of it, but he said he'd rather not be a regular part of what we're doing. Those papers Solomon left with you, I need them now. And then you should light a candle and come down to the cellar with me. I'll explain and then go straight back through the tunnel. Best to be back there

235

before they know I'm missing."

From the pantry, I fetched the small leather satchel. This must be what Solomon's letter meant when he wrote "and to any who should know enough to seek it." That was Matthew. Then with a lit candle stub in hand, I followed Matthew into the cellar. He had one also, that he had extinguished before opening the door into the kitchen, and he re-lit his from mine when we reached the tunnel entrance. The match to the muddy boot that had held the other door was holding the tunnel door open. Dampness rolled toward us from the dark space. Matthew sneezed twice, removed the boot, and pulled on both that one and the one from upstairs, then pressed the door nearly shut to stop the draft.

"The papers," he began. "You knew we were moving papers, didn't you?"

I hadn't put the pieces together that way, but instantly I recalled the bundle that Solomon had first left in our barn, for my father. And the parcel he'd asked Matthew about, when we were all in Glover. And now, of course, the satchel. Reluctantly, I handed it to Matthew.

He continued, his voice hoarse and low: "It's papers for apprenticeships, at the Gilman Mills and others. It was Dr. Jewett's idea: we had no way to get or make letters of emancipation, of course, but Mr. Gilman and a few others can issue apprenticeship notices, with indentures to go with them, to bind the men to labor for seven years. It wouldn't pass in the worst of the Southern states, but in Pennsylvania and Indiana, our papers give a man a chance to convince others that he's properly hired and bound up North. You see?"

Whispering excitedly, I added the next part: "And Senator Thaddeus Stevens gets the papers to the fugitives, so they can escape northward?"

"No, no, the senator has nothing to do with this. I see why

you're guessing that, because he helped with Sarah, but he's not really part of all this; he's too easily seen. No, it's another fellow in Philadelphia, a colored man named—No, I shouldn't tell you. Best not to spread information. But he's helped hundreds to head north, mostly to New York. And if Solomon says seven or more, he means there are at least seven men waiting right now for papers. Hush, what's that?"

We stood, listening intently. I whispered, "I think it was just the stove."

"Good. But I must go." He peered inside the satchel, ruffled the papers, then closed it and placed it back in my hands. "There are five sets here already. I'll ride to St. Johnsbury tonight and see the others, to make sure they prepare two or three more. Time's short."

"What can I do to help?"

"Keep the satchel safely hidden but have it ready for Solomon. I'll bring the other papers to you before Monday morning, for you to add them. And not a word to anyone except William and me!"

"Not a word," I promised. At last, all the pieces were coming together.

Matthew coughed sharply as he opened the small wood-framed door and stepped into the tunnel, then turned back to me. "I almost forgot." He sniffed and cleared his throat. "Jerushah says you can write to her this way—seal up a letter and put her name on the outside, and then leave it at the other end of the tunnel. Don't ever open the door at our end, mind, for there are too many people there. She says she'll send me to look inside the door once or twice each day. She says to give you this, too. Dear heavens, she'd have skinned me if I'd forgotten it."

He tossed a small fabric-wrapped object toward me, closed the door behind himself, and was gone.

At that moment, I heard footsteps up in the kitchen. I placed the satchel of papers into the top of one of the potato bins, where I could retrieve it later. Hiding Jerushah's little packet in my pocket and lifting my candle, I looked around for a quick reason to have come down the stairs. There, the milk. I seized the small covered can by its handle and returned to the kitchen, where my father stood next to the stove, warming his reddened, wet hands.

He gave a nod and a tired smile. "Where's your mother?" he asked.

The outer door opened, making an answer unnecessary. "Ephraim—good; our supper will be ready as soon as Alice lays the table. I just went to see Helen and begged a bit of butter."

"Well, I'm glad to say you'll soon have your own again," my father announced. "Cow's sure to calve tonight or tomorrow. Most likely sooner than later, so I'll be in and out of the barn tonight. Alice, you heard your mother: hand me that milk can, and you can lay the table."

The bustle of supper turned merry with news that Helen not only felt herself again but had launched whole-heartedly into spring cleaning, and when my mother read the letter from Charles and John, she reached the same conclusion I had: that John was sweet on the Paddock girl he'd found in California. Good things were blossoming.

All the time, the sense of sitting over a cellar of mystery distracted me. Now I was party to all the important secrets of the village, I was sure! Should I tell my father that Matthew and William included me in their secrets? No, Matthew had said my father didn't like to be very much involved. Of course, he must have passed along the bundle from our barn, in early spring, to William.

The other distraction for me was Jerushah's mysterious package in my pocket. I wanted to open it and discover what she had sent, and my heart sang with the knowledge that she wanted me to write to her. At least my best friend didn't hate me any longer!

Outside, a roll of thunder echoed, and a cascade of raindrops splashed against the window. I prayed Matthew didn't catch his death of cold, reaching St. Johnsbury tonight.

CHAPTER 27

It rained and blew all evening. My mother, tired from the day's labor, took to her chamber early. My father visited the barn, found no calf yet born and joined my mother, saying as he saw me in the kitchen that he expected to go to the barn again at midnight. I lit a candle to take to my upstairs bedroom, explaining that I planned to write letters. With paper and ink set out on a small table, I followed Matthew's example and set a shoe against my chamber door to wedge it snug, so that if anyone were to start to open it, I'd have time to put away anything that shouldn't be seen.

Then at last I opened Jerushah's packet, smoothing out the scrap of soft, rose-hued silk she'd used to wrap it.

There was a letter in it, and from within the folded page, out tumbled a golden chain with a square locket hanging from it. I eased my thumbnails into the slit to open it, marveling at its tiny hinges. Inside, an ornate panel, pierced decoratively, protected something shadowed and soft behind it. I pulled the panel open, and discovered a curl of dark hair.

What did this mean? I fastened the locket shut again, spread out the page, and began to read what Jerushah had written.

My Dearest Alice,

How could I ever have been such a harridan as to shriek at you, as you brought me home from our northern journey? Please forgive me, and if you write to Solomon

McBride, tell him that your own Jerushah begs his pardon
for her unpardonable rudeness. I can only plead the
distress of illness and the fever of my heart. You are always
and ever dear to me.

A letter from Sarah arrived here today, although I have
not had time to give it more than the briefest of readings.
She sounds well and happy, and seems to have taken to
her new family. She sends you her affectionate greetings,
Alice. She longs for her own parents, of course, and yearns
for the happy day when they are re-united (which I pray
will be soon).

I too yearn for the company of those I love. Sarah's
absence grieves me. I read to the children here, but that is
nothing compared to the pleasures we all had as girls
together. Your own absence, dearest Alice, is also a great
loss to me. I would urge you to come to my side, but you
must know that my mother is not yet willing to forgive the
hardships that this return has imposed upon her. Wait then,
dear one, until I can tell you that her heart, like mine, has
relented.

Alice, oh Alice, how I have dreamed of a cottage to share
with you at some distant time, as we might both become
schoolteachers and savor our independence together. I
could be all to you, I know I could, for I love you with all
my heart. To see you drawn to some foolish young man is
near unbearable for me. You too must know that you and I
are fated for each other. There is no man good enough for
you, Alice. I wish you could see this as I do.

But if you cannot, then this shall be a burden even on
my longing soul, but one that I will face and carry until I
am able instead to honestly wish you great joy in your
choices. In token of this promise, I send to you now a lock
of my hair, that you may carry me with you in some sense

as you find your life's true path. "Remember me, when this you see."

Though I hope yet to recover much of the function of my physical heart, and thus to be of assistance again to my mother, it is clear to me that I have given my love to you always. May God bless and keep you, and may our lives adapt such that you may soon come to visit here, to sit with

Your longest, truest, most loving friend,
Jerushah

Twice over, I read the letter. The relief of the peace offering at its opening eased my own heart, but much of the rest of the letter gave me deep concern. Had I in some way suggested to Jerushah that such a future, the two of us as spinster teachers in a cottage together, was a dream of mine? Had she conveyed her own dream to me in some way, and had I been blind to it? Even as a dream, the notion sounded girlish to me, childish. A woman's way meant growing up, changing, finding a man to share her life. Perhaps Jerushah believed herself to be unmarriageable, due to the rheumatic fever—a worry that could have some grounds. I must encourage her instead to recover and look to her own future.

I penned a careful reply:

My Dear Jerushah,

What joy there is in reading your letter. Your forgiveness of me is a gift that I treasure, for I regret all the hardships of our journey from Coventry and wish only that you may swiftly regain your good health.

What may come in both of our lives, as we find the loving husbands that I trust Providence may ordain for us, is yet far from today's sight. But it comforts me to know that in all our lives to come, we shall treasure our friendship.

I will wear the lovely golden chain always, knowing that the soft curl within the locket belongs to the truest and sweetest of friends.

Though the weeks to come are sure to fill with the tasks and delights of springtime, I assure you that I look forward to the equal delight of being able to visit with you again, when your recovery and your mother's softer opinion shall both permit.

Meanwhile, know that you are in my prayers each night, and that I seek the blessings of good health and sweet comfort for you, as I am always and ever,

Your true friend,
Alice

I inspected my letter. There was nothing in it about Solomon. Should I have said something? But what could I say—that I shared a secret with Solomon and William and Matthew, one that I dared not share with my own best friend? I thought it was wiser to speak only to our friendship and hope that time would ease Jerushah's sorrows. The tangle of her hopes and my own must sort out later.

Carefully, I unfastened the clasp on the delicate gold chain and held it to my neck. Fastened in place, it hung gracefully, with the locket exactly fitting into the hollow of the bone at the base of my throat.

Must I take my reply into the tunnel tonight? No, I decided: The morning would be soon enough. I hung up my skirt and petticoats and also my blouse, blew out my candle, and eased into bed. Even with the window nailed shut, the pounding of the rain and the repeated heaving of the wind told of the continued April storm. I had so many people to bring into my prayers that I lay awake, hands folded, for a long time, hoping all was well for the ones I cared about.

My father's midnight barn visit did not wake me—but in the

morning, news of the calf took me to the barn before breakfast, to marvel at the perfect little creature with her wide brown eyes, wobbling beside her mother.

Chapter 28

Saturday's tasks included gathering a dozen eggs, as the chickens seemed to recognize that spring had arrived. Despite the storm's end, clouds still scudded across the sky, and a warm wind held a hint of more rain to come. I could hear the roar of the river even when I was inside the barn or house.

I found my father among the sheep, checking on the lambs. Only two ewes remained in the lambing pen now.

"Are the other men still clearing the dam for William?"

My father shook his head. "No, the water's so high now that there's nothing able to hold at the sluice. It's all washing over the dam."

"Is it dangerous? Could the dam wash out?"

"It might. Here, hold this lamb's head; I want to feel the hind legs. Hmm. A bit lame. We'll keep an eye on him. Don't worry about the dam, Alice. Either it holds or it doesn't, and if it washes away, we'll all help William put it back when the waters are lower again." He wiped his hands on his trousers and stood up. "So, you shouldn't be here in the barn when you could be in the kitchen." My face must have shown how I felt about that, for he added, "Or you might walk to Wilson's store for me and get a penny sack of tobacco. I'll use it to make an ear wash for the lambs, to rid them of mites. Will that suit you?"

I agreed, and my father said he'd let my mother know, so I could leave straight away from the barn. "More rain coming soon," he added with regret as he held the barn door open for me. "Hurry and you might not get wet."

At the village store for the first time in weeks, I found a hand-ful of neighbors in conversation that ceased abruptly as I entered. Mr. Wilson said a quiet hello and asked what I needed, and as he packed a paper sack, I turned to say hello to Adeline and ask after her brothers.

"Oh, they've been well for ages," Adeline confirmed. "My mother says it might not even have been the spotted fever that they had. How is Jerushah?"

There it was, the dangerous question, and I felt the silence around me as others waited for me to answer.

I tried to keep my voice calm as I said, "She's not fevered any longer, of course. I believe she's coming along as best she can. Her mother is a good nurse to her."

The oldest Hopkins boy, Samuel, kicked his feet in the far corner and called out, "Maybe she's slow to recover because she misses that little girl that stayed with her, Sarah. Why did your father make you take her away, anyhow? Can't stand to have a colored child in the village? I hear he wants to send them all to Africa or something."

All the frustration of being blamed by Mrs. Clark rose up in a blinding anger, and I hurled a reply to Samuel: "My father didn't make me take her away. Jerushah and I helped her stay safe. There was a bounty hunter investigating the village, thanks to Mr. Cook telling everyone's business around the county."

This exaggeration would surely count against me at the Judg-ment Day, although it was not exactly a lie. At any rate, it stopped the Hopkins boy for a moment, until his father defended him by saying, "Sure, and we all know what happened to the bounty hunter, too. You Sanborns don't care who you hurt or what you do. And your cousin, the judge, will always let you off. One of these days you'll hurt the wrong person; you'll see what happens then!"

Mr. Wilson stepped forward quickly, preventing me from answering. "Now, Giles, you're barking up the wrong tree; you know you are. Everyone knows you're sore because the Sanborn sheep make a profit and yours don't. Stop trying to hurt the girl, would you?"

The room spun around me. I felt as though I'd found the center of all the old sour darkness in the village, in what Mr. Hopkins had hurled at me. Mr. Wilson's defense didn't matter, if people already believed such awful things.

I stumbled from the store and ran home, falling twice in the mud along the way. When I tumbled into the kitchen, my mother grabbed my arm and said, "What is it? What's happened?"

But I couldn't even say it, I couldn't repeat it. I simply burst into useless tears and pounded my hands on the table. "I hate this place, I hate it, I hate it!"

My father told my mother, "It's my fault. I sent her to the store. I'll go find out who said what to her."

"No! Don't go there!" My throat ached from the hurt inside me as I cried out.

Eventually I laid out the words more or less as they had come. How could anyone have twisted the month's events so horribly?

In my father's face, I saw a dark melancholy as he told me, "This happens sometimes among people. Some of it's my doing, for being too private in my ways."

"But we held the sugaring-off gathering here," my mother protested. "We included them all. Just the way we always have."

"Once a year doesn't make for friendships," admitted my father. "And it doesn't erase the envy, either." He propped his arms on the table and laid his head on his worn fists.

After a long moment of silence, my mother said, "We'll have to walk with it and just take care of each other. It's not your fault, Ephraim. Nor yours, Alice."

The words hung in the air, weak and unconvincing. I wished

that North Upton had someone like Charles Hayes, who could lay his hands onto people and call them back to health of body and spirit. The tasks of the spirit are as necessary as those of the body, I realized. "The minister?" I asked aloud.

"He'll do his part," my mother agreed with a bit more confidence. "I know he heard the talking last Sunday. Give him time to reach out to people."

Time. I wanted to insist that people understand me and my family. But instead, we had to wait for someone else, and some other pace of change.

The three of us drifted in different directions, my father to the barn, my mother to her baking, and I to my chamber to read again the letter Jerushah had left for me. Even my closest friend seemed to have stepped apart from understanding me. I felt desperately that I had to transport my own letter to her. But the opportunity to slip unnoticed to the cellar and enter the tunnel didn't come until late, when my mother called from the kitchen to say she'd go to the barn to see if she could find two more eggs. "And I want to admire this fine calf your father's been talking about," she added, as I heard her pull on her cloak and step outside.

As soon as the door shut behind her, I padded down to the kitchen, pushed my feet into William's cast-off boots, and lit a candle stub. I remembered the mud on Matthew's boots—who could tell what there might be in that tunnel?

First, in the cellar I made sure that Solomon's satchel was still hidden among the potatoes. Then I pried open the small door to the tunnel, and looked for something to wedge into the opening to make sure it didn't shut tight again. I couldn't leave one of my boots! For lack of anything better, I used a large potato, wedging it between the door and the frame.

Holding my candle in one hand, my letter to Jerushah in the other, I stepped into the uneasy darkness.

The smell of damp assailed me powerfully, and I edged forward with care. The tunnel height varied as I went, and the boards of its roof wore dark stains of water, as well as trailing cobwebs. A small spider dropped onto my hand, and I shook it off with a shudder. I held the candle in front of me, and it lit the walls closest to me but not the floor. One cautious sliding step at a time, I felt with my feet in the oversized boots.

How long was the tunnel? It had to go the entire length of our lane, and under the road, and then beneath the dooryard of the Clark home and tavern. If only I'd been counting my steps from the doorway; yet they were such small steps, I might still not know. I began from where I already stood, counting aloud in a whisper: "One, two, three, four . . ." Not until I'd passed two hundred did I dare to hope I'd passed the middle point.

Trickling water echoed in the tunnel ahead of me. The passageway tilted downward. As it did so, I saw water running down the walls to either side. This must be the portion under the road.

The further I went, the deeper was the water at my feet. Now I wedged the letter into my skirt pocket, so I could hold up my skirt with the hand that wasn't gripping the candle. A bit of hot wax dripped on me, and I straightened the candle to stop it from dribbling. The water was two inches deep. Now three. Nearly four. Ah, now three again, and the tunnel tilted upward noticeably.

A mere twenty-two steps further brought me to its end, at the doorway into the Clark cellar. Following Matthew's instructions, I didn't open the door. An empty pail sat on the floor, and I presumed he meant it for a delivery station. I left the letter there, turned, and began the return.

Just as I reached the far end of the wettest portion of the tunnel, I slipped and nearly fell. Although I caught myself in time, I dropped the candle, which at once blew out, the hot wick hissing as it struck the soggy ground.

I froze in place. The dark surrounded me. Only the sound of water behind me assured me of any sense of direction. Slowly I reached my hands outward until my fingers brushed the damp, cold walls.

Shuffling carefully, half a step at a time, I moved forward. I wanted to scream or at least whimper. But who would hear, if I did? Instead, I counted my steps again. When my counting went past two hundred, I thought at first I was almost done, then recalled that half steps would be shorter, and besides, I hadn't begun to count right at the start, had I?

Three hundred and sixty-three: I saw a change in the darkness ahead. It wasn't exactly light, but I knew it must be the opening into our cellar. A moment later and I stood erect with the large potato in my hand, shutting the door behind me, leaning on it in relief. I vowed I'd never enter the tunnel again, no matter how much I missed Jerushah. There had to be some other way to exchange letters.

I placed the potato back in its bin, then changed my mind when I heard my mother's steps in the kitchen above. I regained the large potato and, by feeling among them, three others. I would need an explanation for being in the cellar, and potatoes would have to do. My fingers touched Solomon's satchel. My heart jumped, and I felt my face heat.

Upstairs, my mother said only, "Oh, thank you, Alice, I can use those in the morning. What made you think to get them now? Did you leave a candle down there?"

"I dropped it," I replied honestly enough. "It went out. I'll go back for it later."

Only when I glanced down did I realize I still wore the muddy boots, and that my skirt hem showed clear evidence of dragging through the dark waters below. Fortunately, my mother's supper preparations absorbed her and allowed me to place the boots behind a chair, and I turned my skirt to get the driest portion to the front.

"How did you like the new calf, Mama?"

"Oh, she's a lovely dear thing, isn't she? And look, I found four more eggs, so we'll have griddle cakes in the morning."

I discovered something I'd never known before about secrets, as well as secret passageways: When you know things that you can't speak to the people in the room with you, you feel alone. Very, very alone.

And though Saturday crept to a close, it seemed to have been days long already. I excused myself early for bed. Upstairs, I sat holding the letter from Solomon, wondering: If I had such discomfort in simply taking care of things here at home, what was happening to him in far-away New York, or on his way back to Vermont?

CHAPTER 29

The Reverend John Dudley, as "supply minister" to the North Upton pulpit once again, dropped his voice to a near whisper. I braced in my seat for the roar that would soon follow. He had done this twice already during his sermon, drawing people toward him as if to impart a secret or a narrative too shocking to be spoken aloud, then infusing us all with power and certainty as he proclaimed his strongest points.

"And even in the halls of politics and privilege, I tell you, even among these leaders in our nation's capital, comes a voice in the wilderness, crying, 'Make straight the way.' And that," said the quiet, insistent voice, "that voice is of William Seward, addressing the Senators of this Union of states." The minister paused, then elevated his voice to a natural speaking level. "And Mr. Seward has declared that there is no Christian nation, free to choose as we are today, which would establish slavery. And why is that? Slavery, says Mr. Seward, is incompatible with the security of natural rights, the diffusion of knowledge, and the freedom of industry."

A rustle of approval came from the congregation at the term "freedom of industry." As if their approval had fed his own confidence, the minister rose taller, projected his voice more loudly among us, and erupted into his finale.

"For Mr. Seward has proclaimed in the halls of Congress that there is a higher law than the Constitution. A higher law than the Constitution! And what is this higher law? We know it!

We say it with him. We pledge ourselves to the brotherhood of all mankind, all mankind indeed, a heritage bestowed upon us by the Creator of the universe. For we are that Creator's stewards, says Mr. Seward, and we must so discharge our trust as to secure in the highest degree the happiness of our brothers."

He paused, drew breath, and in loud, deliberate syllables thrust forth the finale of his sermon: "Into our hands the Creator has entrusted this: a higher law. May God bless this to our understanding and send us forth in God's holy and necessary work."

Women and men alike nodding, the people in the church lifted their voices to join his: "A higher law! Amen!"

Above us, suddenly, the church bells began to toll. Everyone stared upward and at each other. The bells rang to call us to the services but never to dismiss us. I clasped my hands over my ears to mute the din and looked to my father. He, in turn, was pointing to the rear of the church, where Deacon Stuart had climbed upon a chair and with hands cupped to his mouth shouted, "The dam at the Sanborn mill has given way! The river is over its banks. Flood! All men to the river—women and children should stay in the church!"

"Stuart's a fool," my father growled as he bent close to my mother and me. "Come on. We need to move the sheep up into the barn. I'll need both of you to help."

As a group, we pressed out the side door, running up the road toward the farm. Giles Hopkins and his twins, running as though they'd never been fevered, came with us. So did one of the Wilson boys at first, until Mr. Wilson called him back to help move stock at the store.

As I ran, I rolled the waistband of my skirt, to lift it higher. What matter now if I showed my ankles while moving sheep? I saw my mother doing the same.

As we ran past the Clark home, Mr. Clark came out to meet us. "Why are the bells ringing?" he called.

"Dam broke at William's," my father shouted back. "There'll be water up the road any minute."

Mr. Clark shouted over his shoulder to his family, then hurried toward us. "My place is high enough, but yours won't be. How can I help?"

With that instinct for danger than animals possess, the sheep already were bleating loudly. Under my father's quick commands, we divided into groups of three, to herd them from the low paddock at the bottom of the barn, up into the structure. The Hopkins twins and their father seized pails, shovels, and barrels, making an impromptu set of barriers to guide the animals. My mother and I dashed into the flock, reaching for stumbling lambs and making sure they climbed the slope upward.

Less than half an hour later, thanks to so many hands, all the sheep were secure, although still bleating. One lamb had gone lame, and my father separated it and its mother to their own stall. Water and grain quieted them some, and I realized my mother had vanished—into the kitchen, no doubt, to add to the noon meal and set an extra kettle heating.

Ruefully, I examined my Sunday best skirt, smudged with mud and sheep waste. Cleaning it would have to wait until later. I pushed through the sheep to find my father.

"William and Helen? What should we do about them?"

"They're higher than the mill and will come to no harm, as long as William doesn't take any fool notion to chase after the pieces of his dam. Go help your mother. I'll finish here."

From the dooryard, I could hear the arriving waters, hissing over our best hay field and surging toward the paddock where the sheep had been. I stole only a moment to run behind the house and see. Then I splashed through the puddles and into the kitchen, already reaching for an apron.

Although Mr. Clark did not stay for dinner with us, Giles Hopkins and his sons accepted, saying they'd be safer with us than daring to enter Mrs. Hopkins's kitchen in sheep-soured clothing. One of the boys ran down the road to assure his mother they were safe. She was still at the church, with a dozen other families; the rest had ignored Deacon Stuart and gone to their homes and farms, and quite a few were helping move the store goods upstairs, reported Edward Hopkins when he rejoined us for mutton stew and biscuits. I marveled at how the bitter exchange of words from the store had vanished in the crisis of William's collapsed dam and the flooding of our farm.

A rhubarb pudding concluded the meal. As my mother poured mugs of hot tea, a pounding at the kitchen door announced more news.

"The bridge upriver from the Four Corners side has washed out," reported Mr. Clark. "No harm done, but the stage won't be able to get through in the morning. Just as well for my part, I've got my son in bed now too, with a spring fever and cough. It never rains but it pours," he grumbled, declining a mug of tea. "But yes, I'll gladly accept some of that pudding. My mother-in-law has taken over the cooking at my place, and she's not much for sweets."

Around me, people talked and laughed, general relief fueling a neighborly satisfaction in helping each other.

But it took only a moment for me to realize that a detour for tomorrow's stage, coupled with Matthew being ill in bed, meant a disaster for the papers that were supposed to connect with Solomon on his way through North Upton. Did Matthew have them? And, even if he did, who could take them to Upton Center?

For a long moment, I couldn't think what to do. With Mrs. Clark still blaming me for Jerushah's illness, and now another of her children sick—and, though she might not realize it, I knew that Matthew's condition was partly my fault—it seemed unlikely she'd even let me talk with her son.

There seemed only one answer, and it was an answer I hated: the tunnel. I would have to use it tonight, to reach Matthew and the papers of apprenticeship that should be sent to Pennsylvania and southward.

I took advantage of the general commotion around me to find William's cast-off boots and place them at the door to our cellar stairs. Then I retreated to my room, to consider and plan.

CHAPTER 30

Waiting that evening for my parents to take themselves to bed and fall asleep came more easily than the next step: waiting for all the lamps and candles at the Clark home to be extinguished. I could not watch from my own chamber, as it faced the wrong way, and although I tiptoed to our front room I doubted that I was seeing all the distant windows at the other house. With my skirt already belted up, and a carrier bag slung across one shoulder, I crept outside and walked partway down the lane, to inspect both the tavern and the house windows across the way. The air clung, warm and humid; an unexpectedly gentle night, and without rain. The moon, just past full, lit the landscape brightly each time the wispy clouds slipped away from it.

When I was satisfied that the remaining gentle glow from the tavern window was only from the remnants of its hearth fire, and no candles showed at all in Jerushah's house, I returned to my own and lit two candles: a tall one in a heavy candlestick, and a stub. Careful not to trip on the steep cellar stairs in William's old boots, I reached the potato bin and set the taller candle in its heavy stick upon the floor, a little ways back from the tunnel door so the damp draft would not extinguish it. Holding the other candle, the lit stub, I stepped into the tunnel and again set the door to nearly closed, with a large potato holding it. Yes, I could see the flicker of the tall candle through the gap, so I would have a light to walk toward on my way back.

This time, I counted steps from the start. At two hundred

twenty-seven, I began to hear the trickling water. At two hundred forty-five, I stepped into it. Oh my—it was deeper than before. The river's overflow must be feeding the underground seepage. Grateful to have my skirts lashed up, freeing my left hand, I clung to the wet wall on one side, edging cautiously into what was now a flowing stream. My right hand held the candle steady.

At its deepest, the water came nearly to the tops of the boots I wore, and I moved on tiptoes to prevent water flowing into them. Two hundred ninety-eight, two hundred ninety-nine, three hundred. At three hundred and five, the depth of the water eased. By three hundred and twenty, I had reached the upslope of the tunnel and forgot to keep counting, as I hurried my pace toward the exit into the Clark cellar.

When I emerged from the tunnel, I took off the wet and heavy boots and left them to hold open the wood-framed door. I set my candle stub beside them, leaving it burning, and by its light I padded in my stockings up the stairs toward the door that would open into the hallway that joined the Clark house and tavern. I crept out, eased the cellar door shut behind me, and stood in near darkness, listening.

A faint red glow from the kitchen side showed there were still coals in the woodstove, leaking some light past the grates. It was enough to maneuver by. After making sure there were no movements above me, I tiptoed to the chamber beyond the kitchen, where Jerushah should be sleeping. Entering it, I closed its door to the kitchen, eased toward the bed by feel, and listened to the quiet breathing of my friend in sleep. The sound guided me to her face, and I knelt next to the bed, placed a finger lightly to her lips, and whispered, "Jerushah! Hush, don't make any noise, it's me, Alice. Jerushah, can you hear me?"

"Alice!" She was instantly awake but barely made a sound. She breathed out, "Alice, what are you doing here?" Her hand reached out of the covers and seized mine. "I went to the cellar myself for your letter—Matthew is too feverish. I haven't yet written you a reply."

"Hush," I repeated. "That can wait until later. Jerushah, Matthew has papers that I need to get from him. They're for the fugitives. I've got to take them to the stage tomorrow, and it won't be coming through the village, so I need to find the papers now and convey them to Upton Center."

"For the fugitives? What fugitives?"

"Colored people who've reached Pennsylvania. There's no time to tell all of it now; make Matthew explain to you in the morning. But they're depending on us. Can you tell me where Matthew sleeps?"

"He sleeps most nights upstairs with the little ones," Jerushah whispered. My heart instantly fell, for how could I go among all the other sleeping members of her family? But she continued: "You know he's fevered? His cough has been so loud that tonight he's in the tavern, bedded by the fireside there." She scrambled against the covers, emerging from them. "Alice, I'll go there. If someone sees me, they'll think only that I'm checking on him. How did you get into the house?"

"Through the tunnel." I agreed to her suggestion and told her I'd wait in the hallway, behind the cellar door, where I'd be unlikely to attract any attention.

The moonlight through the window lit Jerushah as she stood in a white nightgown. She wrapped a shawl about her shoulders and took my face between her hands. A kiss to my cheek, and she was out the door of the chamber, gliding across the kitchen. I followed her to the hallway and stepped aside into the cellar stairway, while she continued to the end of the hall. I could hear, from my hiding place, the faint creak of the tavern door opening, then closing. How good it was to see her again, and to have her touch me in friendship. I shook with emotion, marveling also at her moonlit beauty, a vision I knew I would never forget.

Although it felt like an hour, I am sure a bare four minutes had passed until Jerushah opened the cellar door and handed a folded stack of papers to me. I placed them in my carrier bag, fastened it shut, and looked up into her dear face.

She gave a faint smile. "I don't think he'll remember in the morning, but I'll remind him when his fever eases, and I'll draw the full explanation of this matter from him. Stay safe, Alice. Come back to me soon."

I took her hand and kissed it lightly on the palm, and replied, "Be well, Jerushah. Be well and be blessed. I'll be back."

She drew a wavering breath, and I could hear the thinness of it and feared again for her health. But she only whispered, "God keep you. I'll place my return letter for you soon, Alice," and gently shut the cellar door.

I hurried down the steep steps, grateful for the light of my candle stub. I fitted my feet back into the boots, made sure the laces were securely tied, and seized my candle. Though the tunnel breathed its damp chill at me once again, I almost felt accustomed to its length. I shut the wood-framed door and moved forward. How many steps to the rushing waters? No, I didn't know that number—I'd neglected to count them in this section. Never mind, it couldn't be long.

Indeed, I reached the underground stream sooner than I'd expected and eased into it. Now that the precious papers hung at my shoulder, I mustn't tumble—I must keep them dry at all cost. Slowly I moved through the waters. A sudden movement and splash startled me, and I gave a tight shriek, but it appeared to be a frog jumping from the far edge of the waters into the stream. A moment later I reached the far edge myself. I was through the worst part. I stepped onto the drier soil of the long second portion of the tunnel and felt hot wax run down my hand. The candle—it had reached its last portion, and I dropped it, flinching from the pain of the burning liquid.

This time I told myself that I'd managed the tunnel once in darkness and could do so again. Resolutely, I took full-size steps so that my count might still apply. To either side of me my hands followed the walls. Twice, I bumped my head on lower wooden beams. But I kept going. At two hundred and seventy-four—my steps must have been shorter despite my resolve—I saw the flickering light of the candle I'd left behind in our own cellar. I hurried to complete the journey. Closing the tunnel door firmly behind me, I panted and leaned against the wall, gasping in relief.

Next, the potato bin. I removed Solomon's satchel and transferred into it the papers from the carrier bag. I placed the emptied bag among the potatoes, untied the old boots, and tiptoed up the stairs, carrying boots and satchel.

Here must begin the part of the night I'd been least able to plan. I should sleep for an hour or two, at least. But not for too long. I wanted to saddle Ely and start for Upton Center before dawn, so that my parents would not stop me. Already I had prepared a note to leave on the kitchen table, saying I'd be back in the afternoon but giving few details. I hoped my father might understand enough to defend my action, should my mother be distressed.

But how could I be sure to wake so early?

I set the boots to dry, next to my father's ample chair near the stove. I sat in his seat, with the satchel on my lap, my fingers entwined with its leather straps. And I closed my eyes, sure that the discomfort of sleeping in a chair would wake me before long, and sooner rather than later. I was mistaken.

When a touch to my hand woke me with a start, dawn's silvery light showed my father kneeling next to me, deep concern etched in his furrowed brow and pursed lips. "Alice," he whispered. "What are you doing here?"

CHAPTER 31

Riding on the wagon's bench, rattling over the rutted road to Upton Center, I filled in the details for my father, for there was so much he hadn't heard—how Miss Farrow had known about the Hayes family, how Henry Clinton had pursued us, and what Solomon and Matthew and William were ensuring, with the help of Dr. Jewett and Mr. Gilman. Thank heaven, the little I'd told him in our kitchen had persuaded him of the need to meet the stagecoach on its detoured route. And though he insisted on driving me, rather than letting me leap onto the back of a horse I didn't know how to ride, his swift work in the barn convinced me he understood my urgency.

On the road, he listened intently, asking only occasional questions. When we reached the wide curve of the road outside the village, I remembered at last to tell him about the wolf, and he vowed he'd take a hunting party out for it, later in the week.

"Tell me again how these papers come into it," he requested, shooting a sideways look at me as he urged Ely to keep trotting.

"They're apprenticeship papers," I explained. "Except they're more than that, because they have letters of indenture with them—the kind that say someone is bound to a number of years of labor to pay off the opportunity to learn a trade. Some are for the Gilman Mills, for the foundry there, and some for the ironworks that the Paddock family has. And I saw one for a rake factory like William's mill, but off the Joe's Brook Road in Barnet."

"So, William might issue a set, if he chose to," my father considered aloud.

"Yes, I'm sure he could. But wouldn't he need to have an actual job available, that the person could fill? It might be that someone would want to stay here in North Upton, instead of going on north to the border with Canada."

My father nodded. "No doubt that's why there's not a set from William on hand as yet. When we get home again, I'll talk with him about how it might be done. I could use a part-time hand at the barn, and he could use a few hours a week at the mill, so I venture to think we might share a man."

Relief washed over me at my father's new willingness to take part. I threw an enthusiastic arm over his shoulder and kissed his bristled cheek.

"Easy, my girl, don't startle the horse. About time you learned that anyway, it's something every young woman who might be courted should know: Kisses are all very well, but not when a man's driving, and especially not a young man whose experience is not yet so wide or deep!" The twitch of a smile assured me that my father found no grave fault with me. I wondered whether he had guessed, as my mother had, how Solomon McBride affected me. Or perhaps my mother had told him; there, that must be the case.

The road crested the last hill before Upton Center and dipped down to make one more crossing, this time of the Water Andric, which fed into the Sleepers River. As we came over the top of the hill, my father exclaimed in surprise and drew the horse to a walk. "Will you look at that? A couple of trees must have jammed up against the bridge and torn it loose. We'll never take the horse across that one, will we, Ely?"

By a single support, the remains of the bridge hung over the river, tossed up and down by the rough waters. I cried out, "But we have to cross it! We have to!"

"Hush!" My father's left hand came across to seize my shoulder. "What did I just tell you about not upsetting the horse? We'll find a place for Ely and the wagon, and then we'll consider our possibilities."

The first part was simple enough: an area to one side of the bridge, level and dry, served to rest the wagon, and my father hitched Ely to a large stump that had clearly been cut high enough to serve for other horses before. I examined the satchel on my lap, looking for the best way to carry it. Unfastening one end of each leather strap, I linked the loose ends together to form a long loop that could pass over my head, so that the satchel rested against my chest. Re-setting my cap, I followed my father down to the start of the bridge.

He eyed the mess of bridge and trees with exasperation. "It'll take quite a crew to straighten this all out." Placing one foot on a dangling support truss, he tested it by leaning forward. I gripped the back of his coat.

"No need to do that," he grumbled. "I'm not planning to take a swim." He pulled himself back onto the riverbank and looked around him.

"Rope, or a longer tree perhaps," he muttered. He walked back to the wagon and climbed up, to sort through its contents. I stood by the water, waiting. I could even see the first houses of Upton Center ahead of us. When would the stage come through—how much time did we have?

Jumping down from the wagon, my father came back toward me, carrying a short axe, a board, and four heavy spikes. Again, he tested the truss, leaning to see if it would take his weight. He stepped off it and turned to me.

"I think we can make it, but I don't like the gap where that second tree is leaning. Do you see the one I mean?"

He pointed, and I saw the gap. "I can't cross that," I confessed. "Even if I tie up my skirt, I can't jump that far."

"Nor can I. But if we fasten the board across at shoulder height, I think we can hold to it and get across. I can strap my suspenders over the board for a safety line."

Ah, the way William and Matthew had done at the mill that day. I nodded. "How can we do it?"

"It will have to be you that puts in the first spike. You're smaller, and the truss will bear your weight. Once I step onto it, it would sag too far down for the job. Do you think you can swing the axe well enough to pound in this spike?"

Absolutely not, was what I wanted to say. But instead what squeaked out was, "I can try."

"Good girl. Look, I'll start it into the board here, so you'll just need to strike it two or three times, and then you can come back and I'll finish the task. Ready?"

"Ready." I swung Solomon's satchel around so that it hung down my back instead of my chest, and when my father had the board and spike united, I stepped sideways onto the truss, grasping at a tree trunk with one hand and guiding the end of the board with my other. From the bank, my father took most of its weight so that I could draw it forward.

Underneath me the Water Andric, swollen to a racing river far different from its summer shallowness, tugged in sharp lurches at the tree limbs that dangled in the water. I risked looking down and realized with terror that, if I slipped, I would wash away downriver exactly as Henry Clinton had. I whimpered despite myself.

My father called out, "Grasp the strap on the board, Alice. Take hold of the strap. It's my own best suspender, and it won't fail you. Hold on to what I've given you."

I forced my gaze back to the board and saw the strap knotted onto it, ready to support me. I thought of how William had clung to Matthew's suspenders. I took a breath and thought of Solomon riding in the stagecoach. And I released my grip on the board to slide my arm through the loop, and with the other arm reached blindly behind me to accept the axe from my father.

Ten minutes later, we stood together on the far bank of the Water Andric. I trembled from shoulders to fingertips, and my legs wobbled. My father placed the ax on the ground, dropped an arm over my shoulders, and said, "Don't stop now, Alice. Your young man's on his way and doesn't know you're coming. Let's hurry, or we may miss the stagecoach yet."

The warmth of his arm and the strength of it reminded me of when Solomon had gripped my shoulders outside Jerushah's house. I drew a fresh deep breath, swung the satchel around to hang under my arm, and half walked, half ran the final stretch into the village with my father taking long Sanborn strides at my side.

As we reached the granite post in front of the general store, where two wagons already were hitched, my father pointed up the hill road that led toward St. Johnsbury Plain. "If that's not the stage right now, I'll eat my hat."

I lifted my cap and raked my fingers through my hair, trying to set it in order. My torn and stained skirt appalled me, and when I realized I still had the waistband rolled to keep the hem up, I blushed and quickly lowered it. Several men and boys came out of the general store just after I had done so, as the pounding hooves of the stage horses and their merry bells echoed through the village.

Mr. Simpson, who owned the store, strolled out, wiping his hands on his apron. He looked at my father and asked, "How on earth did you get to town today, Ephraim? Come around the back way, all the way through St. Johnsbury? No, wait a minute, I hear that bridge is out, too." He twisted around, seeking our wagon or carriage.

Helpfully, my father pointed north, toward the torn bridge over the Water Andric, where the outline of our wagon and a bit of Ely's head were barely visible. "I don't think much of how your men are keeping the bridge," came the teasing reply. "My daughter and I very nearly needed a duck's feet or wings to reach here."

"I'll be darned! Did you cross that mess?"

"Sure did. And by the way, I'll take a hundred foot of rope from you before I head back, if you don't mind."

Dust and sand flew up from the road as the team of horses pulled up next to us. Young Sam, his cheeks as red as ever, jumped down from his perch with two canvas mail sacks in hand. "Here you be," he said as he passed the larger one to Mr. Simpson. "And I see we've got a Sanborn contingent to take the North Upton mail directly." Handing the smaller sack to my father, he lifted his hat politely toward me. "Miss Alice Sanborn, a fine morning to be out and about."

A commotion erupted inside the coach, and the door flew open. Solomon leaned out, then leaped down, incredulous. "Alice! Mr. Sanborn! What—" His eyes grew wide as he recognized his satchel on my shoulder.

I drew the straps off over my head and patted my cap back into place. "Matthew's fevered," I said, as if that explained everything. "But it's all there, with the ones Matthew added from town."

Solomon took the satchel, staring from me to my father. "How did you get here?"

"Flew, or swam, depending on which tall tale he tells you," Mr. Simpson inserted. "Climbed like a pair of monkeys is more like it." He pointed up the north road. "Hey, fellows, looks as though we won't need to spend our hard labor on bridge repair, if the Sanborns can get across it in that condition."

As the men laughed, Solomon leaned closer to me and said hurriedly, "I have to tell you, Alice—one of the men waiting for these: it's Sarah's father!"

My father overheard and clapped Solomon's shoulder in approval. "That's the way to move 'em north," he enthused. "And the rest of Sarah's family—her mother and the other children—they'll be next?"

Now everyone was listening. Most all of them knew Sarah, or knew of her, although they might not know yet that we'd taken her north to Coventry.

"No, I'm afraid not, sir," Solomon answered my father. "It's a hard life down there. We've already helped Sarah's father, Mr. Johnson, to send a letter to his former master, offering to pay for his freedom and to buy the others. But the man's asking a thousand dollars for Mr. Johnson, and three thousand more for the others."

The men fell silent. A thousand dollars! And three thousand more! For a farmer, a year's cash earnings might be thirty dollars in a good year, and even in town, a hundred dollars was big money. Enormous money. As I looked around me, I realized each man was counting how long it could take to ransom a person that way.

My father's face reddened. "Selling them high, isn't he? Selling human beings, as if a man could own another soul?" He turned to the others, who shared his mounting indignation. "That little girl deserves her family. Hold the stage."

While we all stared, he stamped across the road and entered the doors of the Caledonia County Bank. Minutes later, he stamped back toward us, waving a fistful of currency. He pushed it into Solomon's hands.

"There's twenty hard-earned Vermont dollars. You make sure it gets to that man. Tell him to start a bank account. We'll send him out lecturing until he can gather the rest."

Mr. Simpson took off his hat, baring his bald pate to the morning sun. "Any others wishing to contribute to the freedom of Miss Sarah's mama and papa?" The hat circulated, each man dropping in at least a coin or two. Mr. Simpson emptied the collection in turn into Solomon's hat.

I didn't know why, but tears were leaking down my cheeks. I could hardly believe such a change in my father, as I heard him call out to Solomon, "And, by gosh, you tell that man I've got a brother who's a newspaperman out West. We'll make sure the story goes along in front of Mr. Johnson as he circulates to tell his tale."

This time, Solomon couldn't wipe my face for me in front of the crowd. But he emptied his hat carefully into his satchel and said in a choked voice, "I thank you all, on behalf of Mr. Lemuel Johnson, late of Maryland and soon to be of New York and Vermont after that. And if it please you all, we'd best be headed toward the Capitol, where I'll meet my southbound connection."

With all the men shaking his hand and slapping his back, Solomon climbed back into the coach, settling the satchel on his lap. Young Sam fastened shut the door and boosted himself up to grab the reins and cluck to the horses, as he slapped the leather straps in front of him. The stage headed off, and the last I saw of Solomon was his hand, waving boldly out the window.

I sniffed and rubbed a sleeve across my wet face. By habit, I reached into my skirt pocket for a handkerchief and pulled it out.

It was Solomon's, with the softly stitched edging and the sweet letter _S_ in the corner. I unfolded it carefully and held it to my cheek.

CHAPTER 32

With rope from Mr. Simpson, we crossed the Water Andric more securely this time, and Ely greeted us with an expectant nicker. We climbed up on the wagon and for a few minutes were silent, as the well-rested horse trotted steadily along the road toward North Upton. Sunshine leaked between the clouds, warming us.

After the long uphill stretch, my father rearranged himself to be able to converse, one eye toward me, the other for the road. "That's a fine young man," he began. "He's a hard worker, and he'll gather plenty of support for Seward's stand against slavery in the territories."

I agreed. "But he's not like Uncle Martin, is he? I mean, he doesn't get into arguments with people. And it seems he's staying in New England. His parents live in Boston, you know."

"Mmm. And you're helping him for the sake of Sarah's family, and for the sake of freedom and duty, I suppose." My father gave a quick smile and nod. "But you're also more than a little bit sweet on the man himself, it seems. Have you thought about what it would mean to let a young man from Boston come courting you?"

The wagon slowed as Ely's feet and then the wagon wheels entered an especially deep muddy section of road. I twisted in my seat to examine my father's face more closely. "It's not something I've thought about yet," I admitted. "But sometimes people from North Upton have married away." As I said the words, my stomach lurched. Leaving North Upton? Leaving all the people I knew?

"Sometimes they have," my father agreed. "But they think hard about it first, or they should. It's not easy to live away from your own family."

"That's what Sarah is doing. So is the Hayes family, sort of—Mrs. Hayes said it would be hard to find wives for her sons, without connections through relatives."

Ely slowed further. My father shook the reins and told him to get on up there. He watched the horse and leaned forward on the bench. This time he didn't look at me as he added, "It's hard in the other direction, too. Your mother misses John and Charles. She'd find it hard to have you so far off. Most likely she'd tell you also that it wouldn't be easy to bear and raise children when your mother can't be there with you."

I clutched the wooden seat with both hands as the wagon lurched and bumped. Just imagining being far way from my mother, forever, squeezed my heart—still, I recalled the hours of watching the Northern Lights with Solomon. I thought, too, of how much I longed to escape the closeness of village life, where people talked about you and twisted their stories of what you'd done and who you were. I fumbled for words. "Maybe there are choices in between," I offered. "Not so far, and not so different. Also, maybe Charles or John or both of them will come home when they've made their fortunes out West. Especially if they're already sweet on girls from Vermont."

"Girls from Vermont whose families have gone West," my father reminded me. "I don't want to forbid this or say you can't see this young man because of your mother. But I want you to think about it. Will you?"

"Of course."

In my pocket, Solomon's handkerchief felt smooth and warm. I wished I could just think about that, and about how good it felt to help with the work that Solomon and the others were doing, to bring more people out of slavery. One by one, that was how my mother had described it—helping one person or one family at a time. Still, I realized that wasn't really Solomon's way, except for Sarah and her family. Solomon, as Seward's man, tackled change for the laws and government of the land. I felt small and unimportant in comparison.

We took the last turn and could see William and Helen's house. The roar of the Sleepers River made more conversation impossible. My father gave my hand a quick pat, then concentrated on making sure Ely stayed on the driest parts of the road. The view from the wagon was better than from the ground, so I could see William and the Hopkins brothers down by where the dam had stood, inspecting the rushing waters. I pointed, and my father nodded.

Beyond the empty schoolyard, and past the turn for the store, the road led to Jerushah's house and our lane, opposite. My father sat between me and the view of the windows and yard of the Clark house and inn. Leaning forward, I saw no faces at any of the windows.

Ely turned down our lane. A moment later, my father stopped the wagon in the yard and told me he'd take care of the horse. "Go help your mother. She's sure to want news, too. And tell her I'm headed back to William's, on foot, to take a look at the damage and see what he has in mind."

Perhaps my mother knew what matters my father had spoken of. But she only asked whether we'd been in time to reach the stage in Upton Center, and since she knew nothing yet of why we'd gone, I told her the long tale of the papers and how they needed to be taken to Solomon, including the good news that Sarah's father would receive a set of them—and leaving out the part about going through the tunnel to get them. I didn't want to mislead her, and if she had asked, I would have told the truth, but it seemed like a truth that belonged in part to others. It was a relief not to speak of it.

"What a good young man that Matthew is," my mother commented. "Riding all the way to town like that for those papers, after going through so much with William last week. I wouldn't have guessed how much strength was in him."

"But he caught cold," I worried. "He won't get ill the way Jerushah did, will he?"

"I doubt it. The weather's warmer now, and he's at home, not riding around the countryside in an open sleigh the way she was. Watch the stove for me, and I'll take some honey across the road, so Mrs. Clark can use it in her tisanes."

"Are you sure? Mrs. Clark is so angry with me. Maybe she won't want you to visit her." I choked at the idea.

My mother brushed it aside. "I've told you, Alice, give her time. She won't mind a bit of company for a few minutes. Mind the fire, now. I'll need a good hot stove when I come back, to fry up ham for tonight. There's wash water staying hot on the back burner, too."

The late afternoon sun's heat threatened to overheat the kitchen, so as my mother departed for her visit to Mrs. Clark, I set a chunk of firewood by the back door to hold it open. Mud surrounded the house—I could see no snow at all, not even next to the barn where it piled up from sliding off the roof— and the scent of wet earth declared that spring had arrived. I stood at the door to savor it and saw a bird fly past with a tuft of hay dangling from its beak, a sure sign of nest-building.

In that sweet moment, I thought of Jerushah and the letter she had promised me. If only I could go to her, to sit in the kitchen as we used to do, with Sarah between us, our sweet shared lamb. Shouldn't spring's warmth feel more joyous than late winter's ice and cold rains?

Back in the kitchen, I realized the stove fire had dwindled

while I lingered in the sunshine. I snatched several lengths of thin, dry wood from the box and placed them on the remaining coals, then stuffed in two good-sized split logs of maple. With a clang, I shut the front door of the firebox, then slid open the draft at the side to encourage the fire to catch again.

Jerushah's letter: what if she or Matthew had placed it in the pail by the far door of the tunnel, early this morning? She would have waited all day and still would not have a reply—in fact, she might see that her letter sat neglected. That was what decided me: thinking my friend could feel alone and ignored by me. Seizing two candles, regardless of whether my mother might notice their use, I lit one and bolted down the cellar stairs, confident that my familiarity with the tunnel would allow me to quickly reach the other end, fetch the letter that surely waited there, and return, before my mother came home again.

Indeed, experience is a good teacher: With my skirt rolled up to keep it dry, the door propped carefully open, a candle placed where I could see it from within the tunnel, and the other in my fist, I hurried along the underground passageway without even bothering to count my footsteps. Splashes underfoot told me when I'd entered the stream, and soon I felt the uphill change that signaled the approach to the Clarks' cellar. There was the pail—yes, there was a letter waiting. Poor Jerushah, unanswered all this time! I thrust the folded paper into my pocket and raced back home, replacing my potato doorstop and remembering to bring both extinguished candles up to the kitchen.

A roaring surge in the stove told me immediately that my kindling and logs had caught fire all too well. I dashed across the room to bang the draft shut, but it was so hot that I came near to burning my hand before I grabbed the iron poker instead and used that to slide shut the metal covering over the air grating.

Still the roar of flame continued. My mother ran in through

the door, out of breath and calling to me, "Alice! It's a chimney fire! Come outside, right now!"

A chimney fire? They almost always took place in spring, but never to us. I stumbled out the door, dragged urgently by my mother, as my father pushed us both out of his way. He ran inside, calling over his shoulder, "Fill some pails from the trough at the barn, just in case!"

We ran for the barn, and fumbled to fill pails with water while staring back at the house. My mother whispered, "Dear merciful heaven!" Sparks and black smoke poured from the chimney, scattering black cinders over the roof and toward us as we labored.

The house door banged as my father came outside again. "Never mind the pails! Help me with the ladder."

Under the shower of hot cinders, he seized the wooden ladder from the barn and carried it to the house. My mother held it in place. My father carried a large stone up with him and shouted to me to find more stones.

The base of the barn had stones against it, and I grabbed two of them and stood at the foot of the ladder, uncertain whether to climb it. When I heard a loud crashing sound followed by my father's shout of pain, I dropped my rocks and began to climb. But I was barely halfway up when he reappeared at the top of the ladder, calling, "Where are the rocks? Bring them here!"

I backed down and collected one—all I could manage while gripping the ladder rail—and started up again. My father came down partway, seized it, and soon another crash and an added gust of cinders revealed that this one, like the first, had gone down the chimney. The third rock followed.

The smoke thinned out, although small cinders continued to fall and to dance in the air.

"Now the water—pour some out; don't try to carry the pails any more than half full. Don't climb the ladder; just put the pail upward with the handle upright. Good, that's right." He snatched the first pail, and we could hear him tramp across the roof with it, to splash it over any places where the flaming cinders could have caught.

A roughened voice behind my mother asked, "Do you need more help? We saw the smoke."

It was Matthew, coughing between sentences. Mr. Clark came running also, a pair of pails dangling from his hands.

Above us, my father leaned down to accept another pail. My arms ached from the weight of them, and my sleeves were wet and speckled with black.

"It's about done now," my father called down. "I'm just wetting down the roof, to be sure." The smoke indeed had dwindled to a thin stream of gray and brown. Mr. Clark took his two pails and filled them halfway at the horse trough, then passed them up to my father.

"We'd best go inside and see what kind of mess we need to clear up." My mother swept a hand over my hair and shoulders, brushing off ashes. "Come on, Alice. Thank you, Matthew, I think we can manage from here."

Matthew nodded and, still coughing, started back down the lane. Mr. Clark stood talking with my father. I followed my mother into the house.

Black drips of melted creosote had spattered over the kitchen floor, along with bits of cinder. The stove hissed malevolently, its roar quenched by the stones that had knocked loose the flaming material inside the chimney. My mother handed me a cloth and a pail, and we both knelt to scrub the floor.

Half an hour later, assured that there were no fires on the roof, my father came inside and kicked off his boots. Our floor was nearly cleared, although some of the black stain still clung to the boards closest to the cookstove. My mother looked up from the corner where she'd ended up and said matter-of-factly,

"Supper will be cold bread and applesauce. Ephraim, will we be able to make tea?"

"Not here, tonight. I'll need to brush out all of the chimney and stove parts before we light a fire in it again."

I groaned. "No fire at all tonight?"

"There's the hearth in the front room. Abigail, you could heat your kettle over the hearth."

My mother agreed. Moreover, the kettle of hot wash water provided for a warm cleansing all around.

Only when I climbed wearily to my bedroom did I rediscover Jerushah's letter in my pocket. There was just enough light left to read it, if I sat by the window.

My Dearest Alice,

Your letter assures me of your affectionate friendship, and for this I will always be grateful. Although I wish we could share more, I must accept this as it is, I know. How I would have loved to sit with you in the quiet of my room last night, so that we might hold each other and thus capture the warmth of our two hearts in one sweet moment of peace!

But for you, last night, there was an errand to be done, a righteous cause to be pursued. I see that you resemble Mr. Dickens's David Copperfield, who set himself to be the hero in his own life. What call can I have on you, when I am neither a fugitive slave nor a leader of the cause against slavery? How necessary it must be that you abandon me, to seek what Providence intends for you.

As for me, it appears that a lifetime of faint heart and frail condition awaits me, and I am unsure that I have the temperament for such a future. Be sure to reply to me soon, Alice, so that I may feel the pulse of life in you, for my own is so quiet that I barely hear it whisper in the stillness of each night.

> I remain always Your Friend, and more,
>
> Jerushah

There it was again: the resentment that had surfaced in Jerushah's illness, the night that Solomon attempted to break our journey at the inn at South Walden. "Neither a fugitive slave nor a leader of the cause against slavery." She meant Sarah and Solomon, I knew. Was it so terrible that I wanted to help each of them, and that Jerushah had not needed my assistance in the same way?

Irritation rose in me, along with a sharp impatience. I wanted my own life, as it seemed to be forming out of the shadows around me. The drive north with Sarah had given me a bond with Solomon, and a partnership of sorts with William and Matthew, so that I felt of use, and vital. How could I step away from all of this, to nurse the insecurity in Jerushah's heart and attempt to wean her from her jealous petulance?

Exasperated, I re-folded the letter and set it aside. I needed to rest. I would say my prayers and include Jerushah in them, but all else must wait until the morning. As I lowered my head to my pillow, I realized that the window of my chamber showed a speckling of black cinders stuck to the outside, but beyond them, a starry sky glittered. How sorry I was that no window of my home permitted a view of the glories of the Northern Lights! Recalling the shifting red and green curtains of wonder, I drifted willingly into sleep.

CHAPTER 33

My father needed assistance, drawing me out of the kitchen at the start of the day. Helping him with morning chores among the crowded sheep and lambs, I found the oldest lambs already large enough to bump into me with force—keeping my footing in the slick muck underfoot was a challenge. While my father distributed grain to the feed troughs and threw down some of the oldest hay from the top of the barn, to toss onto the mud for better footing, I passed my hands over each lamb, checking for any that seemed too thin or lame. They crowded thickly around the troughs.

"Can we let them back out to the paddock now?"

"No, give it another day to dry out," my father answered. "Did you see all the mud that the river left on our field? I may try it with corn this year. I'll talk it over with William if he comes for dinner."

"How will he build the dam again? It must require a lot of wood."

"That's so. But it happens he's piled up quite a bit at the mill, and with just a few more tree-length logs, he'll have plenty. Most likely he already has someone out cutting for him. By the time the logs arrive, the river will be down quite a bit."

While my father tended the cow and calf, I grained my mother's chickens and gathered the eggs: a dozen, a sure sign of spring-turning-to-summer. So was the riot of bird song in the air as I walked back to the house.

I pondered Solomon's words from Monday: that Sarah's father needed to raise a thousand dollars to buy his freedom, and three thousand more for his wife and children. Was Sarah included in that number? The very amount staggered me. My father's gift of twenty dollars must have nearly emptied his savings. It would take fifty times that much just to pay the first thousand dollars. What Henry Clinton had shouted from the top of the mill about "thieves" suddenly made sense: if a "master" from the South thought a slave was worth a thousand dollars, no wonder he would send a slave hunter to re-capture his property.

How many colored slaves were there? How many people's life savings would it take to convince all the "owners" to emancipate them?

At breakfast I asked my father for the number of colored slaves, and his face grew somber with concern. "More than three million, I've heard," he told me.

My mother gasped. "How do they do it? How can so many be held captive?"

"Fear, and power, and brutality," my father replied. "Greed is a mighty incentive for evil."

" 'For the love of money is the root of all evil,' says the Scripture," agreed my mother.

Stunned by the enormous number, I only shook my head. I stared at the food still on my plate. Three million people, daughters and sons, mother and fathers, babies and grandparents. My father's former passion for sending all the coloreds to Africa, to form their own colony there, seemed suddenly dwarfed. Surely great sin had led to this condition.

My father soon left to work on sheep fencing that must reach from the barn to the lower fields. In the kitchen, once the plates were clean and stacked, my mother began to mix the day's bread. I withdrew to my chamber to write a response to Jerushah's letter. Already our secret set of exchanges felt wrong, adding to the uneasiness of the morning.

Dearest Jerushah,

I hope indeed that Providence will never require me to abandon my friends, and I do not mean to abandon you. Let us seek permission from your mother to exchange letters in a more normal fashion, perhaps through Matthew's hands. If you share with her our correspondence, it may be that she will allow her heart to soften so much sooner, and we will spend hours in each other's company again.

Do not fear that I will leave behind our friendship, in spite of the labors I find in front of me. The more that I think about the situation of the coloreds of our land, the more I understand that we must convince the Slave Power as a whole to give up its pursuit of human bondage. Only evil can come of such a terrible institution.

I hope that you are feeling stronger with each day, and that the summer sunshine is brightening your home, as it is mine. Tell me about your grandmother and her visit with you, and what you are stitching—for I know you so well that I cannot believe you are idle, even if your health is not yet recovered.

Let us think of Sarah today and celebrate what God has wrought, that Sarah has already attained the freedom with which her life should ever have been endowed, and that her father and family are soon to follow her into this happy state of affairs.

Fondly, and with deep affection, I remain Your Friend,

Alice

There. I folded the letter, pleased that I had found words for what I wanted to convey to Jerushah. Should I take the letter through the tunnel? In the morning sunlight, the answer was clearly "no;" I should carry the letter instead to the Clark home and ask Mrs. Clark to allow Jerushah to receive it.

Informing my mother of my destination, I stepped out the door and to the back corner of the dooryard. Ah—a branch of a willow tree erupting with catkins, each soft gray strip of fuzz set in a tiny green cup. I broke off a small length of the seasonal promise and carried it with me down the lane as if it were a blushing flower.

Mrs. Proctor, Jerushah's white-haired grandmother, came to the door. I reminded her of our introduction when she had arrived with the stage, and I asked, "May I leave a letter with you for Jerushah?"

"Jerushah!" she called over her shoulder. "Your friend Alice is here with a letter for you."

Mrs. Clark called back, "She's still in bed, Mother."

"No, she's not in bed, for I just set the covers to air in her room."

I stood waiting, while one of the little girls was sent to the outhouse, to see whether Jerushah could be lingering there. But, again, Jerushah wasn't present. Another little one went upstairs to the other chambers, and Mrs. Proctor called into the tavern.

No Jerushah.

A creeping panic infused the household. Mr. Clark came in from the tavern, asking what the commotion meant. Upon hearing the reason, he pressed past me to examine the dooryard of house and inn, then to circle the house, calling Jerushah's name.

Foreboding struck me, and I stepped into the hallway and turned away from the kitchen, toward the door to the cellar steps. It was not fully closed. I called out, "Here!" and flung the door wide, to feel my way down the steps in the dim light that penetrated from above.

I found Jerushah collapsed at the foot of the cellar steps. Others rushed down to join me there, and to lift her and cry out in concern. She made no sound, and her eyes were closed, a heavy bruise to her forehead explaining her still form. Her hair hung limp and so did her arms. As her mother and father carried her past me, I reached impulsively for her hand and felt the chill of the skin—how long had she been in the cellar, to take such a chill into her?

I leaned against the cold stone wall of the cellar, dazed. When I looked up again, I saw Matthew at the top of the stairs, looking at me. He whispered: "The tunnel?"

I looked across the cellar. The door into the underground passageway was closed. Careful not to stumble in the near-darkness, I felt my way across to it and pressed the thumb latch. It opened with a soft click. I felt for the pail inside the doorway. There was nothing in it. I shut the door.

From the foot of the stairs, I told Matthew, "It wasn't open."

He shook his head but didn't speak until I reached the top of the stairs and stood next to him. He cleared his throat and whispered hoarsely, "I told her I didn't have time to go look for your letter."

Numbly, I held out the folded page that I still clutched in one hand. I told him, "I brought it over here myself."

CHAPTER 34

The darkest hour is just before the dawn—people say that. But every hour of that dreadful day grew darker, with no dawn in sight.

First, Jerushah's father and mother laid her onto the bed in the back bedroom, and the one fragment of hope of the moment came when her mother confirmed, "She lives! I can feel her heart, and there is a breath from her lips."

Matthew and I, each wrapped in our own guilt, stood outside the room. He heard the news and whispered in that hoarse voice, "Thanks be to God!" and fell into a chair, curling his chest over his knees, eyes closed. I stood next to another chair, unable to speak.

Mr. Clark came out of the bedroom and shook Matthew's shoulder. "I'm riding to fetch Dr. Jewett. You go find the minister. And Alice," he said turning to me with urgency, but without the ferocity that I felt I deserved, "Alice, fetch your mother to help my wife. Run!"

Seizing his cloak and hat, Mr. Clark ran out to the stables of the inn. Matthew and I followed him out the door, and Matthew headed down the road toward the church and neighboring manse, where the minister lived. Why should he fetch the minister? Was it because Jerushah was so close to death? A new thought struck me: Perhaps our own minister could lay his hands on Jerushah after all, the way Charles Hayes had offered to do. Charles's touch surely had healed our Sarah—why did I not let him do the same for Jerushah, all those weeks ago?

Even as I ran to fetch my mother, I blamed myself again for failing Jerushah in Coventry. Maybe she would have wanted Charles to do the same for her as he did for Sarah. Maybe I had failed to see the hand of Providence in the gleaming dark hands of Mrs. Hayes's son.

With so much blame choking me, I could hardly tell my mother why I'd run into the house. "Jerushah—she fell down the stairs—barely breathing—help her mother!"

Swiftly my mother seized herbs and flannels, thrust them into a basket, and raced out of our kitchen, saying only, "Don't try to start the stove! Mind the hearth, keep the fire low, and stay put until I'm back."

Next to the hearth in the front room I sat on a low stool and looked at the small fire under the two kettles in which dinner simmered. When I tried to say the Lord's Prayer, I reached "forgive us our trespasses" and couldn't go any further. So I just rocked back and forth, one hand clasped around the dangling gold locket with Jerushah's lock of hair within. Over and over, I said, "Please, Lord, please," with Jerushah filling my heart.

Eventually my father came into the house, calling out, "Abigail? I need William's help soon; is dinner about ready?"

I tried to call out to him. He walked through the empty kitchen and found me, and immediately placed a hand on my shoulder. "What is it? What's wrong?"

"Jerushah," I croaked. "She fell. Mama's over there, helping."

"How long ago?"

I shook my head and pressed out, "Not long after you went out."

"I'll go see what I can do." He set a small chunk of wood on the coals and poked them to start the flames again.

I watched the hearth fire and waited. In the orange and yellow flickering flames, I imagined the fires of hell. Surely that was what I deserved. If I'd gone to get Jerushah's letter sooner, if I hadn't waited until morning to answer her, if I hadn't agreed to the secret exchanges through the tunnel, if I hadn't turned away Charles Hayes, if I hadn't gone north with Sarah and Jerushah and Solomon . . .

But here I stopped. Henry Clinton, the slave hunter, was no imagined demon. His arrival, his hunt for Fred Johnson, the risk of his seeing Sarah, were all too real. The evil of the Slave Power and its minions, at least, could not be my fault.

The kitchen door opened. Slow steps crossed the kitchen. It was not my father. It was my mother instead. In that moment, I knew what she had come to tell me, before I even saw her tear-streaked face, her arms extended toward me.

Jerushah, my best friend Jerushah, the most beautiful and kind and beloved friend in my world—Jerushah was dead.

I stood and cried out, "Couldn't the minister save her? She was good! God loved her, always!"

"And God has taken her home," my mother told me as she crushed me to her chest. "She is in a far better place now, Alice. You must know that."

"No," I said, over and over again. "No, no, no!"

"Yes," came the whispered reply. "God bless her and keep her, and may God comfort her family, in this great sorrowful time."

"It's my fault," I whispered. "It's all my fault."

CHAPTER 35

The graveside service took place at the end of the next day. I wore my misery as a cloak that covered my face as well as the rest of me. Silent, curled inward, I stood next to my parents and William, and my Grammy Palmer stood behind us. Each time that the Reverend Alexander said anything, I saw a black shadow of anger: why had he not saved Jerushah? For Doctor Jewett, also in the gathering, I felt no such rage—he had arrived too late. But if a colored man could lay on hands and bring God's healing for Sarah, why not our own minister for one of us? Jerushah was so good, so good.

Mrs. Clark and the small children sat on an improvised bench during the service. Mr. Clark and Matthew, still coughing occasionally, stood next to the board coffin. Out in the churchyard, when the sexton and my father and two other men lowered the coffin into the hole in the ground, Mrs. Clark wailed, and all the smaller children began to sob. The women of the village, including my mother, pressed close to gather them up and nursed them through the slow walk back to their house. The men followed, except for my father and the sexton, who stayed on to finish filling the grave.

Nobody needed me. I stumbled away and found myself climbing toward the ridge above the village. A few small trees lined the route. Small golden-green leaves on the tips of their branches mocked the day, pretending some kind of blossoming could come from such darkness. I wanted to howl in pain like a wolf, but my throat remained sealed in silence. I had not loved Jerushah the way that she loved me. This, too, I knew, was my fault.

I stared at the village below. Its sunny, orderly line of homes and barns and the wisps of smoke drifting from several chimneys made no sense to me. With Jerushah, I'd lost everything, it seemed.

A rustle from the path below drew my slow attention. Someone was coming—no, two people were coming. The first was Matthew. The second was—how could it be? But it was: Miss Farrow. She herded Matthew in front of her, and the two of them stood with me, silent for a few minutes.

As I looked at the tall colored woman with her dark skirt and jacket, her hair covered by a neat black hat, I saw Sarah in my mind: those small dark hands, her sweet face and trusting smile. I remembered how happy she had been, settling into the Hayes family, comforted and useful. It struck me all at once: I must write to Sarah and tell her of Jerushah's death. The thought robbed me of breath, and I doubled over as though a fist had landed on my stomach.

Miss Farrow caught my shoulders. "It's time to sit down," she said quietly. "Matthew, is there a bench?"

Matthew shook his head, his thin face pale and desolate. He coughed into his hand, then pointed toward a large rock, a boulder of granite resting at the ridge. "There?"

The three of us arranged ourselves on the cold stone. I noticed Matthew avoiding me, sitting at the other side of Miss Farrow. I choked out, "It's my fault. I should have been a better friend. I should have loved her better."

Matthew shook his head. "No, it's mine. I should have gone down to check the pail for her, so she wouldn't have been on the cellar stairs. I knew her heart hadn't recovered."

Miss Farrow put one hand on my knee, the other on

Matthew's shoulder. "You both have a lot to bear," she agreed. "Terrible things happen in this life. Good people are hurt, and children die. Families are riven asunder, and love fails to preserve us."

As she spoke, I heard the double description of her words: they described our loss of Jerushah, but they also called out the dark shadow of the enslavement of three million colored people like her.

I asked, "Is it always like this? Knowing you haven't done the right things, or done enough, and seeing how it all ends in death?" I heard Matthew sob.

"But it doesn't all end in death," Miss Farrow asserted. She gazed out over the village and waited.

After a long moment I replied, "For some people, it does. For Jerushah. For William and Helen's baby," I added. "For the slave hunter."

She nodded. "That's the part of death we bear more easily: when evil leads to its own losses. But when it leads to our own losses—even the loss of a very young baby not yet fit to survive—when it strips us of the people we love, we blame ourselves, and we blame our God. We ask whether truth and justice will be upheld for us. We ask why life is fragile."

Letting go of me, she reached downward and plucked a small white flower from the grass at her feet and lifted it toward me. "Is it fragile?"

"Yes," I agreed, unsure why she'd asked.

"Yet precious, and lovely, and worth loving?"

"Yes."

Matthew said, "Like my sister." He pulled out a handkerchief and blew his nose wetly. "She was precious, and lovely, and worth loving. I loved her so much!" He wailed, his voice catching between gravelly deepness and a broken, thin cry.

"I don't know why," Miss Farrow continued, "but Creation

comes to us this way, in both strength and weakness, life and loss. I hear each of you listing the losses. Can you name instead the life that Jerushah has given to each of you?"

Matthew answered first: "Caring about my mother and father, about my family. Caring about my grandmother. Caring about fairness and kindness."

"Sarah's life," I added. "And Matthew's. She loved you so much, Matthew. And your word is so true: she always cared— she cared about stories, and laughter, and keeping warm when it's cold, and how the village joins in services on the Sabbath. If there was goodness in something, whether of body or spirit, she cared about it, and she smiled and held it." I reached up and fingered the locket at my throat. Jerushah held me also. Did that mean there was still goodness in me?

The sun shone more brightly, heating the air around us. It must be noon. The realization made me stand up all at once. "Everyone's eating at your house, Matthew. I should be there, helping."

"I should, too." He rose, panicky but certain. "My father needs me to help. So does my mother."

"So does Jerushah," Miss Farrow murmured. She patted his shoulder and said, "Don't go too fast on the path. Steady is better than hurrying. I'll follow soon."

Matthew left us. I repeated, "I should be there, helping." But the black guilt rolled back over me, as swiftly as a cloud over the sun. I gulped and spoke a part of it: "You only told me to drive them to the Four Corners. It's my fault that we turned north. Solomon wouldn't have done that if I hadn't been so afraid of the slave hunter. And then Jerushah wouldn't have been ill."

"And now the slave hunter is dead, too," Miss Farrow agreed. She actually sounded sad about it. "It's a dark and spreading poison, this buying and selling of men and women, girls and

boys and babies." She paused and waited for me to think
through what she'd said.

"The Slave Power," I mused. "Is that where the evil comes
from? Does it taint us all, all the white people who haven't put
an end to it yet?"

"It might," Miss Farrow said softly. Her words plunged me
into deeper despair.

"It's too strong and large for me to fight. What can I do?"

"You can come to town with me and labor with many others,
you know. Every set of papers sent South, every merchant and
wife convinced to take a stand, every person sure that slaveholding must end, it all becomes another power—a power of
freedom and justice."

For a moment, I heard hope, even for myself. Then I
remembered again how Jerushah's death lay on my hands and
in my heart. "I can't," I whimpered. "I'd ruin things there, too."

Miss Farrow looked past me, down the hill, and lifted a hand
to beckon to someone. Out of the trees stepped a tall young
man with broad shoulders and a gleaming dark face.

"Charles?" I asked incredulously. "Charles Hayes? But how?"

"I sent for him," Miss Farrow said simply, one hand on my
arm, pressing me to sit where I was. "As soon as I heard about—
about Jerushah. I knew you'd need what he could ask for, for
you. Charles is here for your sake today."

I stood and cried out, "But I didn't let him help Jerushah!"

A gentle sadness on the face coming toward me stilled my
voice, and I heard him say softly, as if to a lamb, "You were
afraid, then. I understand. Sister Alice, will you sit with me a
moment? I've ridden a long journey today, and I'd like to sit
down."

Good manners took over by habit. "Please sit down," I
choked out as I seated myself again on the stone. Between the
two colored people, the older woman and the young man, I felt

strange and alone. My familiar village lay just beyond this hillside, but how far away it seemed now.

Charles said, "I surely am sorry about Miss Jerushah. I imagine you'll miss her, all your life. That's a good thing, you know. It's a sign of how much you cared about each other, isn't it?" He laid his hand out on the rough rock, palm up. "Maybe you'd be so kind as to hold my hand as we pray for Miss Jerushah."

I hesitated. I'd never held anyone's hand who was a stranger to me. Then again, I'd accepted shelter at the Hayes home with Sarah and Jerushah, when ice and snow still held the land. Now spring sent its softness on the air. I laid my hand on top of Charles's, and he covered it with his other hand and bowed his head. I lowered mine, also.

"Our Father who art in heaven, hallowed be thy name," he began. "Now into thy kingdom of heaven, accept our sister Jerushah, we pray. Bless her with joy and Your constant comfort, and let her know, please, that we miss her mightily. But with Your help, we'll carry on. Take the burdens of sorrow and grief, of failure and despair, of shame from us."

How could Charles have guessed that shame itself choked me?

He continued, "Lift us up into your healing, Lord, for the sake of our small selves and Your large work. Fit us to labor for Your freedom and Your justice."

A vision came to me then: of my brothers John and Charles in California Territory, speaking their minds and finding their new families; of my Uncle Martin, laboring over his printing press, calling out for the end of slavery in the territories; of Solomon, speaking to a solemn assembly in a large city somewhere; and of Sarah, growing into womanhood, with her father to watch over her, and the rest of her family arriving from the South. It wasn't what I'd expected. But there was joy in it, and a sort of song, and something of Jerushah's voice as we'd sung our hymns in the snowy wilderness to the north, all caught up in caring about our lamb, our Sarah.

The spring call of a red-winged blackbird broke the silence around me. I opened my eyes. I was sitting alone on the boulder, warm and comforted as I hadn't been in so very long. Charles Hayes and Miss Farrow stood together, looking down toward the village, and Miss Farrow turned to me and asked, "Are you ready to go help with dinner now?"

"I am. And tomorrow, to help with more than that."

Miss Farrow nodded, understanding that I'd accepted her invitation. She and Charles began to walk down the hill, and after a moment, I followed. I wasn't crying any longer. But I reached into my pocket for a handkerchief to dry the dampness from my skin. I pulled it out, touched it to my cheeks, and noticed again that it was Solomon's.

It seemed I'd pulled out his handkerchief over and over again for powerful emotion. It occurred to me that I'd over-use it at such a rate. I sniffed and determined to spend the next few hours exercising courage and offering comfort, instead of crying.

Courage. And liberty, and labor. The words clung together, giving me a balance to my steps down from the ridge. Who could tell what might lie ahead?

For all the parts of Jerushah's death that were my fault, there was something else remaining: work that needed doing, justice that needed more effort. Jerushah gave her help to Sarah, with joy and love. I could take my part for Jerushah, as well as for Sarah, and for the sake of something warmer and more alive than mere duty.

I wondered what might lie in front of me, beyond the shadow of Jerushah's death. When would Solomon McBride return to North Upton? My father's gentle warning about what that might mean came back to me. But, oh, how sure I felt that my life must go outward from here, toward places where I could see the dance of the Northern Lights, and where I could help more people than Sarah, more than even Sarah's family.

In front of me, I heard the rustle of Miss Farrow's feet on the path. Ahead, the light of the warm afternoon lit the treetops with their clusters of new leaves. Above the village, a pair of bluebirds winged past, bright as a promise.

My feet kept moving down the slope toward the houses and families clustered there. My heart, however, gave an extra beat, then seemed to pause for a moment, considering the adventures ahead. In that moment, I knew I was carrying hope.

ABOUT THE AUTHOR

Beth Kanell lives in northeastern Vermont, with a river at her feet and a mountain at her back. Exploring American history led her into crafting three earlier published books: *The Darkness Under the Water, The Secret Room* (which is a sort of 160-years-later sequel to *The Long Shadow,* also set in fictional North Upton), and *Cold Midnight.* Her books of adventure travel, her regional histories, and most of all her poems all contribute to how and why she writes. Visit www.BethKanell.com to get better acquainted, and to find resource materials for all of her novels.

The employees of Five Star Publishing hope you have enjoyed this book.

Our Five Star novels explore little-known chapters from America's history, stories told from unique perspectives that will entertain a broad range of readers.

Other Five Star books are available at your local library, bookstore, all major book distributors, and directly from Five Star/Gale.

Connect with Five Star Publishing

Visit us on Facebook:
https://www.facebook.com/FiveStarCengage

Email:
FiveStar@cengage.com

For information about titles and placing orders:
(800) 223-1244
gale.orders@cengage.com

To share your comments, write to us:
Five Star Publishing
Attn: Publisher
10 Water St., Suite 310
Waterville, ME 04901